Something caug... missed it, had it n... for there was some... ous about it and a bit repulsive. It was a dead animal. Not a cat, exactly, for it seemed to have little hands; and not quite dead, for it shuddered. What was it doing here?

He reached out to poke it, hesitated, then jeered himself into doing it. A dying animal— what harm could it do him?

His finger seemed to tingle as it touched the odd fur. *Be my host!*

Startled, the boy drew back. But he was not hurt, and he had heard something. Something very like a *shedu*, maybe. It had not been unfriendly.

Cautiously, he touched the cat again.

Be my host!

This time he maintained contact. It was not a voice, exactly, yet it spoke. A soundless voice. The voice a spirit might have.

PIERS ANTHONY AND FRANCES HALL

PRETENDER

TOR®

A TOM DOHERTY ASSOCIATES BOOK
NEW YORK

PRETENDER

Reprinted by arrangement with The Borgo Press

Cover art by Don Maitz

A Tor Book
Published by Tom Doherty Associates, Inc.
175 Fifth Avenue
New York, N.Y. 10010

Tor ® is a registered trademark of Tom Doherty Associates, Inc.

ISBN: 0-812-52396-2

First Tor edition: June 1985

Printed in the United States of America

0 9 8 7 6 5 4 3 2

PRETENDER

CHAPTER 1

The craft was in trouble. It might have been an enemy nimbus-mine, for this was a marginal zone. More likely it was random failure somewhere in this old unit. NK-2 was no mechanic. It would be necessary to dock for repairs.

He sent his host-animal for the local planet chart. In a moment the configuration of suns and worlds spread across the host's visual center.

Few planets in this region were habitable, fewer were actually occupied, and none were civilized. Only three supported galactic enclaves, and one of these was marked with the warner signifying probable enemy penetration. The chart was not new, but NK-2 doubted the situation had changed significantly in the interim.

His most expeditious docking was on the warned planet. His trajectory suited the other two poorly, and he hardly wanted to risk them while the reliability of his craft was in question. In this case it was better to chance confrontation with the enemy, unpleasant as the prospect was. He was no combatant, but he could exercise suitable caution.

NK-2 had the host examine a detail chart of the chosen world. The natives were at the early-cluster stage, and their technology was unevenly distributed and as yet far from the level required for galactic intercourse. Station A-10 was located at the leading cultural and economic center, which was situated beside a river not far from a mountainous region somewhat removed from the planet's sizable oceans.

All he had to do was dock his craft, send out a distress signal, and wait at the station until a repair vehicle responded. The local representative was DS-1, and of course he would be competent to handle this case. That was the purpose of such enclaves.

But if the enemy had truly infiltrated, there could be complexities. Ordinarily he would contact Station A-10 prior to docking—but the enemy would be certain to intercept such a message. He would have to do it blind; that was the lesser risk. And he would signal for assistance while still in space, using a tight beam that avoided the planet.

Too bad he couldn't wait it out in space. But a derelict ship was bad policy anywhere, and there were supplies to maintain his host for only a fraction of the necessary time. The animal would starve—and of course NK-2 would die with it. That was another reason why galactic stations were maintained on primitive planets. Standby assistance was never far away.

*   *   *

The docking was routine. The repulser shield discouraged the local fauna so that no natives poked about the craft, and neither the animate nor the inanimate portions of the team suffered disfunction. He was within manageable range of the enclave. Dockings were never made too near native camps, of course; even the shield could not abate too drastic an intrusion!

NK-2 sent his host about the craft, putting it in order for his absence. He still did not dare signal Station A-10 for fear of enemy monitoring, but his host could easily travel the distance.

According to the subnotes on the chart, the natives were four-limbed, fixed-form sapients of large size, possessing tamed animals one of which resembled his host. With just a touch of repulse to abate curiosity, he should be able to enter the city and connect with the station without even advertising his presence to either natives or enemy. Then it would be all over except the tedious wait.

Perhaps he could use the time to indulge in research relating to the motivations of incipient civilization. Any primitive society offered rich opportunities for such studies, and NK-2 had upon occasion been tempted to enter some other field than radiation prospecting. But he lacked the training for alien ethnology.

The host had completed its chores. NK-2 knew he should review the distress-docking checklist, but he was impatient with the routine. Nothing would bother the craft, and he could return if necessary after establishing himself at Station A-10.

He took the host outside after setting the lock to

reseal automatically. They paused a few paces away to look back. There was no sign of the craft. That meant the repulser was operative; the host's gaze avoided that region even when directed specifically. Excellent. They resumed ambulation toward the station.

The light of the local sun was fierce and the atmosphere was dry and hot, causing his host discomfort. The terrain was not difficult, however. It had been so long since NK-2 had been on an alien world that this was a refreshing experience. Were his host attuned to the specific environment, he might have romped.

The animal, far from romping, was tiring. NK-2 allowed it to rest. There were so many trifling differences between habitable worlds that no single creature could adjust readily to them all. But the pause did not seem to help; when he started off again, the animal stumbled. Something was ailing the creature.

Then he remembered: he had failed to inoculate his host against local maladies before leaving the protection of the craft. This was an elementary precaution the checklist would have covered—elementary but essential. Now the unfortunate creature had been contaminated, and NK-2 himself was in trouble.

There was no point returning to the craft, for it lacked curative facilities. He would have to proceed to the station. His host would probably perish, but NK-2 could transfer to a native host. An unpleasant necessity, but the result of his own oversight. He was sorry the innocent animal had to suffer. In future he would be more careful about such details; there was more involved than personal convenience.

Now the host's strength was failing rapidly, as the virulent microorganisms of this wilderness raged through its system unchecked. The animal became confused, and would have lost the way had NK-2 not exerted firm control. This was going to be closer than he had supposed; there was now no possibility of returning to his craft. The Station was much closer, but any delay in locating it could have serious consequence.

Then disaster. There was no native settlement in the charted location—only a large mound covered with scattered blocks of stone. A city had once stood here, certainly—but it had been destroyed utterly.

NK-2 drove his host to the exact coordinate of Station A-10. There was nothing but rubble.

The host collapsed and lay in the bright heat. It was dying—and there was no alternate host available.

CHAPTER 2

The boy came from a peasant hut on the Tigris River, at the fringe of the mighty Babylonian Empire. This region was increasingly menaced by the barbarian Medes. Yet what was that to his family, already so deeply in debt to the temple of Marduk that the charioteers could hardly bring more sorrow!

He was six. He had been born in the year Nebuchadnezzar died, and already he understood deprivation and hunger. His father labored all day in the hot barley fields, but lacked barley for his own bread. What was there for a boy to do?

He approached the great mound with a certain expectant thrill, though he had been here many times before. It was forbidden; that was why he came. This was the ruin of Nineveh, capital of the ancient Assyrian Empire. Well he knew its savage history, for it was still told by the old men of the region, some of whom claimed to have been there at its destruction.

Where was the god Asshur now, who had governed the world from this spot? Where was his power, his terror, his rows on rows of bloodstained stakes, the ghastly glee of his conquests?

Only these stones remained, the mighty rubble of a god.

The boy was looking for a god, or at least a *shedu*, an invisible winged bull to stay by his side and protect him from harm. And to protect his family too, lest he be forced to spend the rest of his life working off his father's debt to the temple.

Something caught his eye. He would have missed it, had it not been directly in his path, for there was something extremely inconspicuous about it and a bit repulsive. It was a dead animal. Not a cat, exactly, for it seemed to have little hands; and not quite dead, for it shuddered. What was it doing here?

He squatted before it, perversely fascinated. He had schooled himself to look for *shedu* which were always where one never looked. This funny cat was surely hard to look at; could it be a *shedu?* But it had no wings, and it was dying. It could hardly be a powerful guardian spirit.

Unless. A god had ruled this city and the world, and that god had perished. Why could not a *shedu* perish too? Perhaps this was a strong spirit who had strayed into the forbidden region and been smashed by the ghost of Asshur, so that it lost its wings and became visible. If it were taken away from here, would it regain its strength? Would it then be a faithful *shedu?*

He reached out to poke it, hesitated, then jeered

himself into doing it. A dying animal—what harm
could it do him?

His finger seemed to tingle as it touched the odd
fur. *Be my host!*

Startled, the boy drew back. But he was not hurt,
and he had heard something. Something very like a
shedu, maybe. It had not been unfriendly.

Cautiously, he touched the cat again.

Be my host!

This time he maintained contact. It was not a
voice, exactly, yet it spoke. A soundless voice. The
voice a spirit might have.

"Are you my *shedu?*" he asked. "Will you stay
beside me wherever I go and grant my wishes?"

But the voiceless voice just kept begging him to be
his host, whatever that meant.

"Oh, all right," he said impatiently. "But you
have to get money for my father to pay off the debt
to the temple, and give me the magic power to read,
so that I'll be better than all the other boys in the
village, and make me a fancy noble when I grow up,
and, and—"

But the *shedu* didn't seem to be paying attention.
Magic creatures were funny that way. You had to
learn how to handle them.

It was difficult, for this was no tame thoroughbred
host, but a wild alien one, untrained in the preroga-
tives of hosting. NK-2 had made the transfer from
necessity, not choice, for his original host was completely out of commission. The exchange had exhausted him; he required an extended period of rest

while he adapted to the alien configuration and restored his resources. Only his umbra had survived the process; it would take time to develop a new penumbra. Meanwhile, perceiving through these strange senses was difficult; thinking with this unfamiliar brain was worse; and actual control of the unruly host was out of the question. The best he could do now was imprint a single fundamental urge: the need to locate Station A-10 before the relief craft arrived. Then hang on, letting the host take it from there.

Aten. He had to find Aten. Before something happened. Before a long time passed, because that was *when* it would happen. Wherever Aten was.

Enkidu shook his head. He could make no sense of it, but that didn't much matter. He had a mission.

He also had a *shedu*, he thought. It hadn't done much. It was just a kind of presence that resembled the grumbled warnings of a cautious old man: don't do this, don't do that, it might lead to trouble somehow. It was annoying to an adventurous boy, and he tried to ignore it.

One day the priest of Marduk came to his house. The local temple was small, since Marduk himself resided far away in Babylon. But the debt was great—and there was no way to pay.

Enkidu looked at the seamed face and weary stoop of his father as though for the first time. The priest was making some obscure threat, and his father was appalled and his mother terrified, and his younger sisters were beginning to whine because of the general tension, but still there was no way to pay. If only he had found a decent *shedu,* he could order it to lift up that mean priest and cast him headfirst into the Tigris!

"Choose," the priest said relentlessly. "Choose—or I will choose for you!" And he looked meaningfully toward the two little girls.

Then the *shedu* spoke. Enkidu, transfixed by his parents' hopelessness and fear, yielded to the nagging urge and echoed its sentiment:

"Take *me!* I am young, I can work, I can learn. I am worth more than both my sisters—more than all the shekels you have loaned my father!"

Surprised, the priest studied him. Enkidu was almost paralyzed with fear, but the *shedu* forced him to hold up his chin and stare boldly back.

"Perhaps you are," the priest agreed, smiling.

NK-2 was exhausted again. He had been recovering nicely, considering the liabilities of his residence in an alien host, and had been ready to work on his penumbra. He had formulated a long-range three-fold thrust, to execute once his full strength had been recovered. First: strengthen the host's incentive to find Station A-10, so that this became the most important single objective in life. Second: free the host from his circumstantial and intellectual limitations, so that he could indulge that incentive. Third: arrange to travel to Babylon, the most likely present location of A-10.

The first was merely a matter of judicious and continued reinforcement, to be peaked about a year before the repair craft was due. Opportunity for the second had come unexpectedly, before he was ready for it; he had had to exert control for a key moment though it devastated his scant present resources. But it was done: he had transferred the boy from his backplanet habitat to a major artery of this society's power structure: the temple of Marduk.

By this world's time-scale, he had seventeen years in which to accomplish the third. Considering the difficulties entailed, it was an adequate but hardly generous amount. He should be able to train the boy to a certain extent while that boy grew into manhood. Though hardly comfortable in this wild host, he was secure. He would not have to change hosts again. This was fortunate, because he doubted he would be able to manage a second such change if he had to. The near-death of his original host before he departed, the adverse conditions of his transfer, the backwardness of this culture—all these reduced both his capacities and his opportunities drastically. It would be long before he recovered his full powers, especially if he had to exercise control too often. What was routine for a conditioned host was a feat of incredible stamina for a wild one.

He knew now what had happened to the city in which A-10 had been located. Nineveh had been the capital—but Assyria had been overthrown by its subject city Babylon in conjunction with the fierce Medes. This host had been born fifty years after that destruction. NK-2's charts had been about a century old—quaint as it was to date a galactic chart in terms of the revolutions of one inconsequential planet—so had not reflected the local change. Now the effective capital of the world was Babylon.

He would have to rest for a few months, as this recent effort following so close after the transfer had brought him to his dimmest point ever. The host would have to look out for himself until NK-2 was ready and able to make further suggestions.

The temple was strange to him, but the priests were not unkind. They deloused him and oiled him and gave him a bed in one of the many alcoves surrounding the main temple. They fed him regularly, so that he soon grew alert and sleek, and they did not brand him until he tried to run away.

This was Calah, actually quite close to his home village as distances went within the empire. In time his homesickness wore off, but his discontent continued and grew. He did not like the enforced discipline of the temple!

At first he was put to work as a kitchen slave, carrying the great masses of bread from the oven, cleaning the floors and even learning to milk one of the temple goats. But his active mind often strayed from such tasks. He did not always remember to remove the bread from the oven in time, so that it burned and tasted bad. When he brought in a pail of milk with fresh droppings in it the priest in charge became very upset for no good reason. But he did not beat Enkidu, strangely.

Instead, the priest talked with him, inquiring the reason for his carelessness. This was not the one who had taken him slave in payment for his father's debt, but a gentler man. Still, Enkidu did not dare tell him about his odd *shedu,* that had come to him amid the ruins of Nineveh and bade him find Aten. Aten was surely a rival god, and that could anger Marduk. But he did confess his ambitions: to have fine clothing and to be a literate man, set apart from the common peasants.

Intrigued, the priest brought a tablet bearing lines of sharp-pointed imprints. "Like this?" he asked softly, and Enkidu nodded, abashed at his own presumption, for not even his father could read. But the *shedu* was nagging him again, suggesting his answers. The kind priest questioned him further, then led him to another part of the temple, one Enkidu had not seen before. Here clay block-benches were fixed to the floor, and beside each was a large earthenware receptacle. Boys of various ages sat on these benches and worked busily on soft clay tablets before them, while a schoolmaster stood in front and barked directions.

"These boys are learning to be scribes," the priest explained. "It is a very difficult trade, Enkidu, and many years will pass before they graduate. Some will fail to learn well enough and will be sent home in disgrace. Tupshar here is a hard master. But he will treat you fairly if you try hard. Do you wish to undertake this training?"

Enkidu stared wide-eyed at the jars containing clay, at the little water-troughs set in the benches, at the busy styli. He saw a boy sharply reprimanded for an inconspicuous error. Another snickered, and was rapped smartly on the arm. He heard loud instructions: words read by the master, that the boys struggled to record just so in their soft tablets, carefully imprinting the little wedge marks on the surface. He saw the sweat gleaming in the faces of many, though they were only sitting still and the room was cool, and he knew that they were tense and afraid of Tupshar. He had had no idea that literacy was so difficult to achieve.

The *shedu* prompted him. "Yes."

"Then remain here," the priest said quietly. "I will inquire again in a few days. It is a demanding school, and none of these boys is slave."

Indeed they were not. Wealthy men had sent their sons to this school attached to the temple of Marduk at Calah, and these boys did not fancy the equal company of a branded slave. But Tupshar tolerated no inequalities; all felt the weight of his discipline alike.

Enkidu realized that his *shedu* was on the job. He had asked it to repay his family's debt, and the debt had been paid. He had asked it to make him literate— and here he was, in training to be a scribe. He had supposed the gifts would be granted outright, if at all; now he understood that they were given only when he was willing to work for them. The *shedu* merely showed the way. In time it would make him free and rich, also—and then he would go in search of the god Aten.

Beside this dream, the taunts of his fellows were as nothing. He applied himself with gusto to writing and mathematics and all other studies deemed essential to men of quality. Enkidu learned rapidly and became, in time, Tupshar's star pupil.

And the *shedu* was ever there, guiding him through the moments of crisis, nagging him to do better. He cursed it frequently, but in the end obeyed, for when he did what it wanted it left him alone. Without it, he realized grudgingly, he would never have come as far as he had.

As a young man he was given leave to return to his village for a visit. He remained a slave, while the villagers were free—but he wore rich robes now and spoke with eloquence and had a personal attendant, while the villagers were ignorant and poor. His father was dead and his mother and one sister had been sold outside the village in cancellation of new debts dating from the year the barley harvest failed. His other sister was now big with her third or fourth child and barely remembered him.

Enkidu was almost unable to converse with anyone in his home village, for no one there knew anything of mathematics, astronomy, economics or other civilized disciplines. They only knew how to irrigate their fields (incompetently), cultivate their grain (wastefully), and patch their squalid huts (leakily) with palm boughs. He observed the thriving lice that inhabited their hair, the snakes and rodents that shared their sweltering sun-baked domiciles, and their ubiquitous naked and hungry children. He turned away.

Even his old home was gone, the sundried bricks dissolved in one of the floods. He had all his childhood wishes, now—but he had lost the world he had known. Nothing remained for him but his quest for Aten.

When his host was twelve years old, NK-2 took note of a shift in the balance of contemporary power: Cyrus the Persian threw off his Mede overlord and went on to conquer the Mede empire itself. Four years later Cyrus also conquered Lydia, to the other side of Babylonia. Now Cyrus was considering new conquest. It was time to locate A-10.

CHAPTER 3

A newly impaled criminal kicked away his life beside the road to Babylon. The vertical pole on which the naked man was mounted dug slowly into his intestines. Enkidu paused to look, for he had not seen many such executions. This particular punishment was less common now than during the generations of Assyria—but specialists still knew exactly how to mount a felon so that he would not die too quickly, despite the pointed shaft that supported his torso via the anus.

A child dashed up to tug at one of the hanging feet. The mother hauled him back, scolding; she was afraid her baby would get tainted blood on his hands and be contaminated. Genii were always present, looking for a chance to take over the body of a careless person.

Enkidu realized he had led too sheltered a life. He

was sickened by this display. Surely a quick death would have sufficed; why make any man suffer so deliberately?

He turned south and put the matter out of his mind. He had to, lest it torment him unduly. Executions were not his business.

The road to Babylon continued southward from the left bank of the Euphrates River, straight through the open gate of the invasion-proof outer ramparts and on into the ground between the walls. Enkidu was footsore and short of temper, and that roadside scene had not improved his outlook.

It was later than he had planned to arrive at this city at the center of the world. He would barely have time to seek out Aten's temple before nightfall. But Enkidu was glad to be so nearly there. His spirits rose as he passed through the outer gates. Surely it would not take him too long to find it. Once he got on the Processional Way. . . .

He discovered with new wonder that the road stretched ahead for more than a thousand paces before reaching the walls of the city-proper. Already it was clear that Babylon was vaster than he had imagined. Open barley fields, great groves of palms— within the outer walls!

He thought of Cyrus the Persian, whom Babylon had expected for some years now. When he came—if he came—Cyrus would find the walls stout. If he should actually succeed in breaking through the outer wall, he would still be excluded from the city proper. This entire area could be flooded at will, Enkidu had heard, though he had not realized the scope of the project. He saw that ground level was scarcely higher than the river here, and a large canal cut through the center of the enclosure.

Closer to the city proper there were houses and cross streets, the overflow of the original establishment. Traffic increased: tradesmen in yellow tunics, ragged loafers, men on the backs of tall half-wild asses. Two chariots of the city garrison swept grandly by. Enkidu stopped in his tracks to admire the magnificent black horses with their flying manes. A merchant's cart clattered abruptly around a corner on two wheels. Enkidu jumped back, avoiding a leather-bound wheel by a finger's breadth. Ah, commerce!

He looked down when he felt the surface change under his sandals. Large flagstones of fine limestone and red breccia formed the pavement now, and every slab bore an inscription. He squatted, heedless of the jostling, to read the angular wedge-writing: NEBUCHADNEZZAR, KING OF BABYLON, SON OF NABOPOLASSER, KING OF BABYLON AM I. THE BABIL STREET I PAVED WITH BLOCKS OF SHADU STONE FOR THE PROCESSION OF THE GREAT LORD MARDUK. MARDUK, LORD, GRANT ETERNAL LIFE.

Enkidu smiled. Marduk was master of Babylon, as surely as Ishtar was its mistress. But was it for the glory of the god that this inscription had been imprinted, or for that of the former king? This was the beginning of the Processional Way. His heart quickened and his eyes strained eagerly ahead.

The Way stretched before him—magnificent, incredibly wide, lined with temples and what must be palaces. The structures were white and gold and the broad earth between them was alive with red and

-yellow and green paintings, all laid out in leisured order. The sky above looked even bluer here than elsewhere. Truly, this was a city the gods themselves might proudly inhabit. But where was the temple of Aten?

He had realized before he came that Aten's temple would not be great and showy like Shamash's or the others. Yet he was vaguely disappointed to have his expectation confirmed.

But he really couldn't afford disappointment until he was sure. There was still time to search out the temple in the city proper. Perhaps it was farther along on the Processional Way, and perhaps it *was* grand after all. . . .

The renowned inner fortifications rose to the height of twelve tall men and more above the water level of the moat—a massive wall of sun-baked brick, with a roadway on top along which charged a chariot of the garrison. Already he could see what must be the famous lions, and above them frequent towers reared over battlements three times the height of a man. Archers at their summits could peer down some ninety feet. This resembled a mountain chain more than it did any human structure!

Pilgrims and tourists squeezed around him as they crossed the moat. The river wandered to the right, but straight ahead loomed the north entrance to the great city. The Processional Way, he could see, passed into and directly through the gate of the goddess of battle and fertility. The Gate of Ishtar.

It would traverse Babylon's center, he knew, this most famous avenue in all the world. It would be garnished by ornate temples inside; but first it had to feed itself into the tiny mouth of the fortress wall. On each side ran a magnificent enameled frieze with sculptured lions. They looked about to jump out of their bas-relief—some enameled in white, with yellow manes, and others yellow with red manes. There were some sixty on each side. Their jaws were open in macabre welcome to the stranger entering the city.

Enkidu took it all in, hard pressed to keep from running ahead like a puppy to sniff out new wonders. There would be time for such touring, he knew—after he had found the temple of his god.

The ramparts thrust up again, mound on mound, tower on tower. Square. Powerful. Beautiful. At last: the Gate of Ishtar itself. He pressed on in, and found himself between two close walls.

This interval was lighted by sunlight from above. Enkidu looked up—and spied silhouettes of enormous kettles hanging beside myriad narrow slits. He shuddered: in time of war those frightful vats would be filled with boiling oil, and skilled archers would be stationed behind the embrasures. What army would dare to come against these ready instruments? Woe to the soldier who invoked the wrath of Ishtar, most powerful and temperamental of goddesses!

The walls below the skylights were at least forty feet above the stone pavement at the ground level. Enkidu felt like a toy figure in this lofty enclosure. The bricks were glazed, and superimposed on them were fantastic sculptures in relief: great snorting bulls, life sized, brilliantly enameled and seeming to charge out at the intruders. Alternating with these were dragons, their sinuous bodies writhing out, nostrils flaring, fangs threatening. Rank on rank of these captive animals lined the walls, dozens of them, sixties of them, each an individual masterpiece of decoration.

The inner door stood open—solid planks of cedar, covered at the edges with copper, with strong bronze hinges embedded in its surface.

Beyond this door lay Babylon.

And Aten.

Yes, it was impressive, NK-2 agreed. It was amazing what substantial edifices could be constructed of such crude base materials. Yet this society remained at least a millennium from the development of true space travel, unless phenomenal breakthroughs occurred.

He was tempted to extend his penumbra and check for Station A-10 directly—but as always the spectre of enemy presence inhibited him. He would be vulnerable when extended, and an enemy infiltrator would be well versed in detection and combat techniques. Better to stick well within the anonymous shelter of his host until he was quite certain of the station.

It wasn't as though this host lacked incentive. It would be impossible to *stop* the host from searching for A-10 at this point! NK-2 could well afford to ride. What was a few more hours, after sixteen years?

By evening Enkidu had not come upon Aten's temple, but his eagerness had not abated. There was so much to see! He still paused many times to stare up at Etemenanki, the towering ziggurat of seven colors that dominated the city's sky. His footsteps had taken him to the Temple of Marduk the Creator, richest of shrines—and on past it. Time enough later to present himself there. This day he would step up to the shrine of Aten himself, and Aten's would be the first temple in Babylon that he would enter. Yet where was this shrine? Merkes?

The Merkes was a closed residential district, the oldest part of the city. It had been planned in spacious squares—but the ancient builders had not reckoned on its now-teeming numbers. It was packed to overflowing with citizens.

Enkidu gaped at the houses. He had seen double-level dwellings before—but these were three and four stories high, with small walled gardens and, he presumed, deep wells in their courtyards. As he strode on in his quest, the houses became poorer. Some of their walls had partly fallen in, exposing the sun-baked bricks beneath the higher quality facing, and the roofs looked long unclayed. Could Aten's temple possibly be amid such debris?

He became aware that fewer people jostled him. The streets were clearing as men and women disappeared behind their red doors. It was late, and he was tired, and still he had not come upon the temple of his god!

He stepped onto an alleyway paved with flagstones well worn but firm, and saw that it led toward a temple. His spleen glowed once again with hope and he hastened his steps.

The altar faced the entrance. This was not Aten's temple! Alluring priestesses stared at him discreetly from beside it. This had to be the temple of Ishtar of Agade. Enkidu looked at it in mingled appreciation and consternation, feeling foolish. He resumed his search.

Lost in the city's splendors, exalted with his inner purpose, Enkidu had taken little thought for his night's lodging. He had expected to find the temple within this stupefying city, and now that he had failed he was out of sorts. His feet were sore from hours of walking on hot hard pavements. How could the day have fled so swiftly?

The tall, shabby houses cast long, long shadows, and the sky was darkening. Only a scattering of people were still abroad. He intercepted a hurrying townsman—a tanner's apprentice, from his smell and appearance—and inquired directly: what way should a stranger turn his feet in order to arrive at the Temple of Aten?

The youth's eyes widened. He drew back, gave a blank stare, and pushed on past Enkidu quickly.

Enkidu drew similar responses from the other folk of Babylon, what few he could find to ask.

Twilight came over the city. Stars began to sparkle like lamps being lit in distant windows. It occurred to Enkidu that he might be forced to defer his visit to Aten's temple until morning. He began to consider where he might lodge for the night.

The Temple of Marduk, of course. He would go there, present his credentials, accept their hospitality. He knew where Marduk was, at any rate.

Yet he was reluctant to visit Marduk first. Aten was the god who had drawn him to Babylon. Enkidu slowed his pace, considering his alternatives. Could he engage a room at an inn? For how much? He was not sure of the going rates in such a city. Despite his education, he remained a country lad. Still, he reasoned: half a shekel should be more than sufficient for a night's room and a meal or two. He had fifteen of the silver half-sheckel coins on his person, and three full shekels. And other things of value. He tightened his finger on his clay tablet and looked about him.

He saw only closed doors.

It was dark now. Countless stars were out, and the half-moon rode high in the sky. The luminous arch had dimly materialized, spanning the entire sky, fascinating him as it always did. The planet Ishtar glowed in the west, seeming as close as fruit ripe for the plucking.

The street was far from divine, in contrast. Its tomb-like silence was broken only by the scurryings of rats and the barks of stray dogs that competed for street scavengings.

Enkidu had passed one or two places that might be inns. He struck out northward.

But the gate that separated Merkes from the rest of the city was now closed and locked. Enkidu's shouts and bangings brought neither notice nor reply from the gatekeeper, if indeed there were one. Some system!

He would have to remain the night in Merkes.

He headed southward again with some vague plan of walking until morning or perhaps finding some place to sit or lie in the open, though he did not relish sullying his white cloak with the offal of the streets. But he was too tired to walk much longer, and it was not safe to stay out with one's silver. . . .

The streets continued to narrow as he moved on

with something like panic supplanting his weariness. The paving ended and the houses closed in to a solid mass, one connected to the next—windowless, forbidding, gloomy. The only evidence that life went on behind the palmwood doors was the occasional openings and spewing out of table refuse. The street was in fact buried in offal and debris. The leavings of countless eaten shellfish crackled underfoot, and each step was a hazard of broken bricks half buried in settled clay. In some places the street level rose above that of the door stills, for the street was built of trampled refuse.

He had just dodged another post-priandal emission when another footfall crackled not far distant. He peered toward the sound.

A figure was approaching him, but the moon was behind it so that he could not see it clearly.

Enkidu stood very still. No point in inviting the attentions of a possible cutpurse.

As the person approached he could just make out a long, plain tunic, but it concealed the bodily outlines. The face seemed smooth. A woman? He could not tell her age in the shadow.

She eyed him boldly, perhaps noting the richness of his cloak, the quality of cloth in his shawl, his knee-length tunic, his headband, and his soft leather sandals. Or was it his face she contemplated: the high-set eyebrows that people claimed lent his narrow face a look of half surprise, the dark brown eyes, the young man's beard that half-concealed his cleft chin? He knew he was not precisely handsome, of course; still—

"One shekel," she said. Enkidu realized that he had been approached by a prostitute.

He was in no mood for such wares. Moreover, she did not wear the mark of a registered courtesan of the Temple of Ishtar, so she was probably diseased. He turned away. All he wanted was a place to spend the night.

Reacting instantly to his look of distaste, she caught his arm. "Half a shekel."

Enkidu angrily shrugged off her hand. He was not trying to bargain! But then another thought struck him. "Where may a stranger spend the night?"

Her eyes appraised him cynically. "The night? Two shekels!"

He caught her meaning. "Not with you!" he grunted, at once embarrassed and exasperated. "I want to sleep—no more. A room for the night, alone."

She stared noncommittally until he brought out a bright shekel, its head of Nabonaid frowning in the shadow.

She took it without a word and turned. He followed her down the alley and into a nondescript dwelling. Even in the darkness of the inner passage he could see its degenerate state. The thin clay lining the walls had cracked and fallen down to be trampled into the dirt floor, and the unbaked bricks behind it were crumbling. They passed into a courtyard whose stench heralded the stacked tiles of an untended privy. Next to that, great jars were filled with water for drinking and household use. A standard arrangement. Crude steps cut into the courtyard wall led to the upper stories.

Enkidu wondered what kept the top floor from settling

down into the bottom, since the house was so close to collapse, but he took a breath and mounted the steps. It was only for a night. He took his blank room on the second floor, not even asking for a lamp.

Strange that this city, rich with its temples and palaces and ziggurats, should neglect the wants of its living masses. The silver and gold outlay for just one temple, out of the half-hundred in Babylon, could rebuild the entire Merkes. But the voices of the priests were ever louder than those of the needy.

As he removed his rich outer tunic so as not to foul it on the filthy palm-bough mattress on the floor Enkidu was glad he had no light. He could not see the racing roaches that he knew were disturbed and intrigued by his presence. He folded the tunic carefully, brushed a space clear with the side of his hand, and set the material down beside him. He weighted it with the clay tablet. His money pouch he kept on his body, not trusting it elsewhere.

As he lay in the silence, his nostrils pinched by the close odor of cramped quarters in this old city, of stale sweat and rind of milk spilled in the mattress, the droppings of rats and fat roaches, his hand reached out to touch the tablet beside him. As his long sensitive fingers passed over the wedge-shaped indentations in its surface, as he read it in the dark, the discomforts and ugliness of his surroundings faded.

This was the script that summoned him to a new position and made possible his search for a new god.

Babylon, whose ancient beginnings were lost in legend, was the city of gods. King Nabonaid, usurping his way to power six years after Nebuchadnezzar, was a scholarly, unpopular man, more concerned

with the religions of remote antiquity than with the
Persian menace of today. He had ordered the idols of
the realm brought to the capital. He stored the foreign gods in his own palace and allowed only the
deities of Babylon to remain in their temples. Enkidu
well understood the fury of the outlying worshipers
thus deprived of their holy objects, yet he sympa-
thized also with the king, who understood that there
were more gods than Marduk and who claimed to be
protecting them against the onslaughts of the barba-
rous Medes.

If the god Aten were in Mesopotamia, he had to be
here in Babylon. No idol of consequence had escaped
the summons of the king. That simplified his search.
No, Enkidu held no malice against Nabonaid!

Enkidu's eyes closed in silent worship and prayer.
Aten.

NK-2 extended his penumbra. The host was alone
now, making it safe, and asleep, making it easy. It
was necessary to remove his perceptions from confinement within the host periodically, lest he become
stunted. It was too easy to forget, during this extended habitation in a solitary wild animal, that his
essence was not physical. But for the fact that he
lacked most perceptions while discorporate, NK-2
would happily have spent the entire period free of
any host.

The stars were there: the host's recent memory
made them clear. Home!

But first he had to find Station A-10.

CHAPTER 4

Enkidu awoke, chilly and stiff, to the morning light filtering in from the bleak courtyard. He reached for his tunic—and learned the price he had paid for his lodging.

Tunic and tablet were gone.

He jumped up, snatching for his money pouch. It, too, was gone, its cord neatly cut. He was left with no more than his sandals and his coarse under-tunic. What an innocent he had proved to be!

The tablet—an illiterate harlot could have no use for that! Perhaps he could salvage some of his treasure. The money, of course, was gone—but that could be replaced, as could the tunic. But the tablet—

He dashed down the steps, almost tumbling, not pausing in the courtyard to splash his face with water.

He found it by the front door, carelessly tossed aside as valueless. Valueless! He exclaimed joyfully—but sobered instantly, for the cover was broken.

He contemplated this disaster, leaning against the wall in his undergarment. This tablet, stamped with the seals of the priests of Marduk, could not be replaced. It was a letter recommending the bearer as a scribe to the Temple of Marduk in Babylon. Such a letter, sealed in its clay envelope, was an inviolable guarantee. It could not be forged. With such a recommendation, his position in the Temple of Marduk was virtually assured. Without it—

Enkidu pressed his wrist against his forehead, as though to stave off his sudden anguish. A broken tablet was worthless. He would have to return to Calah for another, if he hoped to enter the service of the local priesthood. Calah was a month's journey distant, even with money and a camel.

He brushed off the inner section of the letter and tucked it and the cover fragments under his arm. His only chance was to find the woman and bring her before the priests of Marduk to testify to what she had done: stealing and breaking the tablet. This could hardly be the first time an innocent stranger had been robbed in Babylon; they might accept it, at least until confirmation was obtained from the Calah temple.

Daylight was new, but already the hawkers were in the streets, and with them the beggars and menials going about their business. Enkidu, too, had business this morning. He took note of the house's location and set out in search of authority.

The alleys of the Merkes differed sharply from the splendors of the Processional Way. Were both of them part of the same city?

His mishap *could* be set right, now that he had assessed the situation realistically. Cheered, Enkidu became aware of a wisp of savor. Fresh river fish, boiled in oil. The hearty appetite of youth asserted its claim. He had not eaten since early yesterday, and he was ravenous.

He followed the scent to a bandy-legged oldster hawking hot fish from a big tray balanced on his head. The savory river fish were almost under Enkidu's nose before he remembered that he had no wherewithal. He had a wild impulse to snatch a fish and make off with it. He half-raised his hand toward the tray. But it would be a great breach of dignity. Besides, the old man turned without warning; his sharp black eyes raked Enkidu up and down. He glared at the disheveled young man abroad in his undergarments, and moments later he was several paces down the street.

Enkidu found time to marvel as he passed up one smelly street and down another that the city was going about its business just as though Cyrus the Persian were no threat. Yet Cyrus was a fact that Babylon must one day reckon with. Probably soon. Even a futile siege was no laughing matter.

He found authority. Burly guards in the uniform of the King's service marched down the streets, herding before them a ragged multitude of beggars and thieves. Enkidu waited for the wailing multitude to pass, then stepped up to the nearest guard. This was a full-bearded veteran, scarred on bare arms and legs, with a conic helmet and a military tunic extending halfway down his brawny thighs. Heavily laced boots came up to the man's knees, and indeed his tread was solid.

"Well, what is it with you?"

"I must take a woman to the temple," Enkidu

said, finding the explanation awkward. "Her house is down the street, but she's gone—"

The trooper was unimpressed. "Plenty others," he grunted. "Just as good. Try Ishtar's temple."

"No. You see she broke my tablet—"

The soldier looked him over, noting his partial dress and tousled hair. "Broke your tablet?"

"She stole my tunic and my money, but it's the tablet that hurts the most," Enkidu explained. Then he began to understand the expression on the man's face.

"Broke your tablet!" the guard repeated. Laughter rumbled up from his deep throat. "So *that's* what you call it. Was it too brittle!"

Enkidu took his first serious look at the guard, instead of the uniform. He saw the incipient brutality of the man, the hard, glittering eyes, now screwed up with cynical mirth. He should have been alert for crude interpretations.

"I'll *bet* it hurt. . . ."

"My identification document," Enkidu said with what dignity he could salvage, and showed the tablet. Everywhere, it seemed, the unlettered were lewd. "The envelope has been violated. That's why I need—"

"Yeah," the guard said, still grinning. "That's what happens when you fool with these peasant sluts. Violated—" His face sobered at last. "All right, boy, we've had our little joke. Now just you get in line with the rest."

"You don't seem to understand—" Enkidu protested. But the man put his hand behind his pointed helmet, tilted it forward, and shoved him into the center of the street.

"What are you—"

He was rewarded by a sharp slap on the buttocks with the flat of a sword. "Get along now, boy," the guard said amiably. "Good food, good wine, good bathing up ahead!"

Enkidu found himself brutally herded with the motley crowd scrambling before the soldiers' prodding. The people were not, he now saw, quite the rabble he had supposed. Some men were emaciated, some diseased. One was too old to walk upright, another was blind. There were a few women: old, snaggle-toothed, bitter. The thing they all had in common was evident: extreme poverty. Bare feet, hollow cheeks, the men without headcloths and the women in rags, clad worse than slaves. Thieves were far better dressed than these!

Now he was one of them. Where were they being driven?

The stumbling group was herded out of the Merkes district to the avenue of Sin; it jogged south to the avenue of Marduk, out the gate of Marduk through Imgur-Bel, the lofty inner wall of Babylon, and on to a part of the outer city Enkidu had not seen the day before.

Enkidu took the blind man's arm, guiding him safely beyond the wide moat. The guards seemed indifferent to the fate of the ragged group of human refuse so long as it kept moving. Now they left the street and approached the dilapidated huts between the walls. Here was the slimy bank of the Kebar Canal.

"There!" a guard guffawed. "Eat and drink your fill!" A shove sent Enkidu sprawling knee deep in stagnant water. He choked on the overpowering stench of human excrement and other filth. All about him were mounds of sickening refuse. This, it was obvious, was the dump, the sewer, the emptying place for putrid garbage, animate and other. Vultures circled above.

"Mercy!" the blind beggar cried. "I will die here!"

The guard Enkidu had first encountered grasped the man's frail tunic, tearing it. He shoved, and the victim tumbled backward into the canal, there to splash helplessly until others waded into the foul water to pull him out.

Enkidu had been too stunned, too confused, and too ignorant to protest effectively when first mistaken for these people. Now he realized that he *was* one of them, in spirit, and this treatment was beyond toleration. Before he could think things out properly, he was charging up the slippery bank, sandals lost in the muck.

The powerful guard was just turning away as Enkidu bashed at him with the tablet and knocked that conical helmet askew. The hardened clay shattered, forever destroying the message upon it, but he was too excited to care. He grabbed for the guard's sword, looking into the man's dazed and angry face.

Something struck him from behind.

The soldiers were methodical and very careful. Enkidu never quite lost consciousness. Only when they stripped him and spotted the mark on his shoulder did the expert application of pain cease. Then, finally, they allowed him to slump to the ground, retching and spewing up the watery contents of his unfed stomach, while they huddled in conference.

They had not suspected that their captive bore the spade—the brand of a slave to the Temple of Marduk.

CHAPTER 5

The Southern Citadel was a vast complex of buildings set in the northern section of the city not far from the Ishtar Gate. To the west was the Euphrates, to the east the Processional Way. Enkidu, filthy, bloody, and bruised, was taken to the Citadel and on into the palace of the King by the Gate of Beltis. Basalt lions crouched at this main entry, silently roaring their defiance at the passers-by.

They passed directly into the first of five great open courts. Here there was frenzied activity as guards and royal servants rushed about on urgent errands. Tourists gaped at the brightly colored lion friezes done in enameled brick. Free-lance scribes, both Babylonian and Egyptian, squatted near the gateway. Passages led off in all directions, opening to the quarters reserved for the palace garrison, domestic and administrative offices, and the King's private apartments.

". . . but I cannot possibly pay five shekels a year!" a citizen protested as they passed. "My donkey is lame, it has been a poor year for barley, irrigation is silted . . ." But the stern tax assessor was unmoved, just as a similar official had been to Enkidu's own father. As such officers had always been, Enkidu thought, and always would be, as long as empires existed and there were men to be exploited and gods who were not merciful. The regime *wanted* to keep the peasants in debt!

The gods must approve, for they were not far away. These were some of the trophies of war and policy, making the palace of Nabonaid beautiful at the price of distant anguish. He glanced at the plaque under one: a stele of Teshut, bearer of the North Wind—a Hittite deity, according to the inscription. But he saw no representation of Aten.

A guard jerked him savagely forward. "Move!" Enkidu's hands were bound now, and he stumbled to keep the pace. They entered one of the bordering offices, and there at last he was allowed to rest.

The ceiling was high and the room, though dwarfed by the larger space of the palace, was spacious in its own right. The magistrate's desk stood against the far wall, facing wooden benches. A heavy metal ring was set into the floor before it. Unruly prisoners, he realized uncomfortably, were likely to find themselves securely fastened there.

The magistrate was a substantial figure in an elaborate silken robe, his head bound in a small turban. Wealth spoke in his clothing, his ornate copper bracelets, his well fed and superior demeanor. There would be little mercy from this man for those who could not buy it.

A few spectators sat on the hard benches and a young court scribe squatted with his jar of moist clay beside him. A few guards had stationed themselves in the back row near the door. A woman sat a little apart, her face shadowed. Her clothing concealed her figure; he could not tell if she were young or old. For an instant he thought it was the thieving prostitute, but quickly saw that it was not. A man stood in the rear, robed in black, invisible in the depths of a black cowl.

The magistrate lifted a bored countenance as Enkidu was hauled before the bench. Thick fingers toyed with the embroidery on the breast of his robe. "What is the charge?"

"Runaway slave, sir," the guard replied respectfully.

"Oh?" The little eyes lightened with sudden cruel interest. They appraised Enkidu. "Worth much?"

"I'm no slave!" Enkidu protested angrily.

"He bears the brand of Marduk," the guard said, spinning Enkidu around so that the magistrate could see his shoulder. "A northern escapee, from his speech."

"This whole thing is ridiculous!" Enkidu cried.

"Well fed, healthy," the magistrate agreed, ignoring the prisoner's outbursts. "No outdoor menial."

"The Temple should offer a handsome reward," the guard observed. "We can turn him in to the local office."

"Why won't you listen!" Enkidu shouted, flustered. "I'm no slave! I—"

"The Temple of Marduk can afford the best," the

magistrate agreed. "But there appear to be some bruises."

The guard smiled. "He—fell. That's why he stinks so. Nothing serious."

"That's a lie!" Enkidu yelled. "I'm here on legitimate business. I asked this oaf for help and he threw me in the Kebar Canal and beat me. Now he's trying to—"

The guard's hand fell heavily on his shoulder. "Slave, are you accusing an officer of the King's Sanitation Guard of abuse of his authority?"

Enkidu glanced wildly at the magistrate and saw only amused interest in the porcine countenance. The spectators were openly eager; they leaned forward. Justice was a forlorn hope. He tried to think clearly in spite of the rage boiling up in him. Perhaps the truth might spare him further indignity. "I am a temple scribe."

There was a mild commotion in the courtroom. The local scribe looked up. The woman stood, as though ready to come forward. The guard looked astonished.

"He *did* say something about a"—the guard stifled a grin—"tablet. I remember now."

"A temple scribe," the magistrate murmured. "*You*, a slave?"

Enkidu nodded. At last they were listening!

"Are you aware that the sons of kings hardly aspire to more?"

"The class of scribes," Enkidu said, "is open to all who have the talent. Not all kings' sons have—"

The magistrate cut off Enkidu and the growing

chuckle of the audience. "No scribe would remain a slave. Why did you not buy your freedom?"

It was a trick question. Everyone knew that an intelligent slave could be trained as a scribe; even women were not denied, the few who had the necessary capacity. But no scribe of any competence needed to remain a slave, unless so valuable that he was forbidden to earn his redemption. They were casting their net for a large reward.

Enkidu had no doubt of his value. He had paid a high price for his freedom. But it was less easy to cancel a brand than to place it on the skin, and he had balked at the crude and painful surgery required to remove it. He had depended on the sealed tablet to verify his status as a free scribe—the tablet that had been invalidated and lost.

He could not prove that he was not a slave.

"He's lying," the soldier said. "Look at him— you can see he's too stupid to write."

It was a crude gambit that nonetheless angered Enkidu. "Untie my hands and I'll demonstrate."

This was of course exactly what they wanted, and he was soon obliged. He walked to the court scribe, lifted the fresh tablet from his hands together with the stylus, and made a rapid series of characters across its moist surface. *Since when do pigs wear silk and copper?* He placed it on the magistrate's bench while everyone in the room watched curiously.

The official huffed redly. He could not, as Enkidu had suspected, read. He was embarrassed to have this so publicly demonstrated. Low laughter sounded in the courtroom as he summoned the public scribe and returned the tablet. "Read it."

The other scribe looked at the words. He swallowed. "Well?" the magistrate demanded.

The scribe backed off, rubbing the message out with the heel of his hand. "It is of no account."

"*I'll* make the judgment!"

"Tell him what it says," Enkidu insisted innocently.

"I—" the scribe faltered. "It—"

"Idiot! Does it make sense or doesn't it?"

The scribe seemed most unhappy. "Yes, sir. But—"

"Yes *what?*"

The guard stepped up. "I can loosen his tongue," he volunteered confidently. The scribe retreated in alarm.

The woman in the corner spoke. "Why not," she inquired, "put it to the author? Surely he knows what he wrote."

The spectators were openly laughing now, much to Enkidu's satisfaction. He was getting his own back in his small way! "I am happy to honor the lady's request. She is obviously more intelligent than some." He inclined his head slightly toward the magistrate with an implication the gleeful spectators did not miss. Already more were sidling in the door, attracted by the show. "I merely commended his honor the magistrate on his elegant taste in clothing."

That worthy sensed the irony but could not afford to acknowledge it. He faced the scribe. "True?"

"Oh yes, yes, certainly," the man said immediately, anxious to change the subject. "Pig and copper—" he choked, realizing his slip. "He knows the script, without doubt."

"But he's still a runaway—a valuable one," the guard insisted triumphantly.

"I am not a runaway!" Enkidu shouted. He knew it was a mistake to play their game, yet he was unable to school his temper after all he had been through. "I bought my freedom. You can't hold me for reward. There isn't any."

The magistrate glared at the swelling mass of grinning faces. "Fetch me a temple priest!" he snapped to a functionary. He returned to Enkidu. "If you're not a runaway, what mission brings you to Babylon?"

"I came to find Aten."

Most spectators did not react, but the hooded figure stood quickly and came forward. A resonant voice sounded from within the deep cowl. "What is your interest in that name?"

NK-2 realized that something was seriously amiss. His host had rationalized A-10 into a god-figure, having no other way to comprehend the imposed incentive to locate the station. But no other native should react to the word similarly. Unless it was host to a similar entity. . . .

The vicissitudes of primitive police and primitive court procedures had been annoying, though not immediately relevant. His host had handled himself well enough so far. But his use of his vocalization "Aten" should have elicited no informed response. The fact that the cowl obviously recognized the term could only mean that the cowl was, indeed, host to the station representative. His search was over!

NK-2 began to extend his penumbra, for he was unable to make contact without it, except by direct physical contact.

A presence was there.

Enemy!

NK-2 withdrew instantly. Trouble indeed! He had forgotten his caution and exposed himself dangerously. He only hoped the enemy agent had not spotted him, or if it had, had not identified the host. There was no way to locate a specific host from the penumbra alone; only direct touch could verify that. Yet the enemy should have a pretty clear notion from the context, just as NK-2 himself did—if the enemy had been aware of the momentary intersection of penumbras.

But the implication! *The enemy had located Station A-10!*

The cowl-host must have been set to intercept NK-2—or any other galactic who tried to reach the station.

All he could do at the moment was remain tightly barricaded within his host, taking no part in the courtroom activities. Until the cowl was gone. Only after he had eluded the enemy could he set about locating the station.

"What business is that of yours?" Enkidu snapped. For a moment he had felt—something. But that was gone now, and he was thoroughly tired of this court and of his predicament.

The magistrate smiled at Enkidu's words, not pleasantly, but said nothing. This meant even more trouble. Yet if the cowl knew something of his god—

Suddenly the woman was between them. Startled, Enkidu allowed her to take him by the arm as she directed a plea to the bench. "Give me this man—

until the priest of Marduk comes. I will return him to you.''

The magistrate hesitated, glancing at the cowl. But this woman seemed to have some authority, for he shrugged heavily and said, ''Put your seal on this order, then.''

The woman took a small ceramic cylinder from a cord about her neck and pressed it to the tablet that the scribe held out. She rolled it under her finger so that it left an oblong imprint in the damp clay: a miniature picture in relief, the length and breadth of a large toe. Enkidu caught a glimpse of the representation of Ishtar the goddess holding in her two hands Ishtar the planet. Then she grasped his arm again and steered him outside the courtroom.

Had a third party stepped in to save him? He would soon know.

''I didn't know the roll-seals were still in use,'' Enkidu said, fingering his own stamp-seal in some frustration. He did not wish to inquire directly where she was taking him or for what purpose. She was a tall woman, with pleasing curvature hinted by her motions within the tunic. On her wrists were ornate open bracelets, the ends fashioned into the likenesses of lions.

''A few,'' she said noncommittally. ''The Persians use them, and they will presently be coming back into fashion.''

''The Persians or the roll-seals?''

''Both.'' She changed the subject. ''What did you write on that tablet?''

''I wouldn't repeat it to a gentle lady.''

''Such tricks are apt to get you impaled on a very

long, very sharp stake," she said seriously. Enkidu blanched, a sudden vision of the impaled felon on the north highway presenting itself. He hadn't thought of that, and wished she hadn't reminded him.

He had led too sheltered a life. He had to school himself to realize that he was not a free agent at the moment. Justice was hard on strangers, and Babylonian justice could be sharply pointed. He rubbed his rear reflexively.

"I see that you understand," she murmured. "That's one reason I interceded. You are too independent for a slave. You have forgotten that this is Babylon, where runaways are not coddled. Your value as a scribe will not protect you."

"I'm not a slave!"

Her eyes studied him. They were almond shaped, set in a mature but handsome face. "You are *now,*" she pointed out. "They won't let you go without their reward."

"There *is* no reward!"

She cautioned him with a gesture. "In a moment. Now—follow me and try to look like a eunuch."

Astonished, Enkidu did his best to comply. After the recent beating he had absorbed this wasn't so much of a feat.

She had taken him to the northwest section of the palace grounds, where a small hill rose—the only hill he had seen in this flat land. They mounted a long series of steps to a walled structure about fifty paces long. The wall was of stone—unusual in this rockless land of the twin rivers.

The steps climbed the side of the wall, turned, and

passed through a gap. Guards stood aside and Enkidu's guide passed through. Inside was foliage.

They were in the hanging gardens! Palms grew in alcoves set in an inner wall, and exotic plants flourished in carefully tended plots. Steps went up to a higher level. The woman took her seat on a sheltered bench and gestured for him to join her.

"Who *are* you?" he asked. "I thought only the King's harem was allowed here."

She smiled indulgently. "Have I given you cause to think otherwise, innocent outlander?" Her features were delicate and fair in this light, her hair like barley before the harvest. She must be of northern stock; he had heard these people were fair. She was comely, certainly.

"Am I still a eunuch?"

She laughed. "Perhaps when you are clean I shall be able to tell." She summoned him to a fountain springing from the wall nearby and made him duck his head in the flowing water. "I am Tamar. That is much of what you need to know." She cleaned his face and hair with a delicate cloth. "You have been beaten," she observed. "What was the provocation?"

He told her of the events of the night and the morning. As he talked he became acutely conscious of the nearness of her body as her tunic pulled tight beneath her reaching arms. Once her shrouded breast brushed his shoulder, and he knew that the contact had not been accidental.

"Those are the scavengers of Rimut, watchdog of the King," she said. "Every day they comb through the city searching out the poor, the infirm, victims of plague or other useless creatures and herd them out of the city. This is lawful. Stay clear of them. Now the feet.''

It was a bit late to advise him to stay clear; he had already been dumped in the Kebar! Enkidu dipped his bare and battered feet into the coolness. Tamar rinsed her cloth and to his great embarrassment began to wipe away the crusted dust and dung. He had been barefoot since the canal episode, and the gentle cleansing was a luxury.

''Why was your tablet so important?'' she asked next. ''Perhaps it was broken—but couldn't someone have put the pieces together in order to read the message?''

''It is plain you are no scribe,'' he said. She shot him a sultry look and began to scrub his knees. He went on quickly, before she could decide that his tunic also needed washing. ''I mean, you probably believe that a person's signature, the stamp of his seal, is a guarantee that the document is genuine. It is true that the signature of the originator and of the witnesses cannot be forged; but the document could still be altered. Any scribe could scratch in an extra wedge or two and change the entire meaning. Must you do that?''

She was now well above the knees. ''No,'' she said judiciously, ''I don't believe you are a eunuch, after all.'' But she had mercy and ceased her upward spiraling.

''So the original tablet is protected with an envelope,'' Enkidu continued, all too conscious of the truth of her observation. ''This is merely another layer of clay, the thickness of a wafer. It is wrapped around the original and sealed. Then the identical document is inscribed on the surface of the envelope, and the witnesses impress their signatures just as before. Once letter and envelope harden—''

Gently she led him on around the tiers of the garden, past strange blooms and flowing irrigation channels. Where, he wondered, did the water come from? And why was he allowed here? He glanced about, half expecting the guards to realize their mistake and come to make him a eunuch in fact as well as name.

"But it should be easy to break open the envelope, change the message, then make a new envelope to match," Tamar pointed out. "Oh—but I had forgotten the seals."

"That's right. An unprotected document can be forged—but not the seals on the envelope. And since the clay shrinks as it dries, a fresh envelope on a tablet already hardened always cracks open. You cannot tamper with such a document."

"But the envelope on your tablet was destroyed—''

"Making the document suspect. The temple priests would not even have bothered to read it."

"It follows, then, that you are either an unemployed man or a runaway slave."

"It follows," he agreed, glumly.

She brought him to a halt beside a leaning date-palm. "My handsome young friend, you are in even greater trouble than you suspect. Let me explain."

"But the priests at Calah will inquire if they do not hear from me, and they will verify that—''

She grasped his elbows with both hands and brought her lovely face close. "Listen to me, innocent scribe," she said quietly but rapidly. "I know Babylon as you do not. You were a fool to delay your approach to the priesthood here for even one day. You could easily have toured the city after you were settled, with your money and your position secured. You were twice a fool to dally with a common harlot"— she waved aside his attempted disclaimer—"and to spend the night at her mercy. You were thrice a fool to argue with the sanitation squad, which brooks no interference in its purging of the city. And four times a fool you were to make the magistrate in court look like the fool he is. He will now be your enemy. But your crowning idiocy—"

"Aten protect me!" he murmured contritely.

Her eyes flashed. *"That* is the stupidity that will cost you everything," she cried, then immediately hushed her voice. "You uttered that name in public, where Amalek heard you. Where is your sense of—?"

"Aten? But he is my god!"

She dipped her head and beat gently against his chest. "Ten times a fool!" she exclaimed. *"Don't* say that name again. There is no temple in Babylon for this god you seek. Instead there is a mystery cult, nameless and obscure, that will stop at nothing to stamp out that name from either public or private knowledge."

NK-2, deep buried yet listening, came abruptly alert. This was the action of the enemy, surely—but to what conceivable purpose? Station A-10 would under no circumstances indulge in local politics; it existed solely as a contact point for galactics. The enemy should have no need to expunge it this way. Far easier to dissipate the galactic representative outright, irrespective of native repercussions. What was going on?

"The hooded one—Amalek you called him?—just what is his authority?" Enkidu asked after a pause.

Tamar shrugged. "He is the go-between—the emissary of the nameless temple to the palace of the King. He will surely buy you and take you to their chief inquisitor, Sargan. You have uttered the forbidden name. You will not be seen on the streets of Babylon again. That's why I—"

"Buy me? Kill me?" Enkidu was horrified. "How can he get away with that?"

"The magistrate is greedy, and you have embarrassed him. He will declare you to be a runaway slave. Amalek will offer a generous price. The priest of Marduk will stamp his approval, since you bear the spade of Marduk, and he will pocket a share of the profit. That way there will be no loss if you turn out not to be a slave: the transaction is complete and authorized by all parties. I have seen such things happen before. Your little temple at Calah will not venture to oppose that of Babylon."

There was a dismaying ring of truth to her words and logic. "Why did you bring me here? To help me escape?"

She sighed. "You are a country innocent, and I would like nothing better than to take you away to safety. But I would be in rather hot oil myself, since my own seal is on the record. Nevertheless I am going to help you. The chance of success is narrow, but—"

"Who are you?" Enkidu demanded, suddenly

suspicious. "Why should you interest yourself in helping me, especially if my prospects are as poor as you say? What brought you to that court in the first place?"

"Let us just say I have a foolish sentiment for fools. It is fortunate that King Nabonaid has thrown these palace gardens open to, uh, us, during Marduk's festival; it gives me a place to try to talk some sense into you. Now we'll have to do this immediately. Much longer and they'll be suspicious."

"Do what?"

"Get married, of course. Fortunately I know a priest of Marduk who will—"

Enkidu was too astonished to say a word. Could this woman actually want to marry him, after calling him a five-fold fool and proving it? She would be marrying a slave, and one with bad prospects. It did not make any sense at all.

She mistook his expression of doubt. "I am a free woman, and unmarried, I assure you. Now we must hurry."

Enkidu tagged after her, finding his tongue at last. "But there has been no betrothal," he said stupidly. "Your father—"

"I have no father, no brother," she replied sharply. "Ishtar will give me away—the goddess of love."

"And of battle," Enkidu murmured.

They came to a break in the beauty of the terraced gardens. Leather pails, heavy with water, dripped as they were hauled up along a system of pulleys. Slaves guarded their journey, sweating as they transferred the pails to a new pulley and hauled on the ropes. This was the origin of the irrigation streamlets trickling down the conduits: ropes and muscles. All the laborers were eunuchs.

Tamar found what she was searching for: a sheltered alcove cut into the wall beside the bucket system. Inside was the overseer, a priest of Marduk, with his clerk. Tamar explained her business tersely.

The priest seemed to be a friend of hers. He nodded. He then barked orders to his clerk, who set to work imprinting a tablet. Tamar took Enkidu by the hand and led him before the tiny altar set into the stone.

"But—?" Endkidu began.

"We don't have time," Tamar whispered. "Save your questions for later."

He marveled even as it was happening that he accepted her initiative so readily. How could he understand her motives and his own? Perhaps he was merely responding to her certainty, since he had been raised as a slave. He took the loose veil of Tamar in his hand and put it up to cover her face in the symbolic gesture of marriage. "She is my wife," he said. That made it so.

They stamped their seals in the tablet together with those of the priest and the scribe. The seals were stamped again in the soft clay envelope. The priest gave them the blessing of Marduk, greatest of gods, and the ceremony was over. Enkidu had a wife.

Tamar took the tablet in her hands and hid it under her tunic. "Now we must return," she said.

"You worship Ishtar," he said as she urged him along, remembering the bracelet. The lion was Ishtar's symbol.

She glanced at him, amused. "If it has breasts, it

worships Ishtar.'' Then she became serious. ''You'll find that Ishtar can do more for you—and in more ways—than Marduk, king of the gods though he thinks he is. Ishtar is the true ruler of Babylon. Remember that, when you need help. Ishtar is always present.'' She halted, struck by a new thought. She removed her bracelet and handed it to him. ''My dowry. Keep it with you always, Tammuz.''

CHAPTER 6

The cell was dark and dank and silent. Its gray gloom was broken only by the scuffle of rats' feet.

For a long time Enkidu lay where he had fallen when the eunuch had shoved him into the black hole and departed with his stone-oil lamp. His bruises weighed heavily on him now. He clutched his seal, the most positive token remaining of his identity.

Why had he fought the court proceedings, antagonizing the fat magistrate? Why did he always fight? Why was he unable to accept his lot, just or unjust, as other people did, and make things easier on himself? He had been raised as a slave; why did he persist in thinking of himself as a man?

In the darkness he saw the shape of his answer: the great beneficent outline that was all he could now picture of Aten. A lesser god, a tortured god, a suppressed god—but still a god, a genuine one, whose radiance would rise again.

"Aten," he said. But there was no answer.

He tried to see Aten more clearly in his mind. This was not easy, for he had no brazen idol to recall. He could command only sensation, an urge to reach that sunlike presence. But it seemed to him that he felt Aten—faintly, distantly, an impulse in the air, the walls, even within himself.

"I will always worship you, Aten," he said. "I will always search for your radiance. As a foolish child I believed in a *shedu*, but now I am grown. I will find you and swell your power again with the fatness of many worshippers."

A nameless unease pervaded the recesses of his mind at the thought, but dissipated before he could examine it. There was much he did not understand about his god.

It was time to explore his prison. His hands slid about on the floor as he tried to lift himself. His fingers flinched from the cold slime. What dung was he touching?

He gained his feet and stepped carefully back to the door by which he had entered. He found it: clammy immovable metal. His fingers explored the wall on either side, feeling the ridges outlining the small bricks. Baked bricks, too hard for him to attack with his bare hands. No use trying to wash these away with water.

He was hungry; he had not eaten this day. Was he to die here of starvation? "Aten," he said; but the god was prisoned too.

Disheartened, he felt his way around the cell. It was lower at the far end, and here his toes squished in slime. This disgusted him, for he had some idea of its nature and there were cuts on his feet that might offer entrance into his body to the evil genii that lurked in such refuse, but he made himself go on. There was stench as of the Kebar Canal.

He knew that breathing became difficult in a confined space, though why this was so was a mystery. The stink here was bad, but he had not felt that peculiar discomfort of the sealed or overcrowded room. Some breath might come from the door—but was there some other opening? Some escape?

He continued the search. There was no exit below; otherwise the rank offal should have drained and become firm. But there did seem to be a slight breeze, just enough for his wet fingers to detect. If only he could see!

How had he come here? The priests of Marduk he had known at Calah would never have treated a man this way! Even the one who had taken him into slavery as a child had acted wholly within the law, canceling the legitimate debt of his father. And the local priest who had blessed his marriage to Tamar in the gardens—*he* had not sneered at a seeming slave! Why, then, had the priest who arrived at the court been so callous? That one had not been at all concerned with the truth. He had been eager to sell Enkidu for a fee that surely exceeded that recorded on the tablet. Corruption reached even into Marduk's temple, where the god was certain to know!

How could Marduk smile on both just and unjust? One priest or the other should have been struck dead!

Enkidu could not doubt either Marduk's existence or his strength. Marduk had overcome savage Asshur in battle. He had granted his people of Babylon power to destroy Nineveh. He had sent Nebuchad-nezzar to conquer the city-states of the west. He had razed the walls of Jerusalem and forced its people into bondage, while their ally Egypt feared to intervene.

Those Hebrews even now resided in squalor and slavery along the banks of the Kebar. They clung to their quaint customs and to their own little god, Adonai, despite his impotence before Marduk. One had only to look at Etemenanki, the towering ziggurat, "House of the Foundation of Heaven and Earth," to realize that the works of Marduk dwarfed all else.

Yet—how great was a god who permitted such corruption? Marduk's house was divided and it was bound to fall. Marduk might well follow Asshur, and mighty would be the crash thereof, and great the anguish of fair Babylon.

His thoughts were interrupted by the metal gate. He had completed his circuit of the cell and found nothing. No break in the hardness of the bricks.

"Ah, Aten," he whispered, "it goes hard with us." He listened for some response, but heard only the scrabble of rats.

Rats! As if he didn't have problems enough! The scavengers were busy the moment he stopped moving. They were living creatures like himself, but here by choice.

His breath caught. Surely the rats had some entrance! Legend had it that they were generated from the heat of the refuse in which they dwelt, but he didn't believe that. Maggots, yes, rats, no. They were too big. They must have a passage.

They must have a hole at ground level. Perhaps a

little tunnel leading from cell to cell and terminating in the sunshine. . . .

But he was too tired to make another circuit, especially one through filth on hands and knees. He had to rest.

What a day it had been! Robbed in the morning, driven to the Kebar, beaten, hauled into court, married to a lovely but mysterious woman he had never seen before, and finally sold back into slavery and thrown into this cell!

Was he really a husband? Or was that ceremony a dream born of his confusion? He had no need of a wife, particularly not one who called him a fivefold fool and made him a sixfold fool by sending him on to such a cell without even a kiss. What possible motive could she have had? Did she *want* a husband she would never see again? To stave off a forced marriage to some foreign dignitary, perhaps?

The more he thought about it, the less he liked it. He might have misjudged the priest at the gardens; the man might have abetted what he had known was some rank political maneuver. Yes.

His hand touched the lion bracelet of Ishtar. Why had she given him a thing of such value, then? She had claimed to be marrying him because it was the only way she could save his life—yet she had not kept him out of prison. And what had she called him, there at the end?

Tammuz.

He knew that name, of course. The legend had been one of Tupshar's favorite writing assignments, at the scribe school. Tammuz had been Ishtar's beloved, but he had died. She had descended to Hades to reclaim him for the land of the living.

But of course Tamar was no Ishtar, and he was no Tammuz. She would hardly brave this Hades to rescue him!

Yet the memory of her stirred his senses. Her face was flawless, and so must be her body under the concealing clothing.

NK-2 stretched, extending his penumbra cautiously. He did not want to encounter cowled Amalek, the enemy host, again! Or any other entity. But it was necessary for him to spread out every so often to relieve the confinement of a single host.

That host needed help, obviously. He would never locate Station A-10 while trapped here. NK-2 could probably instruct him how to escape—but that would exhaust NK-2 himself, and leave him helpless against the enemy. That would be no gain! Yet if the host did *not* escape, he might be killed, and that would be the end for both of them.

Compromise was necessary. NK-2 had to conserve his own resources, but he also had to guide the host. If he jogged the host's mental processes at key spots, he might guide him with a minimum expenditure of energy.

Why *had* that native female married his host?

Morning. Enkidu forgot his stiff limbs and sore ribs. There was light! It was a ray of comfort from Aten himself from a tiny slit in the cell's high ceiling.

He was hungry. Now he saw what his hands had somehow missed before. There was a small alcove set in the door, passing through it, and inside it was food. He reached into it and found a gross flat hunk of bread and a jar of water.

Cautiously he wiped his fingers off on his tunic and strained them over the surface. There was, as he had expected, a floating insect or two. The food was very likely corrupted by noxious genii eager to produce disease, but at least they didn't plan to starve him.

He took some pains to repeat the exorcism against sickness of the entrails, flatulency and the rest; it could do no harm to observe this precaution, though he was no priest. For good measure he also said over the exorcism against the various pustules, poisons, and the food that returns after being eaten. Then he drank. The water was tepid but tolerable, and the bread better than he had expected. No doubt the exorcism had improved it.

Ouch! He removed the end of a hard weed stalk from his mouth and flipped it to the floor in disgust. He had prided himself too soon on his exorcisms!

With the bread in his stomach he felt stronger. Should he break the water jar and use its sharp shards to scrape a hole or pry loose a brick? No. Such a tactic would only summon ungentle guards, and he hurt enough already. The same for returning the jar to the shelf filled with urine. Best simply to behave and wait.

Meanwhile there was more positive work to be done. He meant to find that rat hole. He could not see it, but it must be there. How could he run it down?

He now recalled a useful mystery: when one hard

object struck another, sound came forth; and as the objects changed the sound also changed. A hollow jug spoke in a different voice than a full jug. Would the same hold true for hollow bricks, or even loose ones?

Strange he should think of that. . . .

Enkidu took off the bracelet of Ishtar and put his fingers over the snarling lions. He did not wish to damage the craft that had gone into their fashioning, much less offend the goddess herself. And it would be unkind to deface the gift his bride had given him. But the metal backside was suitable, and could not be easily damaged. He stooped and tapped it against a brick.

Tap-tap, tap-tap, interminably. By the time he had covered the wall beside the door his arm was tired. He went on around the corner. All remained solid. His legs and back were now protesting, but he drove himself on. It was the only way he could flee the growing hopelessness of his situation.

He had to rest at last. He was getting nowhere.

Tap-tap, he heard. *Tap-tap*. The search went on, even though he was not—

His breath stopped. Suddenly alert, he put his ear to the wall. *Tap-tap. Tap-tap*. It was coming from the other side!

Someone was answering him!

Why hadn't he thought of signaling? Of course there would be other prisoners here, as anxious as he was to regain their freedom. He had inadvertently stumbled on the obvious.

Inadvertently? He looked at Ishtar's token. Had the goddess herself chosen to help him, then?

The tapping stopped. Quickly he leaned down and rapped the brick, in a different pattern. Tap-tap-tap, tap-tap-tap. . . .

He waited. *Tap-tap-tap, tap-tap-tap*. He had made contact!

A different sound checked his experiment at this point: the heavy tread of approaching guards. Had they come to remove the jar—or to remove him? Suddenly he wanted to stay exactly where he was.

The bar-fastening lifted; the gate swung open. A great man-shape stood outlined in the flicker of a lamp held by another person beyond. Man-shaped, but not a man.

The eunuch had come to take him away. "Come," he boomed, scowling.

"Who summons me?" Enkidu retorted with probative boldness.

White teeth flashed in a dark countenance. *"I* summon you. I, Dishon, torturemaster of this nameless temple."

Suddenly Enkidu did not feel like antagonizing this creature. His bravado deserted him. His heart hammered. He was afraid of physical pain, so that he had left the slave-brand rather than endure the momentary physical agony of its expunction, and thus gotten himself into this fix. He could never stand up to torture.

"Aten protect me!" he implored in a whisper as he came forward.

Dishon heard him. "Better ask the protection of no god, since no god exists."

Enkidu looked at him, surprised. "I—I had thought perhaps you worshiped Ishtar." Some of the rites of Ishtar shocked outsiders; Enkidu was an outsider.

Some men undertook public castration, dedicating themselves to her service. Goddess of love she was, and of fecundity—but also goddess of death. Mutilation and torture were as much a part of her worship as was the passion of her votive temple courtesans.

"Ishtar?" Dishon's laughter barked. His huge hand shoved Enkidu forward. He wore heavy leather gloves, virtual gauntlets. That must be his business uniform, protection against spattering blood and flying teeth.

Enkidu clutched his bracelet, feeling nauseous. Ishtar was present here—but she was not his deity. She had no need of his worship, and would not protect him.

The passage was long and dim. He stumbled after the slack-jawed, narrow-headed lamp-bearer, past other cells, and finally up rough brick steps to a second gate. It was lighter here, but Enkidu had no glimpse of the outside. He was propelled down a wider hallway to a chamber at the end. Here there was a brighter light—but the moving shadows cast by the lamps in the niches only made the room more ominous. Enkidu fancied he saw gouges and knives and hot irons, but those were merely products of his fear.

The lamplight glinted on the wall, on the myriad fragments of some intricate mosaic. There seemed to be some pattern to it, yet when he tried to pick it out his mind balked, for the glints were like stars in the night sky.

Directly in front of the mosaic stood a table fashioned of aromatic imported cedarwood, and on this was—no, not a water-torture device, but a waterclock, a clepsydra. A suspended ceramic jar with a small opening in the bottom from which water steadily dripped. A slender copper tube caught the drops and a float gradually rose as the lower water level climbed. A thin rod passed from this through a fulcrum and marked the time of day against a panel.

To the right of the clepsydra sat a figure he recognized: Amalek. Now his face was clearly visible within the cowl. Before him was a papyrus scroll and a reed pen with a small pot of ink. Enkidu had investigated Egyptian writing as a matter of curiosity, but found it so far inferior to wedge-script as to be worthless. Papyrus would burn, and there could be no genuine protection from forgery since there was no hardened clay envelope. Strange that these people should prefer the foreign script to real writing!

At the other side of the table sat a taller figure, in white, also cowled, and this face was almost completely concealed. Only the eyes peered out malevolently.

Dishon heaved Enkidu forward into a red stone circle set into the dull tiles of the floor. "Stand!" the eunuch directed, but there was nowhere to sit. "Answer when addressed!" but no one addressed him. What was coming next?

Presently Amalek spoke. "Give your name and place of birth."

Was this another trial? Enkidu started to protest, then remembered the torturemaster. "I am Enkidu, son of Hadru, of a village near Calah on the Tigris."

"Your age?"

"I was born the year Nebuchadnezzar died."

Amalek nodded, referring to the scroll. "He would be twenty-two, perhaps twenty-three." The white man neither moved nor spoke in response. "Status and employment?"

"Free scribe of the Temple of Marduk. Prisoner of persons unknown, illegally."

This was dangerous bait, but Amalek did not rise to it. "Why did you come to Babylon?"

"I thought my god was here." Enkidu would not be silenced on this score, and he always preferred to speak the direct truth. "Aten."

The white hood jerked up, its glistening eyes stabbing at him. Amalek lifted his pen, dipped it in ink, and made an entry on his scroll.

"Be advised," Amalek said, "that you have spoken heresy. It is our intent to show you your error and return your attention to matters proper to the laity."

"Because I worship Aten?" Enkidu demanded incredulously. He had hardly believed what Tamar had told him, before.

"Aten is a false god," Amalek said evenly. "That to which you pretend is impossible."

Enkidu looked at the grim figures beside the waterclock, then at the exotic frieze glinting behind them with its alien midnight sky. These must be formless genii, inchoate within their robes, and that must be their true home. Perhaps they had been sent to test his faith. To strip him spiritually naked.

But he was not naked. The cloak of his god was about him. No apparition could breach his defenses so long as his faith was strong. "Aten is *my* god," Enkidu said firmly. "If you say he is false, you lie."

He faced the table and waited, watching the measured falling of the water droplets. Both demon-figures were as pillars of salt. At last Amalek spoke again. "Where did you learn of Aten?"

"I always knew of him."

"You can not have had authentic information. How can you pretend to knowledge of his nature?"

Here Enkidu found himself in difficulty. Amalek was not barraging him with blind abuse, he was asking penetrating questions that put Enkidu on the defensive. How could he present outward proof of what he only knew in his spleen to be true? What argument could convince a determined unbeliever?

"I know his nature because he has revealed it to me in ways I cannot doubt. Aten is good, Aten is merciful. I cannot conceive of him otherwise." Yet that sounded weak.

"I proclaim Aten a false god," Amalek said. "Aten is unjust and cruel. I curse his name." He paused. "If I speak falsely, why does he not strike me down for blasphemy?"

"I don't know," Enkidu admitted, somewhat discomforted. He had never been forced to explore the matter of his worship in this fashion, and he was not well prepared. "I do not understand all of his ways. That is why I came to Babylon to seek out his following—so that I might come to comprehend the fullness of his nature. Perhaps it is not possible for an unbeliever to blaspheme. Or—Aten may, in his mercy, take pity upon the man who speaks against him, because that man is ignorant, he is spiritually ill, he is not responsible for his words. Perhaps he has compassion on the unjust as well as on the just. I cannot be sure."

"Do you believe this god you pretend to worship can protect you from our torturemaster?"

That question terrified Enkidu, but he couldn't deny Aten. "Perhaps it fits his purpose to leave me in your hands. Or your god may be stronger. . . ."

"Do you then deny Aten's omnipotence?"

Enkidu spread his hands in perplexity. "How can he be omnipotent? There are so many gods—"

Amalek nodded. "There *are* other gods. Many others. Why do you choose to worship a lesser god when you know there are greater ones available?"

Here he was on better ground. "Because he is *my* god. I suppose it is a matter of faith rather than power. The mighty gods—Shamash of the sun, Sin of the moon, Bel-Marduk—these have many temples, many devotees. My worship is not important to them. But Aten is not known, not famous. And not bloodthirsty."

The white figure abruptly stood up. Amalek immediately followed him. "This session is at an end," he said. He beckoned to the eunuch. "Return this deluded man to his cell."

Dishon obliged.

"Who is the man in the white robe?" Enkidu inquired as he followed the lamp-bearer down the hall. "Or *is* it a man? It never spoke."

"That one is chief inquisitor of the nameless temple," Dishon answered. "He is called Sargan."

Sargan! Tamar's information had been correct, then. "How long am I to be imprisoned?"

"Until you recant. You will be granted time to consider. Then a second interview, that you will like less than this one. After that—*I* will persuade you, if that becomes necessary. Consider well, pretender.''

This was rather more information than Enkidu liked. So they planned to torture him to make him deny his god! Yet he felt somehow that the big eunuch slave was not his enemy. At least Dishon gave direct and simple answers to his questions, and affected no air of mystery.

Why should these people hate Aten so? Why didn't *they* merely worship some other god, and leave Aten alone? What was there about Aten that made them determined to hurt him? When he understood that, he suspected he would know why Aten was well worth his own worship!

He would remain firm. If his faith were great enough, he would win through to the true temple of Aten, and stand at last in the company of those who believed as he did, and his life would have the meaning he had long craved.

Aten, he thought, they have raised up awful barriers between us, but they cannot deny you my worship! They can make my mouth cry their words, with their tortures, but they cannot separate me from my god.

"Recant," Dishon advised. "Do not suffer for a god that does not exist."

What use to argue with a godless castrate?

NK-2 was as distressed as his host, but for another reason. He knew there was no god "Aten." This had to be some enemy maneuver to prevent galactics from reaching Station A-10. And the enemy seemed to be in control.

CHAPTER 7

There was bread and water in the alcove, and Enkidu ate again, disturbed in several ways. No gods were banned in Babylon, and Aten certainly should have no enemies—yet here were people dedicated to his interdiction. How could this be?

After a time he remembered the prisoner in the next cell. Was he still there?

Enkidu knelt beside the wall, the bracelet of Ishtar in his hand. Tap-tap, tap-tap, tap-tap.

He listened eagerly for a response. He longed to talk with the stranger, to learn more about this foreboding situation. In the contemplation of another's plight he might find respite from his own fear and bafflement.

But there was no reply.

Enkidu set to work cleaning out his cell, kicking the offal into the lowest corner. During the brightest part of the day—still very dim, here—he searched the walls again. No gaps. He tapped again, hopeful. No answer.

He leaned against the door and stared up at the ceiling, high above his farthest reach. Was there any chance of scaling the wall to reach that tantalizing glimmer and perhaps pry his way out? If this were an ordinary dwelling, with palm-bough roof supports, yes. But here the ceiling was domed, the circular rows of bricks overlapping inward, rank inside rank, until only the tiny circle at the apex was left with its slit of light. The task was hopeless.

"Aten," he prayed aloud. "Give me a sign, that I may recover the confidence I sorely need."

In the stillness he noticed the rustlings of the rats, scuttling in search of provender. He saw one go to the wall, wriggle, then vanish.

He brought his mind back to the problems of escape—but it only drifted again. He did have a friend, or at least a wife—but how could he trust her until he understood her motives? She had come to him only when she heard him utter Aten's name. Yet she worshipped Ishtar.

After a time Enkidu drifted off to sleep. He dreamed of Nineveh in the hour of its destruction; the thunder of the siege machines as they battered down the walls, the flaming pitch, the great stones hurtling over the city from the catapults, the spears and the flights of arrows. The air torn by the screams of dying men, the shrill ululations of ravished women, the bawling of children suddenly orphaned. The ornate temples crashing down, their marvelous stones hauled away, their gods defiled and desecrated. Mighty

Asshur fell that day, his power gone, to become little more than an evil memory.

He stood within the temple of Aten as the city crashed around it. Aten was a god foreign to Assyria and its atrocities—but Nineveh, like Babylon today, had been the center of all religion. Aten's worshippers were slaughtered, his principles ignored, and his idol was borne away in the careless tread of Babylonian vengeance.

His host was correct about that part of it, NK-2 thought as he stretched. Station A-10 *had* been located at Nineveh, and it had surely been relocated here.

Was it possible that this nameless temple was in fact the station, taken over by the enemy? Were regular reports sent out galactically, while the enemy trapped any galactics who docked at this planet? Or was it being set up for an intrusion into the galactic authority itself? If so, it was a monstrous plot, and far more was at stake than NK-2's own existence.

He had to ascertain the truth, and somehow survive to reveal his information. But the chances of his present host were diminishing.

This was a difficult step, and one he did not like at all—but he would have to make preparations for transfer to another host.

If he could find one remotely suitable.

Enkidu woke. Was this dream, or vision? Imagination or history? What did he really know about Aten?

He stood and stretched, feeling better. He went to the wall and poked where the rat had gone—and found the hole he had missed before, hidden under accumulated refuse. One brick had cracked and the rats had chipped and squeezed until they were able to pass.

He put his fingers into the hole and pried. The rest of the brick budged. It was loose, then! He had the beginning of his escape.

He remembered his communications. This was the wall he had been tapping. He took out the lion bracelet and tapped again.

This time an answer came back. A varied pattern of taps established that the other prisoner was back in his cell, perhaps after an interrogation.

But tapping was not enough. There was no meaning to it, once the occupancy of the adjacent cells had been established. An exchange of information was necessary.

He dared not shout; that would surely bring Dishon. He studied the rat-hole. Did it go all the way through?

These brick walls, he knew, had to be very thick, especially at the base. This one had very little slope. Even at shoulder height and above, the wall must be too thick to reach through. Probably the rats lived inside, deserting their nests only for the promise of fresh offal.

He let his fancy wander. Why not catch a rat, tie a note to its tail . . . but no rat could drag a tablet through.

As though nudged externally, his mind started a new chain of thought. Was it possible to communicate through the tapping itself? To set up a code: one tap for "yes," two for "no"? Each word had its own wedge pattern; could he make wedges in sound?

No, it wouldn't work. Taps could not be oriented up, down or sideways; there were just noises. Yes and No were the only practicable words—and even if the other party knew which signal stood for which word, the conversation would be limited. "Yes, no, yes, yes no?" And the reply: "No, no, yes, no, yes!" He dropped the whole idea.

What about a written message, assuming it could be delivered? Would the other prisoner be able to read it? Surely only Enkidu himself was stupid enough to become a literate dungeon inmate. And of course he had no tablet.

"Aten, what am I to do?"

A cake of mud fell with a plop from the far wall. Apparently it had stuck there during his vigorous housecleaning. It flattened and settled in the muck, reminding him for the moment of the surface of a fresh clay tablet.

A sign from Aten?

Enkidu shook his head. Aten seldom gave him overt signals. Marduk guided flights of arrows, assisting the priests in their divinations; Ishtar inflamed the passions of men and women; other gods altered the livers of sacrificial animals in order to make known their wills. But Aten seemed to be a god of the mind. Rarely did he provided physical evidence of his intent.

A tapping inquiry came from the wall. Enkidu tapped back reassuringly, then put away the bracelet. He would have to proceed on his own.

He wedged the two strongest fingers of both hands into the rat hole and tugged at the brick. It budged, protested, slid out part way, braced itself, then held firm. It protruded from the wall no more than a finger's width, while the length of it was well over a handspan. Enkidu pounded it back with his fist, then took hold again. This time the brick came out a little farther.

A third try overcame its reluctance. It popped out of the wall, toppling him into the muck—and landed heavily on his big toe.

He hoped that Aten was not listening for the next few breaths. Then he brushed off the brick, complimented it on its solidity and rigidity, and set it aside. It was flat and roughly square—more than the length of his foot on each side and thin enough so that three piled together would make a fair cube of matter. He now had a creditable hole with which to work, and a creditable tool, too. He could bash out the next brick, if he had to.

Shadow prevented his seeing into his excavation, but his searching fingers found the second row of bricks behind the first. They told him that these bricks were of the softer, sun-baked variety, and no mortar bonded them together. He had only to gain a finger-hold and they should come free.

The rat-hole passed into this cruder wall, providing that finger-hold. But the bricks behind, although loose, were not aligned with those in front and would not fit through the space available. And of course there was weight on them. Somehow he would have to enlarge the opening.

The other prisoner had lapsed into silence, though Enkidu's operations must have been quite audible. Suddenly, however, there came a flurry of tappings.

Enkidu paused. Why this burst of chatter? Did the other man know something he didn't?

The tapping ceased. In the silence he heard the heavy tread of the torturemaster. He scrabbled for a loose brick, jammed it into its place, and trampled down the loose powder. Then he waited anxiously while the fateful footfalls came closer.

The gate jerked and shuddered. The panel to the food alcove slid open. He heard the thunk of new supplies replacing the old. "Recant!" Dishon's bass voice admonished. The steps departed.

After a suitable interval the tapping from the other cell resumed. It was safe to proceed.

Enkidu was beginning to like the neighboring prisoner. He removed the brick again and held it. His fingers passed over its surface. He frowned. The name of the manufacturer was imprinted there.

Enkidu disapproved of such crass commercialism. What would it lead to, should every manufacturer advertise his product by such means? There must be hundreds of businessmen in Babylon, and no doubt the effort of imprinting the bricks with this inessential message added materially to their cost. Such promotion could eventually cost more than the investment in the product itself!

But this reminded him: this brick was very like a gross writing tablet. The mud of the cell was filthy and it stank, but the jellied slop had certain similarities to clay. It hardened as it dried, for one thing, and it held its shape indefinitely until wetted down again. A smooth coat of it on the surface of this brick . . . but he still needed a stylus.

He fetched his bread from the alcove and munched while he turned the situation over in his head. Suddenly he remembered the tough weed-stalk of the last meal. There was his stylus!

He resumed excavation on the wall. Hard labor dislodged a second brick, and with that as an implement he soon freed a third. Now the gap was big enough to permit the removal of bricks from the inner wall.

Easier planned than accomplished! But he finally found one that was not completely pinned by the weight of those above, and pried it loose.

A shower of sand and grit poured out. Enkidu had anticipated this. The substantial walls of large buildings were normally filled with loose matter between the more rigid surfaces. This made his task at once easier and more difficult—easier to clear out, but harder to keep open. He would have to spread the sand on the floor thinly and hope it would not be noticed, and just keep tunneling it out until the hole stayed clear. Well, it should soak up some of the muck underfoot. If the other prisoner had sense enough to tunnel from his side, it might be possible to connect with his cell.

Enkidu was bone weary by the time the thin light overhead waned. He would have to stop and rebrick his aperture before Dishon stomped by to deliver the evening repast. Discovery now would be disaster! And he should mark his tablet while he could still see it. The surface should be nicely set now, ready for imprinting and final hardening.

He filed the hard stem into a wedge-shaped cross-section against the under-surface of the brick. How should he begin? "To Whom It May Concern" or "Please advise if you are unable to read this"? Ha-ha.

As the light faded altogether Enkidu completed his message, incised in crude but adequate wedges:

FELLOW PRISONER: MY NAME IS ENKIDU, OF CALAH-ON-THE-TIGRIS. I AM HELD PRISONER BECAUSE I WORSHIP ATEN, GOD OF MERCY AND COMPASSION. I HAVE BEEN INTERROGATED BUT NOT TORTURED YET. IF YOU ARE ABLE TO READ THIS, PLEASE ERASE THE TABLET AND USE IT FOR YOUR REPLY. WHAT DO YOU KNOW OF AMALEK, SARGAN AND DISHON? WILL THEY REALLY TORTURE A MAN BECAUSE HE CHOOSES TO WORSHIP ATEN? IS THERE ANY ESCAPE? TELL ME ABOUT YOURSELF.

It was too dark now to read it, but he had the sentences by heart. It was not the most elegant message conceivable. How easy it was to make great speeches in one's own mind—but how quickly the splendor faded when these same words were committed to tablet. Was he miscast as a scribe?

He was about to stamp his seal at the foot of the message when he heard Dishon bringing the evening meal. "Recant!" the eunuch admonished. Then: "Pass out your seal."

Enkidu's turmoil could not have been greater if he had demanded an arm. "My seal?"

"Do I have to come in and take it from you?"

Enkidu looked toward the hole. It was not sealed up. It would be the first thing Dishon would notice.

Enkidu handed over his seal. The seal was, after all, only a convenience—not a physical part of himself. The turmoil in his spleen was ridiculous; he did not let it deter him from the tasks he had set himself. He felt somewhat cheered when he was able with his writing implement and a thumb to produce a replica of the imprint of his seal—extremely crude, yet recognizable, he decided optimistically.

There was a faint sound. A kind of scraping from within the wall. Yes! The other man had realized what was up and was tunneling in from the other side!

That revitalized his efforts. What was a seal, compared to human contact? This nameless temple was trying to take away his identity and make him anonymous, but he would not let them succeed!

Much later, weary and numb, Enkidu faced the truth: he had tunneled to the limit of his reach, scooping out dirt and sand by the handful, skinning his fingers—but he hadn't broken through. He heard the soft scratchings as the other man did the same. Their excavations were aligned—thanks to Aten and the rats!—but they simply failed to connect.

Close, so close—but not enough! Probably no more than the thickness of a brick separated them. It might as well have been the thickness of the ziggurat Etemenanki.

He put his mouth to the hole and whispered into it. No response. He tried again, this time calling out as loudly as he dared, not knowing how sharp the eunuch guardian's ears were. He waited. Presently came a sound that might have been a reply—possibly a muffled and distorted human voice.

Voice communication wouldn't work.

"Aten," he prayed, "show me how to complete the tunnel, so that I may transfer my tablet."

In the dark he stumbled over the piled excess

bricks, but Aten did not reply. Dejected and utterly exhausted, Enkidu lay down on the now-gritty floor and slept.

NK-2 had seldom faced such frustration. He was sorely tempted to extend and touch the person in the next cell—but did not dare, because that might be the very thing the enemy wanted. If the enemy pounced while he was vulnerable he could certainly amputate NK-2's penumbra and grievously wound his umbra as well. But if it were *not* a trap, and if that prisoner were a normal, unoccupied human animal—then NK-2 was passing up what might be a promising alternate host. A wrong decision either way could be fatal.

Meanwhile, his own host was being extremely obtuse about the hints presented. He had almost missed the stylus, and *had* missed the potentialities of the piled bricks. But if NK-2 dissipated his strength by trying to control his host more specifically, he would lack the resources to change hosts later.

All he could do was remain withdrawn, providing minimal hints, and waiting for some advantageous development. He almost felt like praying to "Aten" himself!

Tapping woke him in the morning. The other man was warning him. Dishon was coming—and the bricks were still stacked in plain sight! Enkidu scrambled to his feet, grasped a brick in each hand, and began shoving them into the hole. In his haste he jammed some in cornerwise, so that not all of them would fit. Why had he taken out so many!

Dishon's solid feet were tramping toward the door.

Enkidu put his foot against the outermost brick and shoved. It gave slightly. He shoved again, desperation giving him strength. The column of bricks slid back, into the wall—making room for the front layer.

Enkidu swiftly fitted the baked front bricks into their slots—and discovered that one was his tablet-brick. He would shatter his carefully mudded surface, message and all, if he tried to jam it into its original place.

The feet stopped outside. The bars lifted. Dishon was coming in!

Enkidu stood up, trying to kick the damp matting of the floor over to conceal the vacant spot. It refused to kick. The gate creaked open.

Enkidu backed against the wall, holding the tablet behind him as the lamplight spilled in, trying to cover the hole with his heel though it was far too large for that. The light was incredibly bright, illuminating every detail of his cell. Quickly he squatted to cover the gap with his body. He was almost sitting on the tablet now, and hoped the cold sweat of his body was not smearing its surface.

Dishon's bulk was outlined in the bright flicker. "You have been restless, pretender. There have been noises!"

"I've been trying to clean up this filthy cell," Enkidu said quickly, then cursed himself for the half-truth. Did his principles vanish so readily under pressure?

Could he strike the eunuch over the head with the brick and make his escape? No. Too risky. And he had, as yet, no cause to injure the big slave—assuming he could.

"Recant!" Dishon repeated. "You will then be freed."

Enkidu tried to see him better. Was this man actually trying to help him? He sounded sincere. To him, no doubt, it was a simple matter: if the worship of one god offended someone, change to another that offended no one—or to *no* god. Avoid discomfort and stinking cells.

"I'll think about it," Enkidu said. His heel ground sweatily against the wall and the tablet brick almost slipped from his grasp. Had he exposed the gap?

To his immense relief Dishon withdrew, leaving the customary victual and removing the empty jar. It had been a nasty moment.

The tapping signaled all-clear. Enkidu went to his perilous aperture and once more removed the bricks. He had miscalculated, but was still fortunate that he had been able to cram all the rest in. If there had not been that resiliancy—

Resiliancy. Sand?

Unlikely. No, the give must have been a result of the excavation from the far side. The small remaining barrier had given way under the pressure of the lined bricks. The sand between tunnels had been shoved out, displaced by a brick. The other prisoner would have more cleaning out to do.

Enkidu looked at his tablet-brick and thought of the column effect. Push on the rear brick hard enough and the front brick would advance. It had to. It might be possible to ram a brick right through to the other side, if the column were long enough.

Suppose the tablet were the leading brick?

Feverish now, Enkidu hauled out bricks, to empty

the tunnel. But he was disappointed. No bricks had been jammed into the sand; the end brick had merely straightened out so that it was even instead of cornerwise, and another had slid in above it. A neat packing job, the hard way.

Yet the column effect should still hold. Perhaps the idea was more important than the fact. It was worth trying.

He carefully inserted the hardened tablet, which was mercifully free of moisture, and lined another brick behind it. The third brick projected from the wall somewhat.

He tapped to indicate that something special was happening, then pushed. The bricks jostled together but refused to slide as a unit. More power was needed. He braced a foot against the projecting brick and shoved. Still no result. Was he too weak, after all?

"Aten, grant me strength!" he prayed, then placed his heel against the brick again, set himself, and made as though to leap away from the wall. He did not stint.

His body flung back. He slid ridiculously in the slop and crashed into the far wall. But the brick had not budged. He simply did not have the weight to push the column.

Had it come at last to defeat? He saw that no amount of strength would avail him unless he had something to brace against—and there was nothing. If he were to use the bricks, lining them across the cell to support his feet while he pushed with his hands, he would have none left to shove through the wall, unless he excavated a much greater number—but then the wall itself might well collapse, and bring

Dishon galloping. And it would take too much time. He needed something now.

He removed the bricks and explored the dark recesses with his reaching fingertips. Had there been any movement at all? He detected none; the rear of the hole was still within reach. Yet there was something—a vertical crack, a flaw in the packed sand. It must have been there before, but he had been too busy to notice it. He traced it from the bottom to the top of his excavation, then felt for other cracks. They were there—so narrow that his finger could barely detect them, but evidently projecting deeply into the wall's interior. He stopped and thought about it.

How could there be cracks in a solid sand wall? This was no random mudbed!

But perhaps it was! Water could have seeped into the walls during one of the infrequent rains, helping the dirt to pack and jell. Then months of hot sun— and the water vanished in its mysterious fashion and left deep cracks. . . .

Probably such flaws existed throughout the walls. Vertical, of course, because the flat cracks would immediately fill in from above. Too bad, because he needed to push flat bricks through.

Flat? "Aten! I have the answer!"

He scraped feverishly at the hole, this time extending it upward. Soon he had a narrow, high excavation. He set his tablet brick upright into this, so that its sides paralleled the cracks. Now it could work *with* the flaws instead of across them. This should make it much easier to break through; it would have to dislodge a much smaller column of sand, since the

section pressing down from above would be smaller—
he hoped. And the flaws would inhibit material from
caving in at the sides. He hoped again.

He placed another brick upright behind the tablet,
and a third. Once more he braced his foot, leaped—

And accomplished nothing.

His soft foot and inadequate weight simply could
not provide the necessary force. If only he possessed
a heavy hammer, to drive it in like a stake—

And of course he did. He lifted one of the extra
bricks, assessing its weight. Yes—it would do.

But it was awkward to handle. The necessary vertical position and the lowness of the excavation and
the heft of the brick itself combined to make his task
exceedingly difficult. He tried bending over, but was
drawn off balance before he could make an effective
swing. He tried kneeling, but could propel the brick
only a short clumsy distance in that position.

Finally he straddled the projecting brick, faced
away from the wall, bent over, grasped his brick
hammer, and swung it down between his spread legs.
The weight of it sent him sprawling again, as his rear
banged into the wall when it tried to compensate for
balance. But he found that he did have room this way
for a complete, powerful and accurate swing.

He moved out from the wall just far enough for
proper balance, aligned the hammer, lifted it high in
a long stiff-armed arc, and swung it down as hard as
he could.

The noise of contact was horrendous—but he felt
give in the column at last! He struck again, and
again. Yes—the projecting brick was retreating slowly
but steadily into the wall. Success!

Suddenly he heard the running tread of Dishon.

Oops! The noise had given him away! How could he have forgotten that?

But inspiration came, Aten-sent.

"I can't stand it any more!" he screamed, knowing that the torturemaster would stop and listen with professional satisfaction. "I've got to break out of here!" He threw his body against the cell door so that the dull impact was plainly audible. He paused, panting and rubbing his shoulder.

Dishon called: "Now are you ready to recant!"

"Never!" Enkidu crashed painfully against the door again, this time managing to make a sound roughly similar to that of the hammer.

"I have seen it before," Dishon asserted. "You are becoming crazed from your aloneness. Were I to unbar the door at this moment you would charge me like a maddened bull. But you will tire soon, and then you will recant. Your spirit is broken."

"Never!" Enkidu cried again, hoping that his voice cracked with the proper note of desperation.

He listened joyfully as the torturemaster's tread diminished up the hall. Then he returned to his hammering, assured that the noise would go ignored. Perhaps once the channel had been opened it would be possible to force the bricks through by hand, silently. Already the chore seemed easier.

He inserted another brick and repeated the performance. He was getting the knack of it now. Two bricks behind the tablet should do it, three at the most, assuming the other man could pull it free from the other side. Too bad there would be no way to remove the intervening bricks from the tunnel thus formed—but they would be out of reach and could only be pushed out by other bricks, leaving it blocked. No direct talking would be possible.

The third brick went in more easily. Had he broken through? He straightened stiffly and rested against the wall.

If the transfer were successful, and if the sand had not scraped away his wedge-marks, and if the man could read—why then he had established communication. If the other were not a spy for Sargan.

A spy! Why hadn't he thought of that before? Suppose his message were turned over to the chief inquisitor—

He heard mutted sounds, as of a tablet-brick being hauled out. He was powerless to stop the transfer now!

NK-2 was no less alarmed. He had thought host-host communication would be safe, but now he realized that if the enemy occupied the other host the result would be disastrous. No ordinary prisoner would have attempted such a message.

He might just as well have tried penumbra contact. That would have settled the matter far more expeditiously. Now—he would just have to wait, letting the host handle it, while NK-2 conserved his strength for the battle to come.

All day Enkidu waited in anguish, regretting his impetuous action. What had he really expected to gain by contact with another prisoner? His freedom? Hardly. Information? What could the other know that Enkidu did not?

His fingers found the bracelet of Ishtar. Ishtar! Was he wrong to cling to Aten? Why not embrace the goddess, and perhaps be freed to embrace also this mysterious wife of his? Surely he had more evidence of the power of Ishtar than of Aten—and her way was certainly more intriguing.

Yet there was that in him that refused the joys of such a goddess, irrationally. One could not change gods simply because of convenience—not if one's faith were real.

Dishon brought the evening meal. So he was not to be summoned for interrogation today! Was that good or bad? Surely they would have acted by now, if they had the tablet . . . unless they wanted him to incriminate himself further.

He ate and slept. What was to be, was to be.

The next day was long and silent. But towards the end the tapping came. Without pausing for further consideration, Enkidu yanked out the lined bricks. He had to know!

All bricks were clear now except the ones beyond his reach. He could see nothing. The column should move more easily now that he had rammed through the first tablet, and maybe the foot-pushing technique would be sufficient. Unless the other man had been weakened by long confinement.

Presently motion came. The brick edged toward him, touching his fingers. Enkidu clutched at it, pulled, and brought it out of the depths. It was not the tablet-brick; that would be back in the line, two or three bricks.

Bit by bit the second brick advanced until it too was free. The other seemed to have barely strength enough to make the push, but movement continued. The third brick came, and finally the fourth. This one had to be the tablet.

It was! He felt the mud coating. He grasped it with shaking fingers and carefully withdrew it. He tapped on the wall to signify his receipt.

He could not read it, for it was dark. But he could not wait. His fingers told him that there were different wedges in it—larger and deeper, as though the man had fashioned a clumsier tool. Literate! Against all odds: another scribe!

Or was this evidence that Amalek was at the other end? The odds against *that* were not so great.

But he had to read it. The marks had set, their squared-off bases directed toward the left in standard format.

He set his own stylus against the tablet, sliding it along until it dropped into the larger indentations there. This was a clumsy mechanism, but he was able to determine the configuration of the wedge-marks, and so to read.

The message itself, so deviously come by, astonished him. He checked and double checked, making certain of it.

ENKIDU-OF-TIGRIS: MY NAME IS AMYITIS, OF BABYLON. I WORSHIP ISHTAR, GODDESS OF PASSION. I HAVE BEEN INTERROGATED TWICE BUT NOT RAPED YET. I KNOW AMALEK BUT DO NOT UNDERSTAND SARGAN. DISHON HAS NOTHING FOR ME. ANYBODY WHO WORSHIPS ATEN DESERVES TO BE TORTURED. THERE IS ONLY ONE ESCAPE: RECANT. YOU

MAY NOW ENTER MY CELL WITH IMPUNITY,
SINCE I HAVE NO CRAYFISH IN MY HAND.

His neighbor was a woman!

The message had been signed with an improvised
seal, as had his own. He traced it with his roughened
fingers. It seemed to be the likeness of a butterfly.

. . . and a bitter woman. He could not miss the
supreme irony of language. "Interrogated but not
raped—yet." That was a parody of his own assumption of impending torture. "Dishon has nothing for
me"—Dishon being a eunuch. And the reference to
Aten! Finally, the suggestion that he visit her personally. . . .

That bit about the crayfish made no sense at all,
unless it were some code-word that she assumed he
would comprehend. Of course he couldn't!

He pondered the rest again. The implication that
he *could* visit her, as though he were a guard. . . .

She was accusing *him* of being the spy!

Very clever, enemy! But NK-2 would not be lulled
that way! He would stay close and safe within his
host until he was sure—one way or the other.

The sarcasm was too finely edged. This seemed far
too elaborate to be a ruse. A spurious reply should
have been calculated to win his confidence, to allay
his suspicions, while this letter was oppositely slanted.
The sender wanted to infuriate him—particularly if
he happened to be a spy.

Well, he had already incriminated himself beyond
recall in his opening missive. Whether prisoner or
spy, the mind at the other end fascinated him. He

would proceed on the interesting assumption that this Amyitis was what she claimed to be: a woman who worshiped Ishtar.

But why, in that case, was she a prisoner here?

Was Sargan against Ishtar too? He couldn't be; he would have to incarcerate all the women in Babylon, and many of the men also. No—the butterfly was in the cell for some other reason—if this were not the flaw in her story that betrayed her insincerity.

He dampened his tablet, coated it with another pungent layer of mud, and wrote. His practiced hand, he found, did not need light for this.

AMYITIS: EVIDENTLY YOU BELIEVE ME TO BE AN AGENT OF SOME SORT SPONSORED BY THE NAMELESS TEMPLE, SENT TO WIN YOUR CONFIDENCE AND TRAP YOU INTO SOME DAMAGING CONFESSION.

He was, he realized, exactly stating his suspicion of *her!* Perhaps the only way to meet that problem was to extend his own trust, hoping that he would in turn be trusted.

I DO NOT CONDEMN YOU FOR WORSHIPING ISHTAR, BUT HER RITES ARE NOT FOR ME. I CANNOT RECANT MY OWN BELIEF IN ATEN, THE ONE GOD WHOSE MIEN IS MERCIFUL. I DO NOT UNDERSTAND ANY PERSON'S OBJECTION TO SUCH A GOD. BUT AS LONG AS ATEN HAS SUCH ENEMIES I KNOW THAT HIS NEED FOR A FRIEND IS URGENT. I CANNOT DESERT HIM NOW.

There was room left on the tablet. He was unwilling to let it go to waste. Yet what could he say to a person he did not know? A highly distrustful and sarcastic person . . .

. . . and female.

Female. The idea was both fascinating and alarming. He had assumed the other to be a man. What, in Aten's name, was a girl doing in such a dungeon? She could hardly be pretty—not amid such filth. And who would confine a pretty woman in a cell like this, regardless?

He tried to picture the long, straggly tresses, coarse features, bent peasant's body. No, that did not mesh with her message. She was literate, therefore no peasant. The sexual suggestion, sarcastic though it was, indicated a woman who was sure of her ground. Who considered her body desirable.

Or who wished to give that impression. . . .

But such conjecture was futile. He would simply have to inquire—and to formulate his image from the response. If it were invalid—well, he would probably never see her, physically, so what difference could it make? Best to imagine something pleasing.

WHAT DO YOU LOOK LIKE?

Still there was room. What could he say? She was probably an exceptionally bright woman, to have become a scribe. Intelligence in a woman was wasted, of course; but she could still be worth knowing. What would interest her?

Actually, this was *his* message. He would write what interested him. She could respond in kind.

Enkidu began to write—about himself and his god.

He was busy far into the night, too avid to sleep.

He filled the tablet and set about making a second, then a third. He started the first through while the second hardened. Nineveh, *shedu,* slavery, Tupshar, literacy, freedom, Babylon, Aten. . . .

CHAPTER 8

The day passed. Dishon came with the meals, exhorted the prisoner gruffly to recant, and departed.

Why were they ignoring him? They had wholly failed if their hope was to break him down by such sequestration, for he was eagerly awaiting the next message from Amyitis. He readied more tablets so that he could answer her promptly. The hidden inner wall was already denuded as far as his arm could conveniently reach, and great amounts of sand swelled the floor. Much more of this and he would have a cavity large enough to hide in!

At last her reply came through. Enkidu's pulse fluttered as he held the tablet up to the wan light.

CONGRATULATIONS ON A MASTERLY PER-FORMANCE! YOU MAKE ME FEEL QUITE GUILTY ABOUT DENYING ATEN. AS LONG AS YOUR GOD HAS FRIENDS LIKE YOU HE HAS NO NEED FOR ENEMIES LIKE ME.

What did it mean? Surely this was sarcasm—but what was her target? Could she actually believe that his worship was somehow hurting Aten? Was she implying that if Aten had no need of her enmity, she might become his friend? Confusing!

Why should anyone hate a beneficent god? He stook his head dubiously and read on:

I ADMIRE THE WAY YOUR MIND CENTERS ON THE ESSENCE. WHAT IS IMPORTANT ABOUT YOU IS YOUR BELIEF IN THE (MERCIFUL) ATEN. WHAT IS IMPORTANT ABOUT ME IS MY APPEARANCE. VERY WELL—I WILL GIVE YOU ALL THE VITAL FACTS YOU LUST FOR. I WORSHIP ISHTAR: I AM THEREFORE BEAUTIFUL. I BECAME A CONVERT TO THE LIONESS SINCE MY RUSTICATION HERE: I AM THEREFORE STILL A MAIDEN. I WAS NOT IMPRESSED BEFORE BUT I BEGIN TO APPRECIATE YOUR SUPERLATIVE POWERS OF INVENTION.

And her improvised butterfly signature.

What was her purpose? He had tried to respond to her provocation politely, with this result.

He was sure now that Amyitis was no spy. But how could he convince her of his own good faith? He read the tablet again, and grew angry. Her assumption of his basic interests was insulting. Maleness she equated with lust.

He could not deny being attracted by the better looking women. Most nubile unmarried females seemed to have little regard for anything that did not contribute to their erotic appeal. Yet as a slave he had seldom been exposed to the provocative side of any woman he might consider for marriage. As a free man—

As a free man he had come to Babylon in search of his god—and found himself a wife. Now he had the liability of marriage without its reward. And Amys mocked him as a lecher!

Well, obviously she wanted to correspond, or she would never have replied to his messages. She was likely some old harridan whose obsession was the delight she could never bestow upon man.

He had sent his tablets through singly as they hardened sufficiently. He was writing again before he sent the last. This time he described in some detail the adventures leading up to his imprisonment. A prostitute had robbed him of money, clothing and tablet: so much for analogy. He skimmed over the episode of the Kebar Canal to get to the court session and his garden visit with Tamar. A lovely woman—and his wife.

THEREFORE, he finished smugly, PLEASE MAKE YOUR SOLICITATIONS ELSEWHERE. I HAVE HAD ENOUGH TROUBLE WITH YOUR KIND.

This note had to wait until late at night for shipment, as conditions were poor for hardening. In a fever to send it through before he reconsidered, he had another bright idea: make a protective cover for it, similar to a tablet envelope. Then the cover would absorb much of the abrasion, and the messages could be sent sooner after imprinting.

When the time came, he rammed it through noisily, then slept.

*　　*　　*

NK-2 still was not reassured. His host, bemused by the implied sex-appeal of the correspondent, was eager to rationalize her sincerity—but the real question remained unanswered. *Was she host to the enemy?* There was unlikely to be more than one enemy entity on this planet, just as there was only one galactic entity, because this region of space was not important enough. But the enemy could have trained several sub-hosts for alternate use. NK-2 would do the same, at such time as he found suitable material.

Soon he would have to extend his penumbra and check directly, for surely time was running out. Though even that would not be certain, if the enemy elected to hide entirely within the host, as NK-2 himself was doing now. So his wait continued. . . .

It was mid-morning when he woke, much refreshed. The breakfast bread was in the gate—but first he looked to see whether a message had arrived. It had!

YOUR LETTER UPSET ME. I THREW IT TO THE FLOOR WHERE IT SHATTERED. THESE OVEN-BAKED BRICKS ARE VERY BRITTLE AND SOME OF THE FRAGMENTS ARE SHARP. WITHIN A DAY I SHALL FASHION A PIECE THAT IS BOTH SHARP AND STURDY ENOUGH. THIS HAS BEEN AN ENTERTAINING CORRESPONDENCE. THEY WILL LET YOU GO IF YOU RECANT. GIVE MY REGARDS TO TAMAR. I SHALL NOT ACCEPT ANY FURTHER MESSAGES FROM YOU. TELL THEM THAT I SWORE FALSELY WHEN I EMBRACED ISHTAR. ATEN IS MY GOD—THAT ATEN YOU DESCRIBE SO APTLY. I SHALL NEVER BE PARTED FROM HIM NOW

THAT HE HAS ANSWERED MY PRAYER AND
GIVEN ME THE MEANS TO ESCAPE FOREVER
THE CLUTCHES OF THE NAMELESS TEMPLE.

And the butterfly.

A brick blade could not carve a way outside; Enkidu
had noticed the great stones lining the outer wall of
the temple the day he first entered. She could not
hope for any physical escape from the premises. The
knife could be for only one thing: self-destruction.

Enkidu laid hold of a tablet, made ready to write—
and remembered her refusal to accept any further
message. In any event the normal delay of transmission was prohibitive. She would be dead before he
could talk her out of it.

Was she feigning? He doubted a brick would shatter in this muck, and certainly not sharply. She wanted
to shock him, to hurt him, and when one tactic failed
she tried another. After a time she would be more
calm. . . .

But why the statement about Aten? She could not
expect him to believe that her conversion to his god
was the cause of her demise. Aten was merciful; if
she had strayed, he would surely forgive her.

There was a stamp of sincerity in this letter that the
other ones had lacked. She had decided to die; there
was no further point in sarcasm.

What could he do? Tell Dishon? The eunuch would
certainly have to look in on the matter, and perhaps
Amyitis could still be saved.

Saved for what? Torture?

If her message were honest, she now worshiped
Aten. The priests of this nameless temple hated Aten.
This statement, in Sargan's hands, could put her

under the ultimate persuasion of Dishon's instruments. No—if she meant to kill herself, she should be allowed to do so without interference.

Yet how could he stand by and let it happen!

"Aten—" he prayed. But there was no answer.

So that was it! Put pressure on his host, hoping NK-2 would have to investigate directly! And elegant stratagem—and one that would normally have worked, had he not happened to spot the enemy in that courtroom.

Dishon came, left the mid-day staples, departed. Enkidu shivered in his cell, stood, fell back, stood again—and did nothing. He paced before the door, struck his fists together, and sank back, not hungry. Was he doing the right thing? Or had he become answerable to Aten for the death of a woman he had never seen, whose voice he had never really heard? Had he skewered an innocent butterfly?

If she died, and Aten permitted this—what kind of god could he be? Could a merciful god give a worshiper over to death or torture? Did Enkidu worship a phantom?

Yet he had learned through experience that Aten did not work in obvious ways. Developments always appeared natural, as though they would have happened anyway. Why was the god so devious? Why didn't Aten honor prayer dramatically, instantly, thus impressing people and making converts? Surely that would be easier. As it was, Aten had to influence a complete skein of human activity, directing the lives of many people—most of whom actually worshiped other gods. Was this reasonable?

He smiled unhappily. Look not to the gods for reason!

Of course Aten was not the most powerful of deities. Possibly he was able to accomplish his purposes only by selecting the appropriate natural means. It might have been easier for Aten to jog the speech of the child Enkidu and thus put him into the temple of Marduk for education, than to create masses of gold for the family or to impress years of tablet practice into a young mind in an instant.

But a man could scarcely evaluate the potentials of a god, or comprehend a god's motivation. He could only accept the tokens he saw, and hope that he correctly grasped their import. He had to have faith, or his belief was false.

"Aten, I have faith. I know that what you do is right, even if it does seem strange to me at times. But please," he added, "let it be right that she not die."

She wouldn't die, NK-2 knew, for then the artifice would be over. The enemy would hardly give up so soon.

The afternoon dragged mercilessly by. Dishon came, spied the unused bread and water, and opened the door to ascertain that the prisoner lived. "Loss of appetite—the next stage," he boomed approvingly. "Soon you'll recant."

Night. Still no sign from Aten or Amyitis.

Sleep—restless, intermittent, beset by dreams that woke him shuddering. The stink of his residence, the confinement of the walls, the maddening activity of the rats.

Torture, too—horrifying visions of men on tall shafts, kicking, kicking while their lives dripped redly down to fertilize the sod. Great kettles of Ishtar Gate, brimming with bubbling oil, cauldrons of bone-dissolving agony. Water dripping, dripping like thin blood from a water clock. Sharp knives touching private parts—touches that could never be undone. The eunuch heating irons: "Recant!"

In the night he woke, scratching at the wall, tearing out loose bricks, grasping for a tablet that was not there, crying, crying against an evil he could not comprehend. The body of a young woman, hardly cold yet, face against the jellied muck, rats nibbling on toes, fingers, lips. . . .

Yet suppose she were genuine, host to no one, untouched by the enemy. An excellent alternate host going to waste, perhaps forever. So easy to verify . . . *no!*

Morning, unrefreshed and unwanted. Enkidu observed the bricks he had scattered, miniatures of the stones around Nineveh. He rose mechanically to replace them.

A tablet was there.

Almost unbelievingly he drew it out, gazed at the wedging there.

FORGIVE ME.

She lived.

He had to answer immediately, and the tablet was too slow. Forgive her—when he had been the impotent one? He yanked off the bracelet of Ishtar and tapped against the wall. Pairs, triplets—anything to show that he had read the message, that he understood (though he did not understand) that he accepted the fact of her continued life and was glad.

Or had she been asking forgiveness for her suicide?

But even as his breath abated in horror, tapping came back, dissipating his suspicion.

Communication had been resumed.

NK-2 had to know—yet if the enemy lurked, Amyitis was the most likely host of the moment. If the enemy were there, his Amalek-host would be vacant except for the relatively helpless umbra. If NK-2 extended suddenly and touched a host while the enemy was elsewhere, he might set a counter trap.

The best way would be to avoid manifesting his penumbra entirely by arranging a physical-contact transfer. That way the enemy would not know even if he happened to be extended at the time.

Unless the enemy umbra was there. In that case there would be an abrupt struggle for existence: penumbra against umbra. Victory would depend on circumstance—and surely the enemy had arranged things to favor him, here.

Yet the risk had to be taken. NK-2 would try to stun his host momentarily, so that he stumbled and brushed against another person, seemingly by accident. Then—

Dishon came for him that morning. Once again Enkidu traveled the long dark hall, past the cell where Amys waited silently—alive!—and up the steps that led to the far room of the water-clock. He was tired and unsteady, so that he stumbled and almost fell on the stair. The idiot lamp-bearer continued without noticing, and Dishon stepped back, not even proffering a gloved hand to steady the prisoner. Enkidu had to recover his equilibrium by himself. But what did such little accidents matter? Amys lived!

They entered the room. Amalek and he of the white robe sat as before, and the clock dripped steadily, its drop-shadows plummeting as the lamplight picked them out. Stars winked from the wall in back as he came forward to stand in the red circle.

This time Sargan conducted the questioning. The voice inside the cowl was soft, almost a whisper; but in that room it carried easily and seemed to come at Enkidu from all sides. There was the menace of a hissing snake in it. Once more Enkidu marveled that such a person should maintain so firm an enmity toward an innocent god.

"Do you still pretend to worship the false god?"

"I worship Aten."

Amalek rose, but the white robe waved him back. "Insolence will not avail you, pretender. It is our duty and our intent to persuade you of the error of your belief. If you renounce Aten sincerely we will free you and allow you to return to your home in Calah. But the greatest gift we can give you is freedom from false worship. When your spirit is unburdened, the rest follows naturally."

"Aten has sustained me for many years," Enkidu said. "I shall not desert him now."

"Strange," Sargan's muffled voice mused. "His

heresy is very strong." He returned his attention to Enkidu. "Do you realize that you leave us no choice but to put you to the torture if you refuse to recant voluntarily?"

"Why?" Enkidu asked, loudly, because this was the thing he feared. "Aten is a merciful god. He would embrace you also, if you only let him. Why do you hate him so?"

"We do what we must," Sargan said, and his tone was sad but the menace remained. "It is not always easy. We cannot allow a pretender to go uncorrected."

"I am no pretender! Aten *is* my god. I seek only to worship at his temple, wherever it may be."

"Soon we shall show you the instruments. We warn you now, in the hope that you will recant before it becomes necessary to employ such devices. Torturemaster!"

Dishon stepped forward, standing rigid.

"You recognize him, of course," Amalek said. "Dishon is not an intelligent man, or a vindictive one. But his experience in his craft is substantial. In the interrogation chamber, with the instruments in his hands, he shows the mark of genius. Never have I seen defter turns of the knife, a more precise point at which pain draws the shades of consciousness. Seldom does a bone or a tendon snap before he is ready for it to. His touch is marvelous. I once attended while he operated for a quarter of a day—and the subject never stopped screaming for a moment."

Several moments passed before Enkidu could summon the composure to speak. When he did, he tried to make his voice crackle with contempt, but was quite unable. "Aten is my god!"

Sargan sighed. "We shall give you further time to consider. We are not cruel or premature. Consider the other gods. Surely at least one of these is worthy of your fidelity—as Aten is not."

At his gesture, Dishon came up to remove the pretender. Enkidu turned—and felt suddenly faint. He fell against the table, almost upsetting the waterclock, and slid along it toward Sargan. His outflung hand brushed momentarily against Sargan's own.

CHAPTER 9

Contact! And the potential host was empty!

NK-2 left his umbra in the primary host. That portion of himself would be without exploratory capability, but would be safe enough for the moment. *This* portion could not have any influence on the host, but could observe the superficial thought processes.

The two figures remained silent for a time after Dishon had escorted the prisoner back to his cell. The water-clock dripped in monotonous punctuation to their thoughts.

Sargan stood at last but did not remove his cowl. "I look for my god, but I see him not," he murmured. "For an instant, when the pretender touched me—but that is impossible."

Amalek also stood. He was a dark, rather short

man of about forty. His face was unremarkable except for his eyes, which suggested a certain human compassion. "The pretender is obstinate."

"So many give way when their seals are taken. I had hoped this one—"

"Perhaps the Ishtar bracelet is what should have been taken," Amalek suggested.

Sargan shook his head. "No. We *want* him to orient on Ishtar, if he has the inclination. We must remove his identification from Aten."

Sargan stared into the wall. "See the way his myriad eyelets glint," he said, more to himself than Amalek. "They know, but will not speak. Sometimes I think that I can make out the face of Aten—but when I look again, it is only a pattern in the wall, a trick of the lamplight, signifying nothing. How I long for the simple faith, the innocence of a pretender, who has only the name of a god and a personal belief, and neither knows nor believes enough to be gainsaid. But such bliss may not be. Heavy is the burden of accountability my knowledge places on me."

Amalek looked at the water-clock. "Yet this one may be worthy—"

Sargan turned and peered at his second. "He may be worthy and his faith may be strong; but even he admits that Aten is not omnipotent. The line has been drawn for us and it is plain, and once we stray from it we are lost. Aten is not some huge, grasping, indiscriminate deity like Marduk. Aten can commune with only the purest worshipers, and their number must be strictly limited. His essence must not be debased by the ignorant worship of pretenders. Our first and most sacred trust is to shield our god from corruption by strangers. We must allow no exceptions. No pretender to the worship of Aten can be tolerated.''

''Yet in the past—'' Amalek began gently.

''Not in my time!'' Sargan said firmly. ''There may have been some dilution in worldly Nineveh— indeed a god of mercy was much in demand in the face of savage Asshur. Our present problems stem from that period. This pretender himself comes from that region. No doubt the name of Aten still circulates clandestinely among the peasants. But so long as I am high priest our membership will be controlled.''

''Of course,'' Amalek agreed quickly. ''Yet I cannot but wonder at times whether, in our very adherence to the rules we have set to prevent adulteration of worship, we are not in danger of shutting out those very men whose worship would strengthen our god.''

''There is that danger,'' Sargan conceded. He stopped in front of a lamp niche and stared at the flame. ''But consider: if we permit just any man to worship, then we foreclose Aten from any genuine choice.''

''Yet by our indiscriminate *denial* of—''

''It is *not* indiscriminate!'' Sargan cried. Then, controlling himself: ''Your ordinary man-off-the-Kebar is not dedicated. He is spiritually unlettered. What ethics he practices is governed solely by posted statute—and only that which is enforced. His worship goes not to the god who merits it most, but rather to the one who rewards it most specifically. A man who wishes to rise in the councils of government will worship Marduk. When he achieves the power he covets, he then forgets Marduk in his spleen and worships him only with his lips. A man who lusts for a woman not his own will make his offerings to Ishtar. After he has sated himself in the soft flesh of a temple harlot, his need for Ishtar is gone until his desire regenerates. The gods have thus been debauched into panders to the basest desires in man. No! Aten must not be reduced to the purchase of such worship!''

As Amalek remained silent Sargan added: ''Surely you understand that it is not this particular pretender I condemn. Were it within my authority to say, 'Yes, admit this man to the service of Aten,' I would gladly do this. But I dare not set a precedent that would, in the end, destroy my god. For if we relax our standards for this one man, who may be a perfectly upright worshiper in his fashion, perhaps even a credit to Aten, then we must relax them for the next pretender, and for others who will follow. Soon there would be many devotees—and at the last we should discover that by imperceptible stages we had relaxed our requirements to the point of meaninglessness. Then we should find careless, even corrupt worshipers in our number, sullying the purity of our god.''

''Yes, certainly,'' Amalek agreed, but he sounded disappointed.

Goaded by the tone, Sargan spoke again. ''If Aten were omnipotent, the world would completely reflect his goodness. Pain and evil and injustice would be strangers to this city. Since Aten has but limited power, it follows that he cannot be of service to all men. Only a limited few may be permitted to worship him in each generation.''

''Yet we are not within that limit,'' Amalek said. ''A vacancy exists, now that the young woman has been disqualified—''

"Do not speak of that one!" Sargan cried.

"Aten's ways are not man's ways. This man's faith—"

"His pretended faith."

"His pretended faith, though simple and untutored, seems steadfast. He arrived at just the moment the vacancy developed. Can we be certain that Aten has not chosen him to fill this vacancy? Perhaps by excluding him, we—"

Sargan abruptly changed the subject. "This Tamar. She is up to something."

Amalek did not pursue the prior topic. "She has been persistent, certainly."

"This priestess of Ishtar has power," Sargan said. "Moreover, she hates the nameless temple and threatens to destroy it. Now she claims to be the wife of this pretender."

"It may be true," Amalek said. "For weeks she has been loitering about the palace courtroom, though she surely has pressing business elsewhere. When the pretender was brought before the magistrate, and spoke the name of Aten, she stepped in before I could move and took him on a tour of the gardens. She may have seen in him an instrument to attack us from within. Yet I could not let him go—"

"The wiles of women!" Sargan exclaimed. "If we were to accept him into the temple, Ishtar would still have her call on him. If we deal with him as a pretender, it gives her a pretext to bring a mob of women howling at our door. . . ."

"Ishtar into Hades," Amalek agreed. "You are right. This pretender has been compromised. We cannot accept him. If we are fortunate, he will recant before Tamar strikes. Otherwise we shall be forced to give him over to Dishon, though we thus risk his death under torture.''

"It would be unthinkable for him to die as a believer,'' Sargan said. "Then his spirit would burden Aten in the after-life forever, and I should bear the guilt of his death, forever.''

"Not if he is merely the tool of Ishtar!'' Amalek protested.

"He may be a tool,'' Sargan said heavily, "but he is also a man. Ishtar may be using him—but his faith may be genuine.'' He paced the length of the room, finally pausing again before the frieze. "But better even that awful guilt, than the corruption that comes with mass worship!''

Then Sargan crashed his fist against the wall in a gesture so ferocious that blood began to trickle between his closed fingers.

"That accursed vacancy!'' he cried in anguish. "First *her,* then *him* . . . and finally this Ishtaritu whore! It is too much!''

In the moment of physical and emotional agony of the host, NK-2 extended in a tight line like a beam of light and shot back to his primary host. He could do that, now that both hosts had been established, and he would be able to revisit this alternate host similarly, should that become necessary. But such travel was a calculated risk, in the vicinity of the enemy, and he would not do it without reason.

He had learned much yet little. Evidently the native head of this "Aten'' religion was a sincere man who deeply regretted the actions he had to take with regard to "pretenders," male and female. Sargan was even more upset about the girl in the other cell than about Enkidu, but was ready to send them both to the torture if they failed to recant.

The girl, Amyitis, evidently was what she claimed to be. But she could still be host to the enemy.

CHAPTER 10

Another message awaited Enkidu in his cell. He brought it out happily, anxious to distract his mind from the ominous interview earlier in the day.

I DID NOT BELIEVE YOU COULD BE WHAT YOU CLAIMED. IT WAS TOO OBVIOUS—ANOTHER PRETENDER APPEARING AT THE VERY TIME I WAS CONFINED, AND IN THE VERY NEXT CELL. ONE WHO COULD READ, AND WHO HAD THE INITIATIVE AND CAPABILITY TO BREAK THROUGH THE WALL. I KNEW IT HAD TO BE AN AGENT ASSIGNED TO TEST MY RECANTAL, AND ONLY ONE PERSON WOULD SPONSOR SUCH A THING, AND THAT PERSON NOT A MEMBER OF THE NAMELESS TEMPLE. SARGAN WOULD NEVER OPERATE THAT WAY, OR PERMIT IT IF HE KNEW. BUT THIS OTHER PERSON WANTS TO PROVE MY

RECANTAL FALSE, SO THAT I MUST BE TOR-
TURED AND SOLD AS A SLAVE. . . .

And as the tablets were exchanged the next two
days, Enkidu learned the story of Amys.

Her grandmother had been eighteen when her city
of Jerusalem fell the second time to Nebuchadnezzar,
and its inhabitants exiled to Babylon. Amys' mother
had tried to instill the Hebrew faith in Amys despite
her people's captivity. She told her the ancient stories
of Abraham and Isaac, of Jacob, Joseph, Moses,
Joshua and David; the prophets of Yahweh, or Adonai,
the Israelites' god.

But what set Amys' pulses racing were the tales
that her merchant father, a Babylonian, told her of
the city's ancient gods. He smiled indulgently when
her mother took her to an improvised meeting center
in a shabby house near the Kebar where there was
endless talk of Adonai and of prophets and wishful
prophecies of future deliverance of the Hebrews from
their bondage in Babylon. Next day he took her to
Etemenanki.

He led her up the steps built against the massive
ziggurat's side, past the white, black and red stories—
each seven or eight times the height of a man!—until
they came to the half-way point and rested on the flat
terrace provided for that purpose. "At the top," he
told her as she flopped exhausted on the marble
bench, "is the great temple of the gods. Inside that
temple stands a mighty couch with a golden table by
its side. This is the couch of Marduk, ruler of the
gods, and at the moment the new year begins he
comes to that couch and unites with the beautiful maiden

awaiting him from Ishtar's temple. Thus is the new year conceived. . . ."

But her father died unexpectedly. Amys' mother was sold to a minor functionary whose star was rising in an obscure mystery sect.

Her new father was a strong, severe man, far more strict in his standards than ever the old had been. Amys did not like him. He never gave her sweetmeats or pretty things to wear, nor did he keep her spellbound with fabulous stories of ancient heroes. She dreamed fervently of the magic world spread before her by her natural father: the tales of Babylon in its ancient splendor, a dream-city more wondrous than any. She dreamed of Gilgamesh, whose home city she had heard was Uruk, but which in truth must have been Babylon.

As she grew older she pictured Gilgamesh in some detail: towering hero-king, two-thirds a god by birth, so powerful no man could match him in combat. Gilgamesh, who unwittingly inspired the love of the goddess of love herself, Ishtar . . .

She bared her snowy limbs in a forest glade beside a bubbling crystal pool where sweet hyacinth and roses bloomed, where goldfinches, green-plumed parrots and gorgeous herons flew, where woodchuck and wild deer browsed. Queen of the gods, Ishtar waited with all her charms for the approach of Gilgamesh. And the hero came, innocently hunting game, seeking only to quench his thirst—and spied her in rare loveliness.

And then did she blush all over her body, and wrought about herself her golden locks as though from modesty. "Thou seest only Nature's robes," she said, hurling at him a sultry glance as she bounded into the cool water. But in a moment she came again to land and spread her limbs, that her handmaiden might brush the moisture from her and clothe her in fine raiment, while Gilgamesh watched in rapt surprise.

"Come, Zir-ru," he said, mistaking her for a waternymph. "I will please thee with a mortal's love thou has not known before." And the comely queen accepted his hand and lay with him amid the reeds and fondly placed her arms about him . . . while above, the spirits of the earth and forest flew, singing of the wedding of the Queen of Love and the King of War.

Alas, Gilgamesh overheard. "Have I embraced a god?" he cried, springing up in alarm. She nodded, laughing at his horror. He ran from her and fled to his home city, for this thing was forbidden.

Oh, to be a goddess, Amys thought, for now she had some inkling of what a goddess might do with a handsome man. Oh, to smite the mortal hero with longing!

So it wasn't entirely unconscious, Enkidu thought, looking up from the tablet. Women did like to entice men!

Ishtar, unrequited, visited her lord Gilgamesh that night as he lay sleeping upon his jeweled couch, the silken purple canopy hanging about his bed in royal folds. Over his imagination she cast a spell, and nestled in his arms as she had done in the wood, and moved her face to his—but dared not kiss his lips lest he awake.

Overcome at last with longing, she rested her head

upon his breast and kissed him—once. In wild ecstasy he woke and clasped her burning form. But she
faded and hid from him, fearing his fury were he to
learn the truth. She pretended to be a maid of the
palace, and left him to wonder at the fragrant per-
fume that lingered.

In this manner did Amyitis dream as she developed
into young womanhood—but she did not share her
fancies with her stern stepfather. Yet the man did not
neglect her education. When he saw that the child
was intelligent he undertook to train her to read and
write himself, for he was literate. Though she was
but a lowborn girl, he instilled in her the skills
becoming a highborn woman. As she grew and
came to know him well she realized that this stern
man was actually giving her far more of himself than
had her original father. Sweets and tales of adventure
were fun, but education was invaluable.

Her stepfather finally taught her to worship his
own god, for he was now high in the councils of the
nameless temple. Gradually she came to understand
this god Aten and to relegate to the world of heathen
myth her foolish dreams. Aten was a far more select
god than the materialistic idols of Babylon, and his
worship was so privileged that no outsider was permitted even to know his name. Her belief in Aten
became absolute.

Enkidu almost dropped the tablet. Aten was *worshiped* in the nameless temple? By Amalek? By Sargan
himself? Those who had cursed his name, who were
trying to force Enkidu to recant his belief in Aten?

He shook his head. He would have to think about
that later.

Amys, now a young woman with uncut tresses and uncommon grace, presently became a disciple of Aten. She knew the catechisms well and waited only for the death of a Chosen one to take the vow of the Chosen herself.

She was seventeen when such a vacancy occurred. She became a formal candidate as soon as the mourning was over.

As part of her apprenticeship she was taken to see the nether regions of the temple. There for the first time she learned of the pretenders: men and women held prisoner for their sacrilege of professing to worship Aten. She saw the torture chamber. She watched in horror as Dishon poured boiling oil on the belly of a bound man—a man who screamed continuously for the aid of Aten until his gag, which had slipped off, could be replaced.

Shocked, Amys renounced Aten. "No true god of mercy could permit such evil, let alone *sponsor* it!" she swore. And her stepfather's face turned slowly ashen as her words of bitterness and renunciation poured out. He had thought she understood. . . .

But to renounce the god in words was one thing; to obliterate the faith built up over the years was quite another. She had spoken words that must forever cast her out from the company of those worthy of worshiping Aten; therefore her faith must be forever expunged. Amys herself became a pretender.

She was especially dangerous because she knew Aten's name and his ritual, and could easily backslide into imperfect worship unless forced to utter recantal. There could be no halfway measures when the integrity of Aten was concerned. The priests had to be sure of a candidate's absolute belief, or his absolute disbelief. For Aten was more than a god of temporal regions; he cared for the spirits of his worshipers after their bodies died. The worshipers of other gods had to wander the earth as invisible demons, miserable and destructive. Aten's additional responsibilities were great, and the priests of his nameless temple labored dutifully to ensure that he was not overtaxed by the spirits of the unworthy.

"But torture is not necessary!" Enkidu protested by stylus. "They can just bar pretenders."

But it was the inner faith that counted with Aten, not the outer profession. The spirit of a true believer, even one not conversant with the formal ritual, would have claim on the god. There was enormous power in a name, and even more in faith. Since it was not possible, in the present state of the art, to remove a name from memory, it was necessary instead to break the faith. A man who recanted under torture was unlikely to backslide soon, and in time he might forget Aten, or at least find other interests.

Enkidu was coming to understand the mysteries of the temple. These priests were not the evil genii they had seemed. They had reason for their actions. He found that he did not wholly disapprove. He had himself noted the corrupting effect of largeness, or power. Look at Marduk! A religion was only as good as its membership, and a good god was wasted on poor worshipers. The only sure standard of faith was an absolute one. Certainly Aten must not be diluted.

"But how can you defend torture?" Amys demanded. "Aten is benign!"

And there was the pith of that palm. If Aten were

kind, if Aten were merciful—could he sponsor the inflicting of unbearable pain? Could Enkidu himself worship a god whose priesthood employed torture in an attempt to abolish that worship? The object was valid; the purity of the religious body had to be preserved. But how terrible the means! He could not subscribe to both, since he faced that torture himself.

Strange inversion, NK-2 thought. First the natives made a religion of the galactic Station A-10; then they tried to prevent other natives from joining. Probably the galactic representative had become aware of what was happening and acted to correct it—and only succeeded in complicating the problem. Mismanagement there, that would bear investigation.

He knew now, from two sources, that this was A-10. But he had encountered only the enemy penumbra. Could the enemy have taken over the galactic station? Then what had happened to the legitimate representative?

Caution, caution, caution!

As a girl first blooming into beauty, Amyitis had attracted the notice of a wealthy trader and slave-dealer who lived in a neighboring house. This merchant, Gabatha, undertook to purchase the young girl for his personal use.

Here the moral fiber of her foster father balked the merchant. The girl was free, his ward, and a disciple of the nameless temple. Under no circumstance would he permit her to be subjected to the degradations of slavery. If Gabatha desired any further business with the temple, he would take care never to mention this matter again.

The paunchy merchant did desire the business, and he well knew which man he could coerce and which he could not. But young Amys felt his porcine eyes upon her, glowing internally, every time she stepped out of the red door of her house. She knew that there was desire in lesser men than Gilgamesh, that burned as strong.

One day she was chaffering near the clamorous docks, as her mother had done in the years before. She had just purchased several large crayfish from a hawker and had set down the earthen jar she had brought balanced on her head, ready to place the crayfish within. The jar was half filled with water, to keep them alive until she could get them home. The last one was by far the largest, and she was absorbed in the task of trying to fit it into the small opening while keeping her fingers clear of the wicked pincers— when she found herself abruptly face to face with the merchant Gabatha.

She was fourteen and wore no veil. More than one man had turned in silent homage at her passing, and though her face remained serene under the tall jar she took a certain pride in such glances. Now she wished she were ugly.

Gabatha moved with surprising swiftness in spite of his girth. One jeweled hand closed over her wrist cruelly as he jerked her forward. The jar fell on its side, its water gurgling out.

"Ah, flutter your pretty wings, my butterfly!" he exulted as she fought vainly to pull free. "You are about to be treated to a signal honor."

Amys knew that somewhat more than this gross embrace would be forced on her unless she escaped immediately. But the rings on his black-nailed fingers bit into the flesh of her arm, viselike. She screamed as he caught her other hand and dragged her swiftly into a dreary fish-smelling alley. Gabatha stunned her with a back-handed cuff across the side of her neck, and pinioned her hand again. He was expert at this sort of thing. In the noise and confusion of the hawkers no one heeded her scream. Gabatha backed her against the wall and pinned her there with one knee in her belly as his sweaty hands tore into her light tunic.

"You will have my father to answer to for this!" Amys gasped, still trying to fight him off. "He will have your eyes!"

Gabatha brought up one forearm and pressed her neck relentlessly to the wall. He ripped out an oath of shocking vulgarity. Then he lowered his knee, laughing nastily. "A pious hypocrite—and most unneighborly. He never fooled me for an instant with all his noble talk. It will be my pleasure to share his pleasure this day."

Amys tried to scream again, but she could not breathe. She tried to move, but managed only to snatch a breath of air. Then his elbow ground in again and his sour breath was in her face as he savored his coming pleasure while rationing her supply of air.

Then his fingers ripped her tunic and clawed at her breast. He was savoring her rising panic at the realization that she could not hope to resist him.

Amys fought down her terror. Something moved in her hand. She was still clutching the crayfish.

Through a wave of blackness she saw Gabatha's fat face close in on her, its flabby lips dripping with spittle. She gathered all her failing forces, bent her elbow, and rammed the crayfish at the side of his face.

Gabatha dodged automatically. His elbow moved just enough to allow her to slip out from under. But he spun about, closing a hand about her throat, holding her painfully.

He now stood between her and the wall, chuckling at her efforts. He was, if anything, enjoying this more than if she had not struggled at all. Again she rammed the crayfish into his face. He tried to dodge his head again, but crashed it into the wall behind. The outsize claws of the huge crayfish spread wide, then closed reflexively.

Gabatha screeched and clawed wildly at the thing that now hung from his face.

Amys pulled her ripped tunic about her and ran for home. But that was not quite the end of it.

Several days later her stepfather paid the merchant a call. Amys had told her father nothing, but somehow he knew.

Gabatha's face was flushed, and a great bandage covered one eye. He tapped it furiously, not waiting for his visitor to speak. "Your slave-slut—my eye—I demand—" He was scarcely able to speak intelligibly, so great was his wrath.

"I have heard about your accident," the visitor informed the merchant coldly. "I extend my condolences over your misfortune. Of course I do not for a moment believe the foul tale whispered among slaves that a certain disreputable merchant attempted to overcome an innocent maiden in the market place—''

The blubbery lips gaped open, making no sound.

"Nor that she defended herself by striking out his eye with the claw of a crayfish. But I am bound to make this statement: were any man so base as to attempt to impose so on *my* daughter, I would feel obliged to remove from his countenance, with certain instruments at my command, his other eye."

The merchant stepped back, comprehending the threat.

"But first, in leisurely fashion, his tongue, his ears, the fingers of his hands . . .''

The merchant slammed the door.

YOU THOUGHT I WAS GABATHA? Enkidu inquired, now comprehending the cryptic reference to crayfish in Amys' first message. BUT WHAT WOULD HE BE DOING IN THE NAMELESS TEMPLE?

Amys believed that Sargan after satisfying himself that her recantal was genuine and complete would sell her into slavery. This would destroy her self-respect, and help prevent her from aspiring to worship Aten again. If she died soon in that servitude, so much the better. That meant Gabatha.

BUT GABATHA'S AGENT WOULD NEVER HAVE ALLOWED ME TO DIE. HIS REVENGE IS TOO IMPORTANT TO HIM. AND SARGAN WOULD NOT HAVE ALLOWED IT EITHER, LEST MY SPIRIT BURDEN ATEN. WHEN I TOLD YOU I WORSHIPED ATEN, AND THAT DAY PASSED,

AND NOTHING HAPPENED, I KNEW THAT
YOU WERE NO SPY. AND I WAS CHAGRINED—

No reason for that! he protested generously. She
had no way of knowing—

ISHTAR NEVER TREATED GILGAMESH
WORSE THAN I TREATED YOU, she insisted.

That was an unfortunate parallel, as it reminded
him of his Ishtar bracelet and the way Tamar had
called him Tammuz. I AM NO GILGAMESH, he
protested. I AM NOT EVEN ENKIDU, THE HERO-
COMPANION TO GILGAMESH. I AM ONLY
ENKIDU'S NAMESAKE, AN UNCLEVER MOR-
TAL IN THE SHADOW OF HIS NAME. There
were so many legends about the legendary Enkidu,
all embarrassing now.

Her reply was terse.

YOU ARE GILGAMESH TO ME.

CHAPTER 11

Amalek was in charge of the tour of the torture chamber. He stopped at the door before they entered and turned to face Enkidu, while Dishon and the idiot lamp-bearer stood back. Amalek's hood was down now, revealing a face somewhat younger than Enkidu had supposed—darker than the average, but not worth looking twice at in a crowd. He spoke matter-of-factly.

"Torture is generally employed for the riddance of malefactors in a manner discouraging similar behavior by others. The spectators are benefited as much as the felon. Perhaps more so, because there are more of them. A man who sees the flayed skin of a thief stretched upon a frame in the street will think again—and yet again—before reaching for what is not lawfully his. The head of a murderer mounted on a stake outside the city serves as an object lesson to potential murderers."

The eyes fell darkly on Enkidu. "It is the custom
therefore, that the torture be exhibited to many
witnesses, and that it compel their attention. The
effect is enhanced if the culprit screams often and
loudly and if there is an impressive flow of blood.
The beholder must respond, he must feel that *he* i.
the one being corrected, for the evil he harbors in hi
spleen. This is what makes public flogging so
successful. Not to mention impalement."

Enkidu wished Amalek *hadn't* mentioned impale
ment. His posterior winced.

"But our purpose is different," Amalek continued
still eyeing Enkidu disturbingly. "We seek only to
prevent the worship of a certain god. The momen
that is effected, we are content. We gain no persona
satisfaction from such persuasion. Only as a las
resort do we employ physical duress, and only to the
precise extent necessary. We try to avoid mutilation
or permanent injury."

Enkidu let out his breath. That implied that the
would stop short of burning out his eyes or splitting
his tongue. This might not be so bad.

"Nevertheless we have found that pain will achieve
our purpose. It does not have to be impressive o
loud; it merely has to be severe and sustained. Th
very fact that the instruments you are about to see d
not destroy the body means that similar pain can b
repeated and intensified and extended. There is n
practical limit to such duress."

He flung open the door and led them inside. Th
lamp-bearer held his light high, while Dishon's glov
prodded Enkidu forward.

It was not impressive. In the center was a large fla

slab of stone propped waist high. In one corner was an open place for a fire, with a flue leading through the ceiling. Within it sat an enormous metal pot. Against the far wall rested an assortment of smaller crocks, along with thin rods, chains and unidentifiable shapes. That was all.

Amalek tapped the center slab. "The pretender is chained securely to this platform," he explained. "He is gagged so that he cannot scream. The milder measures are begun." He gestured toward the fire corner. "Oil is heated in that cauldron and poured carefully over his body. Because it is much hotter and thicker than water, it burns away large sections of the skin very readily. We use it sparingly, of course, so that its effect is felt over many watches, even days. The effect may be enhanced by quantities of salt applied to the raw surface."

Enkidu reacted less strenuously than Amalek evidently expected. He knew intellectually that the process described would be intensely painful—but it lacked the sheer horror of the impalement stake.

Amalek must have read something of this in Enkidu's face, for he added in a hard voice: "You will find that the agony Dishon can inflict in this way is as great as that of any other torture you know of. But should this be insufficient, he will resort to a harsher corrective. Dishon knows just where and how to place heavy stones on your chest and belly, until the normal processes of your body can take place only with such difficulty and discomfort as you have never imagined. With each breath you will fight for your life. You will disgorge the contents of your stomach and intestines in any manner the weights will permit. Dishon will see to your forced consumption of great quantities of water.''

That impressed Enkidu more specifically. To lie for days fighting suffocation, bloated with water. . . .

By the time Amalek had described the knives and hooks and hot spikes, Enkidu was quite satisifed with the capabilities of this room.

So was NK-2. His host, once subjected to this treatment, would be disinclined to pursue Station A-10 further. He would have to change hosts and re-instill the directive—whereupon the new host would face the same obstacle.

The purpose of the enemy was becoming clear. Had A-10 been destroyed, a new station would have been set up after the circumstance had been investigated and the enemy routed. This way there was no need to investigate. The planet had been quietly nullified by the enemy, and NK-2 was in trouble.

But he had docked here randomly, and he could, if necessary, return to his craft and expose the situation in another distress call. True, the enemy would then discover his craft and destroy it, and probably catch him too in the fifteen or twenty years required for galactic response. But the whole thing seemed far too complex just to interfere with random galactic visitations.

But as preparation for a major enemy offensive— yes. Any number of planetary stations in this sector could have been similarly nullified, so that they would not give alarm when the full-scale thrust came. This preliminary campaign was evidently far advanced.

The strike could come within the century—or even the decade.

He could not afford to gamble that there would be time for his second message. He had to do something now.

"You are Gilgamesh to me," Amys had written. Enkidu paced his cell, mulling over her words. Gilgamesh had been her childhood hero; she had dreamed of him as a lover. She was grown now, but her adult faith had been shaken. She was turning to the little-girl images again. And to Enkidu, her fellow-sufferer.

It was useless, of course. He was no hero, and he could not help himself, let alone her. But he had to deal with her gently, so as not to make her suffering worse. Surely they would be separated soon, one or both going to the torture; better for neither to care about the other too much.

YOU ARE NOT REALLY GILGAMESH, she agreed readily, AND I AM NOT ISHTAR. WE ARE BOTH PRETENDERS SUFFERING FOR OUR GOD. I LOVE YOU.

What?

If the gods were not rational, neither were women! He tried to explain again: love was difficult when two people had never seen each other. He had seen Tamar and even married her, but he did not love her. So how could—

I WILL BE YOUR SECOND WIFE.

Oh, no!

*　　*　　*

What ploy was this? Was the enemy aware of NK-2's knowledge? Was this another intricate pressure on the host? Marriage was a very close relationship within this species, he knew. It was physical, but also mental. Perhaps it would bring the two hosts close enough so that an entity could bridge the gap even without physical contact—penumbra and umbra. Good, if NK-2 wished to expand; bad, if the enemy intended to invade.

Strange pulses and emotional currents were forming in the host. He had been profoundly affected by this female's suggestion. NK-2 would have to exert himself to reverse the trend, for it was dangerous.

He had been a fool to marry Tamar, for he still did not comprehend her devious purpose. Should he therefore be twice a fool—or was it eight times? he had lost count—and pledge himself to a second wife he had never seen?

No.

NO!

And yet—

And yet, though he had never seen her or touched her, he knew Amyitis. In a strange way that defied all his logic, he knew her more intimately than he had known any other person. Her body might be fair or it might not; her mind was still worth loving. His spirit reached out to hers, regardless of the wall. They were indeed two pretenders suffering for their god. Why not suffer together?

Ridiculous!

Yet—

She needed a husband's protection. And she loved

him. She was at the edge of an abyss, and the sand was crumbling away beneath her feet and she stretched out her hands to him, that he might grasp them and pull her free. . . .

And he stood on the same sand, falling into the same abyss. He could do nothing.

The battle had been won. The host understood that the proposed liaison was pointless, even cruel. NK-2 relaxed.

ENKIDU, DO NOT ABANDON ME THUS. WE HAVE VERY LITTLE TIME LEFT. EVERYTHING THAT HAS SUSTAINED ME HAS FALLEN AWAY AND I AM ALONE EXCEPT FOR YOU. ATEN HAS TURNED HIS FACE FROM ME SINCE I DENOUNCED HIM, YET I THANK HIM FOR BRINGING YOU. WE SHALL NEVER SEE EACH OTHER; WE SHALL NEVER BE CLOSER THAN WE ARE NOW. ENKIDU, FOR YOUR SAKE ALSO, BIND ME TO YOU. WE NEED NOT BE ALONE IN THIS. ACCEPT MY LOVE AND GIVE ME YOURS, FOR I CANNOT ENDURE WHAT I FACE OTHERWISE.

No! NK-2 cried. Too late.

They were united by mud tablet in separate and filthy prison cells, invisible and inaudible to each other, with only the rats for witnesses.

I TAKE THIS WOMAN AMYITIS TO BE MY SECOND WIFE, IN THE PRESENCE OF ATEN, THE MERCIFUL.

He regarded the tablet for many moments, then added:

I PUT UPON HER FACE THE VEIL.

He replicated his handfashioned seal and passed the tablet to her. She wetted down a section of the hardened surface with her tears and added her own signature. Below that, he discovered, she had added a line:

THY LOVE IS AS THE SCENT OF CEDAR WOOD, O MY LORD . . .

CHAPTER 12

NK-2 needled his penumbra to the alternate host, desperate for more information. The host was sleeping. But the second time, some time later, he found Sargan alert and was successful. He waited several hours. Then:

In the room of the water-clock the black hood and the white faced the twinkling frieze. Amalek reported to his superior. "The matter of the pretenders has become most urgent. About the young woman . . ."

"Do not speak of her!"

"Sir, we must. She has been long in the cell."

"She recanted fully under interrogation!" Sargan said sharply.

"Sir, are you satisfied that her recantal is genuine? Once the threat of torture is removed—"

"That is the heart of our problem," Sargan

acknowledged. "That is why I have not dared dispose of her."

"Yet even in her cell she could backslide into belief. Should she die with Aten's name on her lips—"

The white robe jerked. "You did not tell me she was ill! We must get a doctor—"

"She is not ill, so far as I know. But prisoners long away from the sunlight can sicken and die suddenly. She is an extremely dangerous pretender. We both know that there is only one possible way to dispose of such a one, distasteful as it is." He paused, but Sargan did not respond. "Two offers have been conveyed to us."

"Her status here has not been advertised!"

"The merchant Gabatha has ways of knowing."

A bitter laugh issued from beneath the cowl. "I chose Aten because he is a god of life and light and gentleness. Little did I reckon, when Aten chose me, that I should be required to sell human beings to feed the lusts of such animals."

"All these transactions involving pretenders are distasteful," Amalek agreed. "Yet better dishonor to ourselves than to our god. The only sure way to destroy her power over Aten is to destroy her spirit before her physical death."

Sargan had spoken similarly many times before, but the concept seemed empty now. "From whom is the other offer?"

"From the keeper of a house of call on the Euphrates."

"Then both offers are from Gabatha," said Sargan tonelessly. "He owns most of those brothels. A shame he doesn't patronize them himself and dissipate his lusts that way. It galls me mightily to cater to him, particularly in this case.''

''I well understand,'' Amalek agreed softly.

''What of the other pretender?''

''The scribe? He has been in isolation many days, and I have shown him the instruments of persuasion, but he does not weaken. He grows more certain of himself, not less. It is as though—''

''As though Aten were with him,'' Sargan finished heavily. He sighed silently. ''What of Ishtar?''

''The priestess has been most persistent. Shc has put her marriage-tablet on display in Ishtar's temple, and she says that unless her husband is freed by the time of the Harvest Festival, she will descend into Hades to rescue him herself.''

''As Ishtar descended into the nether region in quest of her lover Tammuz,'' Sargan muttered. ''How carefully she calculates. Think you she cares one rotten fig for the pretender as a man?''

''A woman like her?'' Amalek smiled grimly. ''She is kin to Gabatha in spirit!''

''What a nuptial that would make!'' Sargan said, smiling momentarily. ''The queen of sex and the lord of lust!''

Amalek almost laughed. Then he became serious again. ''She has long searched for a lever with which to pry open our secrets. In this scribe she has found it. This marriage tablet of hers bears the seal of a priest of Marduk as witness—an *honest* priest. She is now mobilizing her women. She will fortify them with spiced liquor, then inflame them at festival by the re-enactment of Ishtar's descent—and then lead them screeching to batter down our gates. This would not be the first mystery sect to fall before such an assault.''

"I am aware of the danger,'' Sargan said. "The wrath of all Babylon will fall on us if a single one of those holy whores is injured. Yet we cannot release this pretender until he recants.''

"There is also Cyrus.''

Sargan shook his head. "Our problem thus becomes fourfold. Two pretenders, Ishtar, the Persian. . . .''

The priests looked at the wall, and it was as though the surface became a sparkling map, showing the rich valley of the paired rivers criss-crossed by life-giving canals. Already the supposedly impassable northern fortification had fallen to Cyrus, sacrificed by the inept son of the king, Belshazzar. Soon Babylon itself would come under siege for the first time in a hundred years. The city was defended by a series of barricades that even the most powerful forces could hardly hope to storm, but an extended siege would not be pleasant.

"Babylon is impregnable,'' Sargan said. "But the Ishtar rabble rouser may use the Persian presence outside our walls to further inflame her women. I am therefore arranging to have most of the temple treasures removed tonight to a secret place outside of the city where they will be safe for the moment.''

"Outside? Impossible.''

Sargan turned to face him. "What do you mean?''

"He is here already. Cyrus. He is encamping beyond the outer wall. The bridge is up and no one is permitted to enter or leave the city.''

"So? Cyrus moves swiftly.''

"The temple and its treasures are vulnerable so long as the pretender remains in his cell."

"We must act, then," Sargan said reluctantly. "Tell Dishon to prepare the chamber tonight, and heat the oil. He shall begin on the pretender at dawn." He stared deep into the wall. "May Aten grant he recant promptly. Only he can save this temple from desecration."

Amalek nodded. "And about Gabatha's offer?"

"I knew Gabatha as a boy. Animals feared him. He used to shred the wings of butterflies."

"Shall I proceed with the arrangements to deliver the young woman into his hands?"

"No!"

NK-2 had picked up enough. If he were to save his primary host at all, he would have to do it within a day. Enkidu would have to recant. After that, he would see what developed. Local events—such as the coming of the Persian conqueror Cyrus—might change the situation. Should the enemy host be killed by the ravaging Persian troops. . . .

Enkidu woke to the spilling light of a stone-oil lamp. The bars against the door banged upward and the cell became bright. Enkidu scrambled to his feet, shielding his eyes. For an instant he had a wild hope that his rescue had come at last.

But it was Dishon, alone.

The eunuch purposefully closed the gate and leaned against it, setting the lamp in the alcove where he usually set Enkidu's meals. Enkidu clenched his hands at his sides and felt a lump form in his stomach. He felt the hour of the final and most terrible test of his faith racing toward him. His knees went wobbly. He squatted on his haunches to conceal their shaking.

But Dishon's manner, though purposeful, was mild enough. "I come tonight that we may talk sense to each other."

"Sargan sent you here to persuade me to recant?"

"No. He does not know that I am here." Dishon now squatted opposite Enkidu, his eyes studying the prisoner's face in the flaring light. "It is a waste to use physical persuasion when mental persuasion is just as effective."

Enkidu smiled at the eunuch's assumption that he could prevail intellectually. "So you hope to convince me that Aten is a false god?"

"Tomorrow is the festival of the Harvest. Recant tonight; then you and I will both be free to enjoy the celebrations of the city."

So the torture-merchant was willing to pass the savings on to the client in return for prompt settlement. Strange that the eunuch should look forward to the festival; he could hardly enjoy the solicitations of the half-clothed Ishtaritu courtesans.

"Don't you see," Enkidu exclaimed suddenly, "that for you to take my god from me is as great an evil as for the slavemaster to take your manhood away from you! How can you dedicate yourself to such a thing?"

"When I was young," Dishon said slowly, "I spoke as you do now. No one could tell me that I could survive without the constant favors of the full-breasted, fat-buttocked shes of my village. But now I do not miss them."

Enkidu was appalled. Now he did not even miss

them! Was this the way it was, also, to lose a god? Not only the faith, the religious exaltation, but even the desire for both? "If by some magician's art you could be restored—"

"I would not give up the position I have now to return to such an addiction," Dishon said positively. "No art of mine can match the tortures women inflict on men." He looked at Enkidu. "Yet even so, women have their uses, and they are soft. Better that folly than to suffer for a god who does not exist at all."

"How do you know he doesn't exist! What if I denied *your* god like that?"

"I have no god."

"And how long have you had no god? Were you not once a worshiper of Ishtar? Is that why you try to dissuade me from Aten?"

"I worship no god *now*. But if worship of Ishtar is a bar to the worship of Aten, your sojourn here is pointless. Are you not married to an Ishtaritu?"

"What do you mean?"

"The priestess Tamar claims to be your wife."

"Priestess?"

Dishon nodded gravely.

Enkidu tried to absorb this information. She had made their sudden marriage in the gardens known, then. Perhaps she actually was working for his release. "What do you know of her?"

"What does anyone know of her, who worships the lioness? Swiftly she rose from the ranks of the Ishtaritu, for she was beautiful and skilled in service, men say. Many thousands of men she honored, great wealth she brought to the temple of the goddess.

Now she has much influence. Some say she will be high priestess when the elder women slip.''

This was the woman he had taken to wife! The eunuch doubtless exaggerated, but had no cause to lie. The myth of Gilgamesh had given true warning: do not become involved with a goddess!

For what possible reason had such a one chosen to link herself to him? No one had smaller need of marriage than she!

"I see you did not know," Dishon said.

"I see you are smarter than I thought," Enkidu admitted. "But isn't intelligence wasted in your profession?"

Dishon got to his feet, shrugging. "Intelligence is wasted in most professions. Had you been less alert you would never have found your way to this predicament. My first master trained me to these skills. Long ago I learned that life is easier for a slave if his master assumes him to be somewhat simple minded. So I perform my office and keep my thoughts to myself—most times."

"But what an office!"

Dishon ignored that sally. "Ask yourself, pretender: is the evidence for the existence of your god—or *any* god—enough to justify undertaking torture for his sake? If gods do exist, they can hardly care what happens to a man. They will continue to exist, or not to exist, whatever may happen to you, and the world will go on as before."

"I will think about what you have said," Enkidu promised.

The eunuch put his hand on the gate.

"But I will not recant," Enkidu added as the door scraped open. Yet the words came. hard.

Dishon turned. "You will recant—one way or another. Sargan will not stop until you do."

"How can I renounce my god?" Enkidu burst out. 'I don't want to be tortured—but any recantal I made would be a lie." Though something in him suggested otherwise.

"It will be no lie when your flesh sizzles under the oil," Dishon promised grimly. "I have seen it many times. Such faith as could lift Etemenanki itself vanishes like a genie in the smoke of boiling flesh. You will recant. I came here to spare you pain, but I go from here to ready the chamber. Sargan has ordered your persuasion to start at sunrise."

Scarcely had the door banged shut behind Dishon before Enkidu was at work on a tablet. Both he and Amys had learned to soften the surface mud just enough to accept the imprint of the stylus, so that it hardened rapidly. They had also fashioned permanent mud envelopes impregnated with hair to set over the tablets; these did not fit perfectly, of course, but made almost immediate transmission feasible. A reply could be read scant hours after a query.

He had, Enkidu informed Amys, just received news concerning his esteemed and lovely goddess of a first wife, Tamar. Surely Amys, who had spent her life in Babylon, had known of Tamar's business. Why hadn't she informed him? What other secrets pertinent to his life had she withheld from her husband?

I MUST KNOW EVERYTHING IMMEDIATELY, he concluded. IN THE MORNING I GO TO THE TORTURE.

He snatched some sleep while awaiting her reply
but he was restless and tense. Still the dilemma
tormented him. If Aten were real, and Enkidu were
in the hands of Aten's established priesthood, and if
their methods were justified, and they were determined to destroy his faith—then did that mean that
Aten did not want Enkidu's worship? Was it Aten's
will that he recant? Yet if he recanted, if he swore
and believed that Aten were a false god, less worthy
of worship than Marduk or Ishtar—Marduk with his
corrupt priests, Ishtar with her harlots—then surely
the priesthood of such a lowly god was also to be
despised, and their demand wrong.

They demanded that he recant. If they were wrong,
that meant that he should *not* recant, which in turn
meant that Aten was *not* a false god, and—

Which came first: the slave or the slaver? One
riddle was as good as another.

Recant! Recant! NK-2 urged, trying to undo in
hours what he had built up in years. It was pointless
to have his host destroyed so uselessly. But the host
had a mighty will of his own, and progress was slow,
too slow.

In Enkidu's half-sleep he visioned Aten in turn as
a fiery and beautiful horse of finest breed, with mane
radiant as the sun, ready to carry his worshipers to
everlasting joys . . . and as an ugly crocodile, ready
to crunch the foolish mortal in its jaws and destroy
him body and spirit. Which image was the true one?
Surely both could not apply. . . .

He heard the tapping of the neat hooves, or perhaps the great white teeth. *Tap-tap, tap-tap*—which was the proper image? *Recant, recant, tap-tap, tap-tap* . . .

He struggled awake, hearing the signal for Amys' reply.

Her message solved his dilemma.

AT FIRST I DID NOT BELIEVE YOU. THE PRIESTESSES OF ISHTAR SELDOM MARRY, AND NEVER BELOW THEIR STATION . . . Yes, of course she had suspected him of being an agent of Gabatha. A slave-scribe married to Ishtar? Not likely! Any information she might have provided in that situation would have been as useful as an unbridled ass. THEN I FEARED YOU WOULD NOT BE-LIEVE ME—FOR WHO WOULD TRUST THE WORDS OF ONE WOMAN AGAINST ANOTHER? Who indeed? Jealous claims among women were notorious. BUT AT THE END I DID NOT WISH TO HURT YOU, AND SO I KEPT SILENT. And she had accepted the status of an inferior wife—knowing that his first wife could have no inferiors. For Enkidu had married, in the hanging gardens, a woman who had given her body to nameless and numberless vagabonds of the street and who had given her husband: a bracelet.

ONE OTHER THING I HELD FROM YOU, Amys continued contritely. SARGAN IS MY STEPFATHER.

Enkidu dropped the tablet. It fell upon its face in the mud. By the time he retrieved it the final words to him were lost.

The stern but upright man who had raised Amys and defended her from the lechery of Gabatha—this

was now the head priest of the nameless temple? The
one who had ordered Enkidu's own torture?

Why not? It did fit the character of the man she
had described. One who tried to be fair but who
would stop at nothing to achieve the ends he believed
were righteous. A good father at home; an implaca-
ble priest. A man who would be most careful to keep
his bricks lined straight, in a case like this. Yes, it
was obvious—now.

Even so, what sort of man could do this to his own
daughter, or even stepdaughter? After he had nur-
tured her, taught her to read, brought her into his
own religion. The daughter who had known only
kindness from him . . . imprisoned because she ob-
jected to torture in the name of a god of mercy!

Sargan.

A man of demented consistency.

Only a demented god would tolerate this.

Enkidu's struggle was over. Amys was right. Such
a hypocritical god could not be *his* god. The name of
mercy without the spirit. He would have to recant
But not because he had failed Aten.

His god had failed *him*. Aten *was* false.

He planned coldly. He would not recant immediately, for that would be suspicious. They might investigate and discover his connection with Amys, and
put her also to the torture. He could not permit that.

He would have to undergo as much of the torture
as he could bear, before capitulating in such a way as
to convince his tormentors. Never would he betray
what he had learned in this cell.

Once more Enkidu fell asleep, this time dreamlessly.

CHAPTER 13

It was the morning of the start of the Harvest Festival, but Sargan sat beside the water-clock without pleasure. He had kept vigil here since dawn, staring into the sparkling pictures and looking for the sign from Aten that did not come. The sign that he need not do what he knew he must do: be executioner to the living spirit of his daughter. In the name of Aten.

Amalek had arrived periodically with reports: more of Cyrus' army was camped outside the walls of Babylon, to the north, but no one in the city knew what they were doing out there. The women were gathering at the temple of Ishtar to absorb the harangue of the ambitious priestess Tamar. The pretender had undergone the first inflicting of oil, and the second, moaning and retching within his gag but never making the signal of recantal. And Amyitis—

forgotten be her name!—was to be heard sobbing in her cell. Things were proceeding, but nothing was going well.

How could he forget the lovely child, the butterfly, that had brightened his somber days? The regime of the temple was often harsh, but she had been his joy when he went home. That child had grown to an exceedingly comely young woman—a woman Aten himself should have been proud to number among his chosen.

If only he had shown the good judgment to leave the child to her happy heathenhood! She could have lived out a good life as wife to some upright citizen— not a priest, not a merchant, no!—some soldier or scribe. She would at this moment be free.

Instead his touch, his teachings, intended to exalt her to eternal life, had withered her joy in a dark, unwholesome cell. He, Sargan, had done this to her.

Yet did not a part of the blame attach to her? Soon she would have been admitted to fellowship in the nameless temple. *Then* she could have profaned the name of Aten with impunity, since the duty of loyal members was to discourage belief in their god only in outsiders. Sargan himself had profaned Aten many times when interrogating pretenders.

But her exclamation, coming as it did before her final confirmation, had been the ultimate in ill timing. It had betrayed the fatal insecurity of her faith, at a moment when she was still vulnerable. To admit her to fellowship after this heresy would have been a gross breach of his responsibility to Aten. His only recourse had been to try to undo, at any cost, what had been done; to reject her as a candidate, thus forcing her into the status of pretender. To secure a recantal, and then . . .

"Show me your will, my god," he prayed to the wall, while the clock dripped beside him. "The hour of decision is at hand. All that I have labored for is in peril. I know not which way to turn. How may your temple be saved? Is it your will that I do to my daughter what I must do? Show me your will, I implore you."

If there were an answer, he could not fathom it.

"In all ways I have labored to honor your name," he continued. "To your service I have dedicated my life. There is nothing I would not do for you; there is no sacrifice I would not make . . ." He paused.

Was he really prepared to sacrifice his daughter? "Only show me your will, Aten, and it shall be done. Show me your will."

Tears coursed down his face as he stared into the wall. But Aten gave no sign.

"Do not turn from me, my god. If I have offended you, if I have wronged you in any way, show me the nature of my neglect and I will make it right again. My life is yours. Grant me your presence, Aten; without you I cannot live . . ."

Yet how could a man live with himself, if he delivered his daughter into the hands of Dishon or the likes of Gabatha?

Aten withheld his presence.

It was a long vigil for NK-2, too. He could not reenter his primary host during the physical and emotional stress of torture, yet he was gaining nothing here. Both he and this Sargan-host were helpless until the pretender recanted.

Strange that the girl had helped Enkidu make the necessary decision. If this were a device of the enemy, it was remarkably subtle. Could she be host instead to a friend: the galactic representative? Somehow stripped of his penumbra and helpless? Or was that what NK-2 was *meant* to think?

Show me your presence, A-10. . . .

The idea struck Sargan quite suddenly. He sat very still and thought about it carefully. Presently he rose, paced the floor, and thought some more. He was so absorbed that he almost bumped into Amalek coming in.

Amalek said: "The pretender is ready to recant."

Sargan scarcely heard him. "I have the answer!" he cried. "Thank Aten, I have the answer at last!"

But he knew in his spleen that the answer had come not from Aten, but from the depths of his own despair. "Amyitis can be spared. . . . Listen."

Aten had withheld his presence. So be it, then. Sargan outlined to Amalek the answer he had found within himself.

Amalek listened—and remained silent.

"Well?" Sargan prompted at last. "Is this way not better?"

Amalek was doubtful. His black brows knotted. "No such disposition of a pretender has ever been tried. How could it possibly work? Even if you were successful from day to day, still everything—everything!—would depend on whether she cleaved to her recantation. Should she backslide, should she even temporize. . . ."

Sargan brushed this aside. "I would stand warrant for her. It would not be a perfect solution—there is no perfect solution! It would be hard on her, and hard on me. But it would spare her the worst." Then, as if to forestall any further objection Amalek might make: "Bring this pretender to me. When the business with him is settled I will write out the necessary papers, then release my daughter myself."

Alone once more, Sargan paused to offer a prayer of thanks to the god, though distressed that he remained excluded from Aten's presence. He brought a purse from his robe and laid it on the table beside him; it was heavy with silver. He waited.

The pretender was pale and unsteady, his torn tunic filthy. He had to be supported by the sweating Dishon, who still wore his gauntlets. Strange that the torturemaster never suffered himself to touch or be touched, skin to skin!

There was no visible mark on the pretender, but Sargan knew that there would be great red welts on his belly, and that every breath the subject took was excruciating. He was disappointed, almost, that the man had proved in the end to be so weak; he had succumbed in less than half a day. Even though this recantal came barely in time to foil the Ishtaritu raid! Sargan winced at the remembrance that he had pondered this man even for an instant as candidate material. Well, the torture room separated out the real beliefs from the superficial. The pretender's expressions on Aten in the earlier interviews had been remarkably clear and forthright. This was a man

Sargan might have judged fit to wed his own daughter, had things fallen otherwise. A lucid, honest scribe . . . but now he stood revealed as a weakling.

The thought of the girl was like the touch of a red-hot iron. He suppressed it and proceeded immediately to business. "Pretender, do you hereby recant your idolatrous belief in the god Aten, and swear never to utter that name, never to worship that god, never to direct any prayer to him in public or in secret, so long as you may live?"

Enkidu nodded wearily. "I never worshiped an idol, so it wasn't idolatrous. Nevertheless I recant."

"Are you prepared to fix your seal to a statement to this effect?"

"My seal was taken."

Sargan fumbled in a pocket sewn into his tunic. Two seals were there. He brought out the pretender's and set it on the table. "I am pleased that we have been able to save your spirit from the degradation of such a belief," Sargan said, though he found in himself only a ponderous sadness. "Dishon—take this man to the fountain and bathe and dress him suitably."

Actually, the lamp-bearer would do the job under Dishon's supervision, for the torturemaster never soiled his hands on mundane tasks. Sometimes Sargan wondered who really ran the nameless temple: himself or the eunuch.

Amalek wrote up the document, using Egyptian papyrus and script according to temple tradition.

Sargan knew he should be glad to have this business finished. But he still could not feel Aten's presence. The forms had been observed, the recantal had been secured. The raid of the Ishtar zealots was being foiled, and the nameless temple would be preserved sacrosanct. And Amyitis would not go to the merchant of lust.

Yet Sargan felt, quite illogically, as though he had been party to some monstrous evil.

Was this really Aten's will? If Aten had wanted the pretender to recant, why hadn't he arranged for this before the brutal business of torture became necessary? Why didn't he arrange for all pretenders to capitulate so early, so that the persuasion chamber could be discontinued entirely? Surely Aten, in his grace and mercy, could not desire the infliction of pain on any person, even a pretender. *Especially* a pretender!

Strange were the ways of a god. Aten, the benign, yet required torture at his temple—while Ishtar, most fickle and indifferent of goddesses, sponsored in her temple the ultimate joys of union. Could a mortal ever really comprehend the true nature of divinity?

NK-2 tried again to return to the primary host, but there was still an impassable barrier of agony, both physical and mental. Transfer was impossible in such a storm. But this would surely pass within a few hours—and it would be easier when this alternate host relaxed, too.

Enkidu returned. The filth had been washed from his body and face, much improving his appearance. He was now a handsome young man in a plain but clean tunic and serviceable sandals.

Amalek presented the papyrus document; the

recanter, a scribe himself, studied it. He obviously was not well versed in this form of writing, for his brow furrowed in perplexity. "But this is only a disclaimer of Aten!"

"As represented," Sargan said.

"Don't you want me to confess also to theft, unclean living, association with demons—?"

Oh. The ordinary man, in confessing his sins to a priest, habitually admitted to far more than he was actually guilty of, since it was better to be absolved for too much than for too little. This was an interesting insight into the pretender's origins—and perhaps into his assessment of this temple!

"This is not a confession, but a recantal," Sargan said. "Once you renounce Aten you may go to an established priest of the god you select to worship, and confess to him whatever you desire. There would be no point in confessing to Aten, since he is not your god."

The man nodded, comprehending. He took his seal from the table, looked at it, then stared at the document, nonplussed. The seal could not be used on papyrus, obviously.

"You are a scribe," Amalek murmured. "Surely you have also a quill-signature?"

"Yes." Awkwardly the recanter signed.

"To which god will you now repair?" Sargan inquired, touching the purse on the table.

"Ishtar."

Of course. The whore-priestess had married him! The recanter certainly did not look like a giant in lust—but it was never possible to tell. It would be an interesting reunion!

"Ishtar's characteristic number is fifteen. The nameless temple therefore provides you with fifteen shekels for your severance." Sargan counted them out. "We give you also a certificate of your freedom. You are no longer a slave."

Enkidu straightened. "I did not recant for money!" he said angrily. "I recanted because your god betrayed me."

"*My* god?"

The young man seemed to reconsider. "You have taken him from me; he is therefore yours. I was also not a slave. You bought me illegally."

"We purchased you for the good of your spirit," Sargan said, and hated the lie. "It was according to the laws and practices of this city. And you are free now. May you discover fulfillment in Ishtar."

"Show me the way out," Enkidu said.

Amalek moved to guide him. "Take up your silver and your certificate. The nameless temple bears you no ill will, and would not deny you what is yours," he said.

"I will take neither!" the recanter exclaimed. "Nor do I want your good will."

Sargan stared at him curiously from behind his cowl. "But it is our custom. You must accept these things."

Enkidu stepped forward and swept coins and paper to the floor. "You did not buy my god from me!" he shouted. "You showed me your nature, and through yours, his. You helped my unbelief. And now I know what you do not: Aten *is* a false god, a hypocrite of a god, a god no man of integrity can worship. I will not touch the tainted goods of such a monster."

He subsided at last, his face contorted by the pain of his activity.

The recantal was genuine, then; but there were things about it that disturbed Sargan. The recanter sounded very much as though he knew that the nameless temple was *of* Aten, not against him.

"If Aten exists at all," Enkidu added after a moment, "he allowed you to torture me. He was therefore acting through you. Whatever you may profess—you are his agent. He is *your* god, and you serve him well."

Now Sargan understood. The recanter was trying to insult the temple by his implications; he knew nothing. Very good. "Whom, then, do you wish to have this sum?"

"Give it to your torturemaster! Let him buy gold to melt in his pots, that his art may be richer."

Sargan ignored the irony. "So shall it be. And we shall hold the certificate until you claim it. Farewell."

But he was sick inside as he watched the erstwhile pretender leave.

Still too stormy to transfer! Yet the primary host had been saved, and he should be safe enough for now.

It was not too early to consider how he should locate and deal with the enemy. The only time he had touched the enemy had been when Amalek approached his host in the courtroom. Yet there was nothing in Sargan's mind and memories to suggest that the enemy controlled Amalek directly. That could be an alternate host—and NK-2 had to be certain of the primary host before taking action. Elimination of an

alternate would only alert the enemy. It was the
umbra, the heart of the entity, that had to be reached
—either by direct invasion of the host, or by unanti-
cipated and sudden destruction of the host.

Yet how could he act—when he himself was more
vulnerable than the enemy? And if, as he suspected,
the enemy's primary host was this native girl Amyitis—
how could he ever arrange his own host's assistance
in eliminating her?

Sargan reached for writing materials and began
drafting out a memorandum of his intended disposition of the case of the pretender Amyitis for the
temple records. He paused part way through, in growing distress.

It would be hard for the girl, for her proud spirit.
She had left his house one day as Sargan's daughter.
She would return to it now as Sargan's slave.

He would do everything possible to ease her lot.
Never would he remind her of her servitude, so long
as she did not pretend to worship Aten. But still it
would be a very bitter lot for her.

He would have to arrange for surveillance to continue after his own death. Never must she be permitted to have further contacts with Aten's Chosen,
apart from himself or the subsequent guardian. Never
could she marry or be otherwise placed outside the
control of the temple, lest she secretly lapse back into
belief and so regain power over Aten.

Sargan's head throbbed painfully. It was an unhappy arrangement, perhaps an impossible one. Yet
it was the only alternative to placing her into an even
more terrible bondage. It would at least keep her in

the custody of those who would care for her welfare. It would isolate her from Gabatha.

For how long?

Amalek had spoken truly. This whole compromise would turn upon the validity and permanence of Amyitis' recantal. Should she ever temporize or give the slightest evidence that she harbored doubts, the arrangement would no longer be tenable. Her spirit would then have to be destroyed utterly.

On that bleak day would he have the fortitude to do what he could not do now?

His mind turned for relief to the matter of the other pretender. How was it that the man had held out so strongly while confined to his cell—only to capitulate so readily under torture? Why had not his pretender faith sustained him through as many hours of hot oil as it had through days of isolation? This was an atypical pattern.

Where was the missing factor?

Sargan put pen and papyrus aside, knowing this was only a pretext to delay the completion of the damning document, but grasping at it nevertheless. It had become his duty to find the missing information.

He paced down the dark corridors holding the lamp aloft. He hated these dank cells, the stench of their refuse, the misery of their isolated prisoners. Yet such things were necessary to spur recantal. Pampered pretenders never saw fit to change their ways. Once again he marveled at the peculiar mechanisms of the mercy of Aten. . . .

Sargan came to the black door of his daughter's cell. Involuntarily his fingers reached for the lower corner of the voluminous sleeve of his robe. Through the cloth he fingered the small cylinder within. But he dared not tarry, lest he lose control and cry out. He hurried on.

Next was the vacant cell Enkidu had occupied. He held the light high and stepped inside.

The interior was foul and gloomy even in the combined light of day and lamp. The floor was matted with excrement, with only a portion near the door cleared. Little comfort amid this squalor for a lonely prisoner!

Sargan brought the lamp down and studied the floor. An incredible amount of material had accumulated during the last year of intermittent use. Not all was offal—there seemed to be many fingerlengths of gravel laid over the base.

No gravel had been authorized. It would have taken a bucket-line like that of the hanging gardens to fill in this amount. The notion was ludicrous. Yet here it was.

Sargan was not stupid. Very shortly he was running his fingers over the wall surfaces, feeling for loose or faulty bricks. He found them. He pried one out and studied it thoughtfully. A loose brick resembling any other.

But *why*?

He removed two more, then began on the inner layer. One was somewhat larger than ordinary. He held it up to the light.

One face of the brick was covered with a shell of hardened mud formed from hair and excrement. Sargan lifted this free and discovered another face beneath. Set in this smoothed pungent surface were tiny wedge prints. Clay-writing!

I TAKE THIS WOMAN AMYITIS TO BE MY SECOND WIFE . . .

He noted the twin seal-replicas. This was, as far as practicable under the circumstances, a valid document. Certainly it was a statement of intent. But its significance was much greater than its overt commitment.

He stared at it in the lamp's light for a long time, and his fingers became numb. He read and re-read the incriminating words.

. . . IN THE PRESENCE OF ATEN, THE MERCIFUL.

This was a worse thing than he had dared imagine.

Amyitis had backslid into belief in Aten before ever leaving her cell. Her butterfly image was on this tablet, calling on Aten to witness her marriage contract.

But even beyond that, his own daughter had given most intimate aid and comfort to this pretender.

No wonder Aten had averted his countenance!

For if Amyitis had acted with so little regard for the principles of the temple, the fault was not so much in her as in her education and selection.

Sargan had done both.

According to temple regulation, Amyitis would now have to be put to continuous torture until she recanted both the god she had sworn by and the pledge she had given the pretender. Then her person would have to be sold to the most demeaning and brutal bidder . . .

His daughter!

How could he put her under the weights, the burning oil, and all the rest—this butterfly child he had raised from paganism to true religion? The weights he had sought to put on her were earrings, the oil an ointment for her hair.

She was a strong-willed girl. She would never give over under duress what she had refused of her own free will. He remembered the time that obese heathen merchant had tried to make free with her . . . how proud he had been of her that day, when she showed her mettle unmistakably, yet never complained.

Yes. *She* was strong enough. The flaw had been in her tutoring. One did not condemn the crooked stone for being imperfect, but the inept stonesmith.

He paused again outside her silent door.

My daughter! My daughter!

He would never see her again.

Grimly and with infinite sadness, Sargan passed on in silence.

Amyitis host to the enemy! It made less and less sense to NK-2. She had destroyed herself, when she hadn't had to. She could have made up another name to fool Enkidu, arranged it so that all the blame would fall on him. In effect, she had sacrificed herself while helping him go free.

She must, then, be host to a friend. But at this moment, detached as he was from his own umbra, he could not check. His penumbra was entirely taken up with the occupation of this alternate host, acting as a temporary umbra. He would have to return to his primary, recover his unity and strength, then cast out on an exploratory basis.

By that time the girl would be under torture.

*   *   *

Amalek was back in the cloak room.

"She must be sold today!" Sargan said abruptly as he entered. "Delay only long enough to make her presentable."

Amalek made no pretense of misunderstanding. "You have evidence that her recantal was not genuine?"

Sargan nodded beneath his cowl.

"Then we cannot sell her until a firmer recantal is obtained under duress—"

"I will take the responsibility!" Sargan interrupted. "I say this in the presence of Aten: the measure of recantal shall be filled to overflowing."

Amalek departed softly, not deigning to debate, and the drip of the water-clock became loud.

Sargan brought out a new scroll, set up his pen and ink, and began to write. The first letter was addressed to Amalek.

"Sudden business has come upon me," he wrote carefully, "and I find it necessary to depart immediately for Egypt. Until my return I appoint you head priest of the nameless temple, and I ask you to handle its affairs in the manner that befits our god."

He went on to itemize the various properties and monies available to the temple, and noted the members whose contributions were in arrears. He recommended a man to serve as second, in Amalek's old position, and gave sundry other instructions.

"If I do not return within a year," he concluded, "cross my name from the roster and enter a vacancy in the membership. Admit a pretender who is worthy of our god." He thought for a moment, fingering the cylinder in his sleeve-pocket once more. "I have assigned a special project to Dishon. Please close his office to all visitation and inquiry until he has completed his work.''

He signed his name and rolled up the letter. Amalek would be too busy with the affairs of the temple to pay attention to the torturemaster's project for many days. Dishon was quite competent; he needed no supervision.

Dishon. Strange that the most intimate business of the temple—the final purification of pretenders—had to be accomplished by one who believed in no god. Dishon was certain in his own mind that Aten was a false god—false to the point of nonexistence—and that made the eunuch ideal for his position. His hand never held back in the hope that a pretender might endure. Dishon felt a genuine sense of accomplishment when he secured a recantal.

The second letter was addressed to Dishon himself. It would be necessary for the torturemaster to borrow a scribe in order to understand it, of course, but that would only briefly delay the honest slave. Dishon had been given instructions by letter before and would not question this.

''Dishon: You will find a new pretender in the second cell. Take this man immediately and put him to the torture until he recants. Pay no attention to anything he may attempt to claim in lieu of recantal. He is an ingenious and confirmed liar, and should be thoroughly gagged. When his complete recantal has been secured, relegate him directly to the bosom of the Euphrates.''

That avoided the technicality of death, though a man in such condition was unlikely to survive the river. "After this task is done, notify Amalek that some of the bricks in the cells are loose. These must be repaired before the cells are used again." He knew Dishon would take this instruction literally, too; he would not mention the bricks until his subject floated in the Euphrates.

The slack-jawed lamp-bearer arrived in answer to his summons. "Take this to Dishon . . . slowly," he ordered, speaking carefully so that the man would understand.

The dull eyes lighted. "Dishon!" The foolish smile, the departure. Slowly, as instructed—it would take many minutes for the delivery. Any task at all made this creature happy; comprehension and performance brought rare satisfaction. This time Sargan envied the mindless slave.

Alone once more, he stood up, put away the writing equipment, and left the letter on the table where he would be sure to find it. He faced the wall. "May your mercy extend to my daughter," he said. "The fault belonged to another."

The midnight stars glinted, watching him. But Aten was not on the wall.

He turned, sadly, and left the room without taking a lamp. The halls were long and eerie in the scant natural illumination. He found his way to the region of empty cells, not daring to verify whether Amyitis remained.

He re-entered the vacant place of the pretender Enkidu and swung the gate shut. By careful manipulation he was finally able to prop the bar in such a way that it fell into place outside when the gate was slammed. He had locked himself in.

Sargan removed his white robe and folded it neatly. He took off his finely constructed sandals. He pried loose the three bricks and withdrew the marriage tablet, running his fingers over its indentations. He held it firmly and bashed its surface against the wall.

Caked mud shattered, and in his hand remained an ordinary brick. Sargan fitted his robe and sandals into the space he found behind the inner wall, where so much gravel had been removed; then he replaced every brick. Except that one.

He was left standing bareheaded, barefooted, in his coarse white undertunic. After a moment's consideration he removed this also. He dropped it in the dirt at the lower edge of the cell and delicately trampled on it. Then he redonned it. Now he was dressed for the part.

Dishon had never heard the normal voice of his master, or seen his bare face. The torturemaster would discover only another pretender whose disposition was covered by the letter.

He looked at the brick that had been his daughter's marriage tablet, somehow passed through the wall. He picked it up and ran his fingers across its blank surface. He leaned against the firm gate and closed his eyes.

"Not the stone, but the stonesmith," he said aloud.

And as he held the blank tablet and awaited Dishon's footfall in the corridor . . . at last he felt the presence of Aten.

The host slept, the storm abated. NK-2 departed.

CHAPTER 14

Enkidu had reason to regret his imperious refusal of the silver of the nameless temple. It was good to be free again, in the clattering streets of Babylon, neatly dressed. But his situation now was in fact worse than it had been that morning he had waked to find his tablet and money gone. He was without position, money or strength. Every step renewed the striped pain across his chest and belly. Dishon and the lamp-bearer had wrapped him in crude bandages soaked with unguents, but these could not undo the damage of the oil; they chafed him continually. What kind of wreck had his pride made of him?

And Amys, still prisoned in the nameless temple. . . .

It was late afternoon and the Harvest Festival was well under way. Two months had elapsed since his entry into Babylon. The time seemed at once like two

days and two years! Few out here seemed disturbed
by the presence of the army of Cyrus the Persian,
encamped just north of the city.

In a way, Enkidu understood. Why worry about a
barbarian who had taken over a Median empire that
had submitted with almost no bloodshed. Who had
outwitted the money-loving Lydian king. Who had
brought backward eastern tribes to heel. Until now,
Cyrus had never undertaken a siege against a major
city. He had a lesson coming!

Babylon, well provisioned, well garrisoned, had
the most formidable defenses ever constructed. It was
inconceivable that the city should fall within a matter
of years—if ever. Let Cyrus crash his Persian fist
against the outer ramparts. He would retire with dust
and a broken hand. And perhaps an ointment of
rather warm oil. . . .

Oil. Enkidu winced.

Meanwhile, no such thing as a futile siege was
reason to delay the Harvest Festival. Gaily colored
celebrants swarmed the streets and alleys. Priests
emerged at intervals from temples to throw sheep's
heads into the river, the result of fresh sacrifices.
Drink was in copious supply—mead, beer, palm wine,
and even the expensive red grape wine flowed freely.
Tipsy men stuffed their mouths with kidneys, cucum-
bers and palm hearts.

But Enkidu felt a great emptiness within his spleen,
more painful than the outward burns on his belly. It
was the void where Aten had lately dwelt. These
overstuffed tipplers could worship the gods of their
choice. Not he. He suddenly hated all celebrants. He
thought of Amys—and stopped in midstride.

The circumstances of his departure from the nameless temple had forced him to leave the marriage-tablet behind. Now he missed it fiercely—that tangible token of their union. And he had to rescue Amys. But how?

The hawkers were out in force, calling out their wares above the tumult: perfumes, drugs, the tantalizing poppy seed. Enkidu found his nose over a tray of fresh river fish, boiled in oil, balanced on the head of a bandy-legged old man who looked dimly familiar. Oil. Sickening. He averted his face and hurried on.

He found himself at the verge of the enclosed Merkes district, but with no wish to enter. He detoured around its gate—and came upon the temple of Ishtar of Agade. The thinly veiled, thinly clad but full-bodied Ishtaritu girls were doing holiday business. He was hardly tempted.

Yet he was wed to the queen of Ishtaritu: Tamar. He was dizzy and weak and disoriented and dead inside. Why not go to Tamar for help? If he could find her amid this sensual melee. . . .

"No," he refused a perfumed veil. "I seek Tamar . . ."

Perfumed surprise. A twitter of laughter spreading through swinging skirts and high-cut tunics. The toad desired the princess!

Then he produced the lion-bracelet. Gasps; and a way opened abruptly. Such magic in so slight a token!

She was in a private room, dictating rather shrilly to a scribe. Figures poured from her red lips like blood from an offertory bowl after the sacrifice. This was a busy day for the temple and an accurate record had to be kept of the earnings of the Ishtaritu. She did not look up at Enkidu's approach. "I can't be disturbed," she snapped.

Enkidu held the lion-bracelet under her nose. She paused and looked up at him, startled. Her eyes widened in recognition. She snarled—very like a lioness.

It was too late for him to adjust to the unexpected. His stomach knotted and burned. Dizziness overwhelmed him. He fell.

The host wished to unite with Amyitis. So did NK-2—for another reason. He had to know whether she hosted a friend or an enemy. If friend, he had to save her from destruction at Gabatha's hands; if enemy, he had to see that she did not escape. He could check now—but it would be better to wait a few hours, until both he and his host regained strength. So long as the host was unconscious, he could relax; nothing would happen.

This time he woke in comfort. He was on a soft mattress on an elevated and elegant bed. No common man could afford to sleep like this!

Cool cloths were on his stomach, and little else. Someone was fanning him gently. There were tapestries on the walls depicting the adventures of the goddess Ishtar in alarming detail. There were many of them, for the room was spacious and the goddess had a considerable history. Yes—a domicile of the wealthy. Of Tamar, without much doubt.

He turned his head to view the person fanning him. It was a young slave, hardly more than a boy.

"Lie down!" the lad snapped. "You're lucky you

didn't end up floating in the Kebar, with burns like that. Did you fall asleep on a festival pyre?"

Enkidu let his head drop. "Something like that." What use to go into the actual story? Sargan of the nameless temple should have a taste of his own torture. . . .

"Well, you arrived at a busy time. It's a secret, but my mistress Tamar is planning something special for today."

This was evidently one of the snoopy, gossipy breed of household slaves, trained to entertain while he worked. The boy wore the Jewish stigmata—a true child of the Kebar.

"Festivals are always special for Ishtar," Enkidu said dryly, his eyes running over some of the more exotic tapestries. They amounted to an advanced course in sexual performance.

"Not that. She's going to raid some little temple, a mystery sect. Break in with a mob of lush bitches under cover of the festivities—you know, things get out of hand accidentally sometimes."

Enkidu understood well enough. "Would that be the nameless temple?"

"How did you guess? I thought that was original news!"

"I'm her husband—didn't you know? Well, I'll give you some gossip to replace what you lost. Suddenly, now, I know why she married me. And why she was so angry when she saw that I was free. She was planning on doing an Ishtar-into-Hades, and now she has no pretext."

The boy looked blank.

Enkidu laughed. "You mean your people don't let

you listen to the tales of Babylon's past? Don't you even look at these tapestries you clean? You know nothing about the creation of the world, or the great flood, or Sargon in the bullrushes. . . ?

The boy shook his head. "Adonai created the world in six days; and on the seventh day Adonai rested."

"Rested! The other gods feasted! Was your god so weak he—?" But he saw the sober look on the boy's face. "I'm sorry," he apologized lamely. "I did not mean to disparage your god. I'm sure he's a very *good* god. And—"

The boy sat up straight. "Adonai," he said with dignity, "is *the* God. He will still be honored among men long after Ishtar and Marduk and all the others are forgotten."

Enkidu suppressed a smile at the boy's fatuousness. He felt almost jealous. Even a Hebrew slave was permitted his personal god, while the pretender now had none. After his own recent experiences he should be the last man to attempt to come between another man and that man's god.

Dishon was wrong. Enkidu did miss Aten. There was a vast aching emptiness in him, a loss, a sense of great things that might have been, that now would never be; a bitterness of gall at the bottom of every cup of life he would drink.

Yet he might salvage something just as important. "You look as though you're good at finding out things . . ."

"It'll cost you," the boy said without missing a beat of the fan.

"I don't have money at the moment, but I may be

able to get some later. The nameless temple has another prisoner, a girl, Amyitis. If you could find out whether she's still there—''

The boy considered. ''Prisoner in a private dungeon? You don't pick easy assignments! I don't know who'd know—''

''She is the daughter of their high priest, Sargan. The merchant Gabatha has a grudge against her—''

''Gabatha! That gives me a place to start. I know a couple of his slaves . . . five shekels.''

Enkidu sat up indignantly, then winced. ''That's robbery! *One* shekel!''

''Three,'' the boy bargained, pushing him down again.

Enkidu caught a glimpse of a veiled woman in the doorway. ''Two!'' he whispered. Aloud he said: ''Well, I'll tell you about Ishtar's descent into—''

''You'll never convert my slave to civilized worship,'' Tamar said. ''These Hebrew tribesmen will not listen to reason, and their whelps won't either. They'd all be better off back in the wilderness we hauled them out of. Depart!'' she snapped.

The boy looked momentarily rebellious—whether from Enkidu's bargaining or Tamar's tone it was difficult to judge. Then his face cleared, and Enkidu was sure he meant some minor mischief. But he faded out like a genie.

''He's such a good houseboy, but impertinent,'' she said casually, coming into the room. ''I may have to have him gelded for permanent use. Now— what am I to do with you, husband?''

Enkidu found the context a bit alarming. He sat up again, catching at the cloth before it could slide off and expose his geldables, and discovered that he was feeling better. No—she could hardly do that to a *husband* for better performance!

It did not seem wholly wise, however, to ask his imperious first wife for aid in obtaining his second wife. A certain delicacy was in order.

But Tamar had another melon to slice. "Do you realize how inconvenient your escape is right now? I spent two months preparing for this day. Now you—"

"You sound muffled through your veil, wife," Enkidu pointed out.

"I will wear what I choose in my own house!" she cried; but she flung the veil aside. "How did you break out?"

Enkidu started to stand up, then clutched his scant habiliment, changing his mind. If only he had a tunic! "I didn't break out, I—I gave them what they wanted and they let me go. You were wrong when you told me that no one ever—"

"Did I say that? I may have exaggerated slightly," she said, lowering her eyes in a flash of demureness. "But if you could have stayed there just one more day—"

"And let them keep me entertained with hot oil until it suited your convenience—"

She put a cool hand on his bare shoulder, and his flesh tingled in spite of his anger. He knew her now for what she was—and the knowledge translated too much of his righteous wrath into guilty desire.

Salutation, Galactic!

NK-2 whipped into defensive posture. *You are the enemy!*

I am TM-R. Not necessarily your enemy.

Necessarily! NK-2 cried. *When did you take over this host?*

I have been here all her life—and seventy years before that, in other hosts.

But our hosts touched two months ago—

Yes. I felt your penumbra, and investigated directly. Naturally I concealed my location from you.

NK-2 was appalled. *If the enemy could do that—*

I could extinguish you in a moment, TM-R said. *But I need your assistance.*

The strength of the enemy was awful. NK-2 knew that this was no bluff. His existence was in peril—unless he could get his host away, and avoid any further physical contact. He could probably fight off the enemy penumbra, but not a direct invasion.

Tamar paused, conscious of the power she had over him. He knew himself to be an amateur in the hands of a professional. He could rage, but he could not prevail. "Why should I suffer so that you could plunder an isolated temple?"

"It is not a recognized temple," Tamar whispered, seating herself beside him. Her warm thigh pressed against his leg. "It was not for silver . . ."

Were *was* his tunic! "For power, then. With such a thread in your veil, you might become head priestess of Ishtar!"

"You would not have suffered long," she murmured, running her hand down his chest, just short of the angry welts. "You were destined for that dungeon anyway—but I would have saved you, as my goddess saved—"

"Ishtar into Hades," he agreed sourly. "You would exploit the legends of your own religion for—"

Her caressing fingers jumped over the burns and touched his cloth. Enkidu tried to move away, but she held one end of the towel and he was constrained to stay. He had no way to escape—

The curtains of the door parted to admit a slave bearing an enormous tray of fresh fruit.

Tamar bounced to her feet, furious. "How dare you interrupt!"

The slave, a eunuch, retreated in confusion. "But Jepthah said you had ordered food—"

That would be the young house-slave—Jepthah—he had sent to find news of Amyitis. So this was the boy's vengeance on them! Enkidu rather admired the imagination.

"May an arallu take that boy!" she cursed. Then, sensing the disadvantage her temper placed her in, she reversed her mood. "Bring it here, then. My husband is hungry."

He was, too. Enkidu accepted the platter and maneuvered it onto his lap, admiring its gleaming abundance: yellow apricots and purple plums, medlars and bananas, and even a decanter of spiced palm wine. It would not be hard to adjust to such a life. . . .

Yet a tiny voice within him cried *escape, escape!*

Tamar padded restlessly as a lioness before him. "You said something about exploiting my religion—"

Enkidu bit into a plum. "Was it for love of *me*, then, that you planned your foray into the nameless temple?"

She glanced at him with sultry speculation and he realized that he had committed a tactical error. Now

she would feel challenged to demonstrate her supposed love for him, and it would be more difficult
than ever to help Amys. But all she said, with decep-
tive gentleness, was: "You don't understand religion
very well, do you?"

"I suppose not. Babylon has made me very uncertain about religion." Ah, Aten, false god! "All I see
is silver-grabbing and sex and torture, and now and
then an orgiastic festival."

"You think the gods are aloof and distant and take
no part in these things," she murmured. "Supreme
deities that can never be understood, whose needs
and passions are entirely strange. Or perhaps, like
that nervy Hebrew slave of mine, you worship only
one god, lonely as that must be, and see him as
omnipotent and above human emotion—the great judge
in the sky, the eternal provider and defender. You
prefer him far removed."

"He has been far removed from me whether I
prefer it or not!" What was her point?

"You look at Marduk and you see grasping priests
and the wealth of kings. You look at Ishtar and you
see a huge brothel," she continued, with remarkable
accuracy. "You assume that because *you* are able to
see no deeper, there is nothing more to see. Thus you
both magnify and diminish the gods, and you do
them great injustice."

Enkidu remained silent. He was sure there was
more to this than rhetorical debate. *Escape! Escape!*
"If you were to look at a god—any god—with any
real comprehension, to see him as he is, you would
realize that he is very like a man."

"Why bother with him, then?" If only she *could* answer that question!

Tamar seemed scarcely to have heard. "Not only does a god have the virtues of a man, in greater degree; he shares the vices too. The gods *are* like people! It is this that makes it possible for a mortal to worship a god. He worships what is good and bad within his own self, and it comforts him to know that the god does understand. I would not worship a remote, unhuman god, whether good or evil. It would be impossible for me to do more than mouth sentiments my body did not share. I will not be a hypocrite!"

Enkidu chewed mechanically, absorbed by her growing intensity. She was beginning to make sense. He had expected too much of Aten—and too little.

"Ishtar is a goddess—and a great one," Tamar continued, gliding smoothly about the room as though dancing. She was impressive. "But more than that, she is a woman, with a woman's desires, a woman's feelings, and a woman's temper. She is fickle. But though she loves often, and forgets often, she does indeed *love*. And that love is not really so destructive as men claim. It is true that she loved the lion, and led him into the pits set by man. But to this day that lion is immortalized on her gate and in her statues and amulets. She also loved the proud horse—and so destined him for the halter, the goad and the whip. But now he is cared for at night and he need not fear the hunter or the beast of prey.

"But most of all Ishtar loves man—and while she has taken him out of the wild, free fields and mountains and put him in walled cities on the drear plain, she has also given him rich harvests and beautiful temples. She comes to help him when he gets into trouble, even as she came for Tammuz.''

Tamar was beside him again, lifting away the platter of fruit and holding him with eye and hand. Again he felt that excited tingle. ''Even as I come for you, my lover,'' she breathed. ''Even as I—''

You can not escape, TM-R said. *Give me what I want, and I will spare you.*

I will not deal with you! NK-2 cried desperately.

Your ship. Mine crashed before I could summon aid. I will be stranded here forever, unless—

A serving girl glided in with a platter of fresh-toasted pastry triangles, the traditional cakes of Ishtar.

Tamar shot upright. ''By the great stiff beard of Gilgamesh!'' she swore. ''Did I not warn you hence?''

The girl faltered. ''Jepthah told me—''

''By all means,'' Enkidu said quickly. He accepted the cakes while Tamar glared.

NK-2 extended his penumbra guardedly—and met that of the enemy. *You lie,* he said. *You would never have let me enter Station A-10 if all you wanted was my craft.*

I never let you make contact with the station, TM-R replied. *My host put her identification on your host, so that your station agent would know you came from the enemy—*

NK-2 collapsed his penumbra, breaking contact. The Ishtar lion-bracelet! No wonder the station representative had eschewed contact! And NK-2 himself had been afraid to check, because he thought the enemy was hosted in the nameless temple.

TM-R was playing a devious game—and was obviously too strong and too clever for him. Probably there *was* a major enemy thrust in the making, and TM-R wanted his ship not to escape the planet but to destroy. Meanwhile, the enemy agent had tried to use NK-2 himself as a foil against his own kind.

He would be a fool to have any further contact with this powerful and crafty entity. He had to locate and unite forces with the local galactic representative; only together could they hope to overcome TM-R.

He had gained two things from this encounter, anyway: he had learned the identity of the enemy host, and he had verified that another galactic did survive on this planet.

Now he had to get away—and that meant getting his host away from the enemy host. To do that, he had to motivate the male to renounce the female— and that might be the most difficult chore of his life. If only this planet had spawned good, normal, unisexual animal life!

"It seems," Tamar said as the girl disappeared, "that the slavelet is too solicitous of your wants. Eat, then, of the food of my goddess—and I shall dance for you and show you the meaning of my faith." She moved into the center of the room while Enkidu made alternate selections from the two platters.

Twice-thwarted, she was single-minded now, he knew. And she *was* a woman of considerable physical attraction. Best not to mention Amys at all. Not, at least, until—

"Tammuz was god of the harvest," Tamar said, moving about sinuously, "and Ishtar loved him well. And he—unlike the selfish Gilgamesh—loved her for what she was. When he died she was overcome with grief. So great was her sorrow she braved the terrors of the underworld itself to snatch him back from death. Allat was queen of the nether regions, and she hated her beautiful sister Ishtar. By Allat's orders the gatekeeper, Cutha, seized Ishtar as she approached the first gate and tore the golden crown from her head and threw it aside to roll, sparkling like the evening star it was, in the dust."

With a shake of her head Tamar flung off headband and dangling veil and let them flutter to the tiles. Her golden hair, unbound, fell below her waist. She moved more languorously, her body flexing against the flowing lines of the tunic.

" 'Oh why, thou Keeper, doest thou seize my crown?' the goddess demanded. 'It is thus our Queen her welcome gives,' Cutha replied.

"But Ishtar's love for Tammuz made her continue on into the depths of Hades. At the second gate Cutha seized her again and hurled the precious pendants from her ears. And now the goddess shakes with fury. 'Slave, why then mine earrings do you take away?' 'Thus Allat bids,' he says, unmoved."

And Tamar's Ishtar-earrings dropped to the floor.

"At the third gate the Keeper strips the pearl necklace from her throat, and now she quakes in fear. 'And wilt thou take from me my gems away?' she cried; but Cutha shows no mercy. And thus at each nether gate she leaves her ornaments: the jewels upon her breast, the girdle from her waist adorned with fine birthstones, the bracelets from her hands and feet.''

These articles joined the decorations on the floor.

"And at the seventh gate," the priestess said, "her only robe he takes, and sets her before the Queen in nakedness.''

Enkidu swallowed a plum-pit. He had never actually seen a woman in undress before. He had to admit that the goddess took very good care of her own.

Tamar cupped her breasts in the classic gesture of Ishtar. "See," she said. "I am a woman, and this is my body, and my body is of Ishtar. This is what I *am,* this is the goddess in me. Nothing on this wide flat earth can match the gift of Ishtar to woman." She advanced on him.

"No woman has the right to withhold from man the gifts of the goddess," Tamar continued. "When she offers herself to man she offers Ishtar to him. Thus may they both partake of that which is divine—he because he makes offering of his purse and of his seed, she because she makes use of the goddess' gift in the fashion intended from the dawn of man's existence. And Ishtar smiles on them and rewards them both with ecstasy if their offerings are good.

"And as the mating of Ishtar and Tammuz brings fertility to the fields and makes good harvests possible, so does the mating of any man and woman reflect this divine union. If this were not so, there would be no seasons, no time of plenty, no harvests. It would be a terrible crime to deny the race of men its right to partake of this ceremony.

"To this have I dedicated myself. And when the

passion is on me, I know beyond doubt that my god is in this union. There is nothing I can do more holy.''

Enkidu stared at her, her barley tresses wrought about her artfully, exactly as the goddess of legend draped herself in beauty. He saw the flesh of her skin, the radiance of her face, and understood that he had been narrow. Tamar had given herself to Ishtar, sincerely and completely, and her way of worship was as valid as his own had ever been.

"Even so, would I have come for you in your confinement,'' she repeated gently, and this time Enkidu believed. ''And if I could thus advance the cause of Ishtar, it is good. Everything I do is for Ishtar.''

Enkidu might have questioned this last—had he not been dazzled by the splendid body of the priestess. Ishtar had been thrown into a cell in Hades and tormented by every imaginable disease; her gallant rescue operation had succeeded only in making herself a prisoner. In this manner had the first winter come to Earth, for without the goddess of love and fertility nothing could flourish or reproduce.

But Tamar had stripped—figuratively and literally— the pretense from their relationship. What remained was the worship of Ishtar—Ishtar's way.

Enkidu pulled her body to the couch beside him, heedless of the sudden pain of his burns. Again he felt that magic tingle of contact. His lips reached hungrily for hers, and she was warm and lithe and eager.

*   *   *

It was the death-struggle: invasion of host. TM-R had tried to bargain with him and had failed; now the enemy was out to destroy him.

NK-2 had the immense advantage of operating within his own host, whose byways and foibles were familiar to him. But TM-R had such sheer, raw power that tactical nuances became irrelevant. He was being driven back—

He made a desperate effort to invoke a negative reaction in the host, to throw off the enemy host. This failed. He cast his penumbra out, searching for help he knew was not available. TM-R's penumbra was there first, foiling even that effort. All he could do was fight . . . until he died.

The curtains parted to admit yet another figure.

Jepthah, the Hebrew slave, stood over them, not missing a detail. "I had no idea Ishtar was so tired," he observed. "How nice of you to let her rest upon your pallet."

Enkidu, keenly embarrassed, jerked away and dived for his towel. Tamar rolled over on her belly, furious but not in the least ashamed. "I will have you flayed a sliver at a time," she muttered, and for a moment Enkidu wasn't certain whom she was addressing.

The boy, already demolishing a banana from the platter, was not alarmed. "I would hardly be able to redeem my purchase price, then," he pointed out. He dropped the yellow peel on Tamar's left buttock.

"I will use your skin for an offertory bowl!"

The boy selected an apricot. "I suppose you aren't interested in the juicy Kebar gossip I bring . . ."

"Oh?" Tamar's wrath abated miraculously. She was insatiably curious.

"Please," Enkidu said, still glowing with embarrassment, "could you bring me a tunic?"

"Immediately," the boy said, turning to leave.

"Hold!" yelped Tamar. "*What* gossip?"

The boy paused, savoring the moment. "Cyrus is outside the walls. Or at least his army is. Right outside, I mean. The Persian will have Babylon by morning."

"Ridiculous!" she exclaimed. "The city cannot be taken by siege!"

"Who said anything about a siege?" And without explaining himself further, he turned to Enkidu. "Amyitis has been sold."

Enkidu jumped. "To whom?"

Tamar sat up. "What do you mean—no siege? And who is Amyitis?"

Jepthah smiled. "Five shekels."

"You Kebar thief, I *own* you!"

"Three shekels, then," he bargained, smirking.

She puffed up like an overfilled wineskin, but changed her mind before bursting. "Three shekels— but I'll add it to your sale price!"

"His wife," the boy said.

She looked blank. "What?"

"You asked who Amyitis was, so I told you. For three shekels."

Now she did explode. "Pig of a Hebrew! I meant the Persian!" And to Enkidu, dangerously: "Your *wife* . . . husband?"

"His second wife," Jepthah explained helpfully. "Prettier than his first, I hear."

Tamar hurled an apricot at him. It occurred to Enkidu that she would never have put up with such insolence from a slave unless she wanted to. "Who bought her?" he demanded again.

"Three shekels—remember?"

"Give him three shekels, wife," Enkidu snapped. What could he lose?

"Three shekels," she agreed. Enkidu didn't like the sudden intensity of her interest.

"Gabatha."

Enkidu had been afraid of this. The pit of his stomach felt like a stone. "Get me a tunic!"

"Stay where you are!" Tamar cried, and the boy stopped in his tracks. "Why no siege?"

"Because the Persian enters by the nether gate, tonight." The boy left as he spoke.

Tamar wheeled to face Enkidu. "I demand an explanation!"

"I don't know. They must be tunneling under the walls. Though how they could do it with no noise—"

"The *wife*!"

NK-2 saw that TM-R's host was not entirely docile. She had drives of her own. And now he realized how he could force a separation of the hosts. Jealousy!

Tell her! Tell her! NK-2 urged the host. He was weak from the ravage of the enemy's invasion, but there was no point in conserving his resources now. If the two hosts made contact again, he was finished. *Tell her! Tell her! Tell her!*

Why not tell her? She would learn the whole story soon enough anyway. Maybe, just barely maybe, she would help. "In the nameless temple I took a second wife."

"A concubine? You took a concubine—without my approval?"

"You were not available for consultation," he pointed out. But he knew he had to avoid antagonizing her any further if possible. *Tell her! Tell her!*

Tamar said, "Her name is Amyitis?"

He nodded. Why was he so eager to confess, when he knew it would only infuriate her?

"Well, I'll forgive you, I suppose," she said graciously. "A concubine is easily spared, and I've been known to dally with a man or two myself. As a matter of fact, after this hour with you I'm going to be quite busy with temple affairs. I will buy you the prettiest maidens you can imagine. We'll just have time to—"

Enkidu was amazed at her tenacity. Even knowing they would be interrupted in the act, she—but of course, this was her normal business. Doubtless she had performed in public many times, and united with Marduk himself in the Ziggurat temple during the new year's festival.

"I'm out of the mood," he said lamely. "Gabatha will torture her."

"No doubt. Gabatha is a monster. He's cost the temple many a shekel by his illicit competition, undercutting our prices. Who is this girl?"

"Sargan's daughter. Stepdaughter, really."

"Sargan—head priest of the nameless temple?" She knew that name, of course. "That's right—he does have a daughter. And—" Here her eyes lighted as she remembered. "She must be the one who poked out Gabatha's eye! I couldn't have done better myself!''

Enkidu nodded, hardly daring to hope. Had his little *shedu* voice advised him correctly? If Tamar also hated Gabatha, she might be willing to help the girl who had maimed him!

"Well, sometimes a little torture softens a girl's nature. Makes her more pliable. I, of course, have never been tortured.''

"I assumed as much.''

"But you've no doubt had the best of her already. You wouldn't want her after Gabatha finishes with her. You'll find that variety is—'' Enkidu's expression stopped her. "Such sentiment! Was she really so beautiful, then?'' she asked softly.

"I never saw her at all!'' Enkidu burst out. "I married her while we were both imprisoned. We—corresponded.''

Tamar's eyes narrowed slightly. "You never embraced her?''

He nodded innocently.

"Never saw her face, her body?''

Assent.

"And *her* you choose over Ishtar!''

Enkidu looked into her face. Better his head had fallen into the river beside those of the sacrificial sheep! But he blurted out, "I don't think I can get her back without your help. I—''

Tamar's voice, once she recovered it, was hoarse. "You had *better* do it without my help. If I rescue her for your pleasure, I will bring her breasts to you on platters. I will knot her hair around your—''

But Jepthah was back with Enkidu's tunic. The

slave seemed to have a real talent for appearing at interesting moments. "She's already at Gabatha's house. Better hurry."

Enkidu looked at Tamar. She was standing with arms folded, legs spread: naked, glorious, unashamed.

"I must have your help!" he pleaded. But he knew it was useless.

Nebuchadnezzar's ovens raged in her eyes.

So long, bitch! NK-2 cried, extending his battered penumbra just enough to make contact.

The responding blast of fury was amazing!

Get out of here! he prodded his host. Fortunately this was exactly what the host had in mind, now that he had the tunic.

It had been a close call—and TM-R would surely pursue, just as soon as the priestess could be managed. But now he could run!

CHAPTER 15

"Can you show me the way?" Enkidu demanded as he stepped out of the house.

"Yes," Jepthah said, keeping pace.

"How many shekels?"

"No charge. You made my mistress madder than I ever could! That's payment enough. Anyway, I hear Amyitis is Hebrew, so I have to help her if I can."

Enkidu decided not to discuss Amyitis' various changes of religion. She might, indeed, be worshiping Adonai again by this time.

The clamor outside assaulted his ears. Apparently no resident of Babylon remained inside; all had crowded out into the streets to take part in the festivities.

Jepthah guided him out of the wealthy residential section near the temple of Ishtar and on toward the Euphrates. They crossed the Processional Way westward. Even on this great avenue the citizens had set up cooking pots over smoking scraps of palm-wood and dry animal dung, and were heating entrails and joints of rare meat in offerings to their gods. The priests ate best of all, sampling any pots they came across.

Down Adad Street, toward the river; and now they came in sight of Esagila, Marduk's temple, with its gold-leaf cupola dazzling in the last rays of Shamash as the sun-chariot entered the nether world. From Esagila's course to the south came the beat of kettle-drums and hand cymbals, and above that the thin music of pan-pipes. Enkidu also made out the sweet notes of the harpists and cithern-players. If Babylon were about to be conquered, the music-makers didn't know it!

The middle of the street was blocked by lines of dancers facing each other, advancing and retreating in approximate time to the music, while spectators cried and clapped. The wine jugs were passing freely from mouth to mouth.

The two sober persons skirted the main dance and moved rapidly on down Adad—only to be held up again. A stool had been set up, and on this stool stood a naked girl holding a lyre. She was attempting to play the instrument and dance, but the precarious balance of her perch and her dubious sobriety demolished her efforts and left her simply wriggling suggestively. A man in a short tunic crouched with a tambourine, shaking it as he pushed his legs out in a clumsy dance.

Amazed, Enkidu stopped. It wasn't the sight of the bare girl that shocked him, though in other circum-

stances that would have been sufficient. These clods
were trying to emulate one of the sacred dances of
Marduk! But here there was no feeling of sacredness.
Every drunken motion was obscene.

As he watched, the girl lost her balance and fell
off her pedestal. With a cry of glee the man sprang up
and caught her in his arms. She screamed coquet-
tishly and plastered herself against him while he growled
and explored her body with his big hands. The ring
of spectators emitted laughs and hiccupy cheers as he
dragged her squealing into an alley.

Another tipsy woman doffed her tunic and mounted
the stool. Enkidu shook his head and pushed on.
Dance, orgy, or sexual stimulant, this was the inter-
pretation the common folk put on the ideals of the
priests and priestesses. Tamar might talk of the glory
of the worship of Ishtar—but this was what it really
came down to. A drunken man spreading a naked
girl on the filthy streets of the city.

The Euphrates—and parading torches were reflected
from the low, smelly waters. Coracles clustered at
the edge, round basket-boats fashioned of plaited
rushes, flat-bottomed and shallow, but caulked water-
tight with earth and bitumen. It took a clever sailor to
propel these keel-less craft without spinning helplessly or getting swamped by occasional waves.

The boy led him on to the famous bridge of Babylon,
one of the marvels of the modern world, that crossed
the entire width of the river. Five great piers of
tapered stone supported the monstrous wooden span.
The bridge stood high above the water—much higher
than Enkidu had imagined—and the lower planks
bore water marks considerably above the present level.

At the bridge's near end yet another throng of people clustered round a collection of divinators, astrologers and tellers of dreams. Jepthah spat contemptuously. "Charlatans! Don't consult them. Real astrologers do their computations in temple offices, not in the streets! Always the frauds trade on the earned reputations of their bet—"

"Hurry!" Enkidu shoved the boy along, though he was already dizzy with fatigue. He had needed far more rest than he had found. "How much farther?"

"Other side of the bridge."

From the center of the bridge the dark waters were visible far to the north and south, with the myriad wharfs of the waterside market projecting into the river—or rather, the mudbank that was its fringe. Anchored to the ends of the wharfs were the large *kelek* rafts, of strong reed and wood, inflated goatskins attached in clusters to their under surfaces. Such rafts, Enkidu knew, could carry considerable weight—but only downstream. Many of these would be poled on down to Kish, Nippur, Uruk or Ur. Persian siege permitting. The others would be dismantled, the valuable wooden portions sold locally, the skins deflated and packed on the backs of asses and camels for the return caravan north.

"How far *is* this residence of Gabatha's?" Enkidu demanded as Jepthah led him south beside the river. They were now in the new city, the smaller segment of Babylon west of the river, protected by a single moat and wall—but still impregnable.

"Very near," the boy assured him. This part of the city was almost deserted. The sound of the revelers drifted hollowly across the river.

They came at last upon a large estate, its main building extended by walls and closed passages to protect a large central courtyard. Enkidu could see palms rising from its center. The walls marched down to the water's edge; no doubt the merchant maintained his own dock for the shipment of precious wares.

Somewhere in there was Amys—now one of Gabatha's properties.

They were now at the main door: a solid plank of handsome imported wood. "Good luck," Jepthah said, and vanished.

NK-2 extended his penumbra, hoping to check the girl Amyitis, who might be host to the Station A-10 representative. But he encountered TM-R's ambience immediately, and could not reach far. The enemy was already coming after him! If this mission of his host's took too long, he would be trapped again—and no jealousy-ruse would work a second time!

Enkidu's determined banging summoned a timid slave girl. He fixed her with a wild stare and intimidated her into letting him in. He was shown down a long hall, through elaborate rooms and exotic courts, and into the presence of the merchant Gabatha as he sat at supper.

Gabatha was obesely huge. He wore a short red linen tunic and over it an elaborate open robe, richly embroidered. Around his bulging middle was tied a colorful twisted scarf. The fringes of both tunic and robe were embroidered with metallic thread.

His hair was long and dressed in the shape of a

fez, tied back by a knotted cloth. His beard was peculiarly cut; Enkidu realized that it was shaped to take an additional false beard when the merchant went forth on formal occasions. But the face was dominated by what it lacked: the left eye.

This was certainly the man. Enkidu wished there had been more time for him to think out his strategy. Here he stood: alone, weak, without weapon or money. What should he do?

Gabatha was no man to let another carry the conversation. He pushed away the remains of the stuffed duck on his platter and belched loudly. He picked a candied locust off a skewer and popped it into his mouth. Slaves cleared the table and retreated. "Well?"

"I—I have come from the temple of Ishtar on business—"

Gabatha yawned. "I have no dealings with the bitch of Ishtar or her minions."

"If you mean the priestess Tamar," Enkidu said angrily, "she is my wife."

Gabatha scratched his nose, but his eye did not waver. "Ten thousand men have wived her," he said agreeably. "I myself have—"

"She wouldn't touch an animal like you!"

"—often seen the clients lining up before her offices," Gabatha continued imperturbably. "But she and I do not get along. Now: your business?"

"I want to buy a slave from you." He knew even as he said it that this was not going to work. If only he had been able to enlist Tamar's help, instead of infuriating her! But there was so little time—if he were not already too late.

Gabatha's right eyebrow lifted. "For this insignificant matter you disturb me at table? Come to me during business watches, young man, and you can look over my stock."

"This one is special," Enkidu blurted out, and realized that this too was a blunder. The events of the day had dulled his wits, on top of everything else. Was it only this morning he had exchanged his last tablet with Amys? He was living in some dream world, where things happened with impossible swiftness, before he had time to think anything out.

"A *special* slave?"

There was no way of recovering her without identifying her. "Amyitis."

Gabatha's eye did not narrow, but Enkidu recognized the same too-gentle reaction he had seen in Tamar. "Amyitis," Gabatha mused. He tugged at a corner of his beard. "Daughter of Sargan?"

"The same." Woe, woe!

"Sold to me at public auction just this afternoon by order of the nameless temple. Now just what would your interest be in such a girl? Your special interest—when you did not see fit to bid for her?"

Enkidu, hopelessly unskilled at this sort of thing, thought it prudent to remain silent.

"You are husband to Ishtar—you claim. She did have a tablet posted—but her victim, it seems, was hidden away in the nameless temple." He studied Enkidu with new interest. "Your name?"

"Enkidu."

"Of Calah?"

Startled, Enkidu nodded. The merchant had a merchant's mind for names and places.

"So you are the one that that priest of Marduk . . ." Gabatha broke off, snorting with laughter. Some moments passed before he suppressed his private mirth enough to resume speech. "Yes, I begin to see a connection."

Did he guess at Enkidu's real relationship with Amys?

"What do you want with this chattel?"

. . . Still Gabatha could have no proof. The marriage tablet was hidden away safely in a hole in a dark wall. No—to this man revenge was more important than silver. Enkidu must school himself accordingly.

"I have a score to settle with Sargan's house."

The merchant's face became as blank as newly-erased clay. "Really?"

"I was Sargan's prisoner in the nameless temple."

Gabatha's eye became a slit. "So?"

He had to make this speech convincing. "It should be quite plain, sir. Sargan had me imprisoned and tortured—even though he knew I had committed no offense whatever against him or his house. He owes me for the damage he has done me. I have no clay tablet to avouch this debt. Therefore I must collect my payment from his house in whatever way presents itself. You are an intelligent man; surely you have some notion why I want his daughter."

"You are ready to pay out silver to me—and call that repayment against Sargan?"

"The debt is not of silver."

"You intend to hire her out?"

Enkidu managed to answer without a quaver. "No. I will send her body to Sargan."

Gabatha leaned back comfortably. "I see. Your idea has its merit. But you need not purchase her from me to achieve your end, since my intent is the same."

"It *isn't* the same. Vengeance is a personal thing. I must torture Sargan's daughter myself."

"She isn't really his daughter," Gabatha said. "The old fool was obviously enamored of her. He even went so far as to teach her scribe-lore—obviously a waste of effort on a female." He faced away as though dismissing the intruder. "My facilities are undoubtedly superior to yours."

"How so?" Enkidu demanded challengingly.

"I have special quarters for rendering willful slaves docile, and a water-chamber if all else fails. I had that constructed the moment this eye of mine was healed enough for me to attend to such matters. Do you know that I came close to losing the sight of the other eye also? Still, I am a reasonable man."

"You'll sell her to me, then?"

Gabatha appeared to consider the matter. He seized the dangling end of the scarf at his waist, rolled it between thumb and fingers to wipe off the grease. Enkidu had once seen a playmate throttle a bird with that same motion. His ringed hand reached; the black fingernails closed like a hawk's talons on a medlar. "Patience, young man." He bit delicately into the fruit. Satisfied of its ripeness, he took a large bite, savoring it thoughtfully. "I have waited for this day much longer than you have. Even so, I might sell this hellcat to you instead of finishing her off myself."

Enkidu had to say something, lest his face betray him. "I appreciate your unselfishness in this matter."

Gabatha looked at him closely. "Your score is with Sargan, and only secondarily with his daughter. Mine is directly with her. You could waylay Sargan as he leaves the temple, or hire Kebar thugs to do it. Why should you come instead for his fair daughter? You think to spare her, don't you?"

Enkidu was taken aback by the merchant's abrupt and accurate suspicion. "I have never set eyes on the wench. If she is attractive, so much the better; she will not remain so for long."

"Ha! You expect me to believe you have the stomach to do the job, when you can't even lie effectively? You fail by a good margin to look the part."

"You judge by appearances?" Enkidu made his voice angry. "Then see this!" He stepped to the table, pulled open his tunic.

Gabatha eased forward to examine the welts on Enkidu's belly. "Expert work," he remarked.

"These are the marks I bear from Sargan's torture-master. How do you suppose I entertained myself while I smelled the sizzle of my own flesh?"

"How?" Gabatha asked with some interest.

"I could stand the pain only be devising in my mind some worse and longer agony I would inflict in return, on Sargan and all his household. First those he holds dear—then, when he knows what is coming, Sargan himself. Amyitis would be far more fortunate at your hands than at mine."

Gabatha seemed impressed—almost. "Very well, then. I'm not one to deny another man his just entertainments. Let us compromise. We'll attend to her together. That way you'll save the price of her, and I'll have the benefit of your superior devisements.''

Enkidu was trapped. If he refused, he stood exposed; if he accepted, he would have to participate. Either way, Amyitis would die horribly. Gabatha had maneuvered him very neatly.

"I'll consider it,'' he said finally.

The merchant stood ponderously. ''Those irons should be ready by now. Right this way.''

Enkidu could do nothing but follow, filled with gloomy forebodings.

NK-2 tried to extend again, but the enemy presence was even stronger. This was increasingly hopeless. The host would not be diverted from his futile quest, and NK-2 could not even verify whether the girl supported an entity. At this point it made very little difference: TM-R was drawing near, and would not let him escape a second time.

At the end of the hall an armed eunuch guarded a blank door.

Amys' new cell.

At Gabatha's orders the guard quickly unbarred the cell entrance. What, Enkidu wondered sourly, would civilization ever do without eunuchs?

A brazier glowed within, its light smoke suffusing the room before winding its way up through a ceiling vent. Beyond that hole Enkidu saw the faintest twinkle of a few early stars. He wondered briefly whether the star of Ishtar was among them. No, the angle was wrong; but he did seem to hear a faint clamor of female voices. Probably Gabatha's harlot slaves carousing elsewhere in the building.

Glowing iron shafts were embedded in the fire of the brazier, in easy view of any prisoner. Firelight danced upon the walls. Across the back wall of the chamber were spikes and crude metal chains. Gabatha was rich indeed; there would be no running about or prying of loose bricks in this cell!

A single prisoner was there. The one Enkidu had been afraid to look for. She was dressed in a simple gray tunic. She knelt on the paving blocks, her hands suspended at the height of her shoulders by manacles fastened on her wrists and connected to the wall by the short chains. Her head was bent forward; the dark hair fell over her face and bosom. Enkidu was able to detect the gentle motion of her breathing, but she neither reacted nor responded in any way to their entrance.

Was this his wife, then? His lovely Amyitis, she of alert mind and sensitive spirit, passed from one prison cell to a worse one in so brief a time? Who now hung her head and let her long tresses touch the floor rather than look upon the instruments that her legal owner now planned to use on her?

How could Aten—her god!—how could he brook her delivery into this?

And if her own god had passively surrendered her into this evil place, then how could any lone mortal man hope to extricate her—or himself?

Steady. It would be an irretrievable blunder to betray his feelings now. He had to win the merchant's confidence.

Enkidu took hold of one end of a hot iron and

pulled it out. The thing had a wooden sheath on the handle—another expensive innovation. Naturally the torturer wouldn't want to be singed by his own poker!

A youthful slave dashed in from the hall. "Master!"

Gabatha fixed his servant with a one-eyed glare that made him cringe. "Idiot! Haven't I given all of you standing orders never to disturb me when I'm educating a troublemaker?"

The boy cowered. "Sir, the priestess is at the door. She says her—her husband Tammuz—she says he's here."

"Ishtar?" When the servant nodded, Gabatha said: "Bar the door against her."

So Tamar had followed him! She must have started out shortly after Enkidu himself had. She was going to help after all!

The slave backed away but did not leave. "Master— we cannot!"

Gabatha hefted another iron and brandished its glowing end at the boy. "*Cannot*? Do you value the nose on your face?"

The slave retreated further. "The bar—she got it loose before we could—already she is—"

"May Ishtar be fornicated by a leprous camel! Well, brace the furniture against the inner door for now, ostrich-head. Don't let that lioness past!"

The youth disappeared. Gabatha wheeled on Enkidu. "So that was your mischief? Worm your way into my house to spy out my valuables while your slut-queen follows! Well, my silver is locked away where neither of you will get your greedy fingers on it!"

"I don't think she's after silver," Enkidu said. He

had just realized with a chill that Tamar might have come to torture Amyitis herself. Her jealous fury—

"As for this spitfire," Gabatha said, looking at the prisoner, "I will not be made a fool of in my own house! You will take that rod and strike out her eyes—both of them!"

Enkidu stared at him with the cold courage of desperation. He replaced the rod in the brazier. "Don't order me about! What my wife does is her concern."

"Get on with it—if you don't want your own eyes forfeit!"

Was the merchant angry—or nervous? He and Tamar hated each other—and she was now invading his house. Maybe Enkidu could still turn this situation to his advantage, and save Amys!

Enkidu grunted, put his hand on another rod, turned it in the brazier. Its end was white. "Her face is down," he complained, looking up. "Her hands are too close. How am I supposed to get at her eyes?"

"We'll take care of that." Gabatha snapped his fingers and the eunuch stepped in silently. Enkidu wondered if the man's tongue had been cut out, to preserve the secrets of this chamber. "Remove those chains and hold her up!"

Remove her chains. *Some* god was smiling on them!

"Master!" another messenger called, stumping in from the hall. This was an elderly man. Apparently these slaves took turns with bad news, so that Gabatha's wrath would not be concentrated on any one person. "The priestess is disrobing. We cannot stop her!"

"Well, tie her in my bed after she finishes and *I'll*

stop her!'' Gabatha roared, still brandishing the rod. ''With this hot iron . . .''

He gestured obscenely with it.

''Master! She has the Ishtaritu with her—many of them. They are all screaming and disrobing—''

Gabatha clapped his free hand to his forehead. ''Bless me for a winged bull, must I do *everything* myself! Tell the household guard to set up a skirmish line in the first courtyard and skewer the first slut who shows her face—or anything else. What does that woman think my house is?'' he muttered as the slave took off.

''Hades,'' Enkidu answered.

The eunuch had freed Amys and stood her upright. Enkidu's breath stopped. She was slim and fair and firm under the tunic. Almost unconsciously Enkidu reached out to touch the long black hair that still flowed across her face.

''Don't bother with the hair,'' Gabatha advised. ''That will burn away. Just go for the eyes. Now!''

Enkidu hefted the rod.

Noting Enkidu's hesitation with impatience, Gabatha put his own hand on the iron. Enkidu jerked it away.

''The rod will cool!'' said Gabatha with exasperation.

So Enkidu replaced it in the coals. ''How can I be sure this is Sargan's daughter?'' he demanded. ''I don't want to blind an imposter!''

Gabatha was red with anger and impatience. ''Do you suppose I'd buy the wrong girl? This is the one.''

The girl spoke for the first time, from behind the

black hair. Her voice was surprisingly pleasant, considering the surroundings. "I am the butterfly."

Enkidu measured the distance between Gabatha and the eunuch. He would have to deal with both of them.

"Master!" a third messenger called. "Ishtar stands naked, and the guards won't shoot her. They just stare—"

Gabatha mouthed an obscenity that put his prior efforts to shame. "Summon those guards here," he got out finally. "They'll throw their spears when *I* give the order, or I'll geld them with my own fingernails!"

The lad departed.

Enkidu had quietly taken another rod in hand, good and hot. Now he leaped forward, swinging the weapon at the eunuch's neck. Amys was in front, but the eunuch was larger and taller, so that there was room for an angled blow. Flesh sizzled.

The man screamed—no mute, after all!—and seized the rod.

Amys, freed now, instantly leaped for Gabatha. She butted him in the soft stomach so that he skidded back, off-balance. His gross backside barged into the brazier, upsetting it. Bright embers scattered across the paved floor as the merchant landed solidly in their midst. He bellowed.

Enkidu felt a touch. Amys had grasped his hand.

But the eunuch was moving. Enkidu shoved Amys away with a force that sent her staggering—just in time for the thrown rod to miss her. The iron grazed Enkidu's shoulder, burning him, and landed beyond.

"Out!" he shouted at her.

*   *   *

With that contact NK-2 verified that the girl was host to no entity—and never had been. All his trepidation had been for nothing!

But where, then, was the galactic representative?

But more of Gabatha's household guards were there, and in a moment they had both Enkidu and Amyitis captive.

Gabatha was in the process of picking himself up. His face was livid—and so was his posterior, where it showed through the burn-holes.

"Hold her there!" he cried, his flabby lips trembling. He half-stumbled, half-hobbled through the door and toward a wall down the hall—a wall covered by a great tapestry.

"What about this one, Master?" the eunuch asked, indicating Enkidu as he rubbed his scorched neck.

Gabatha hardly paused. "Let him come and watch this," he said without turning.

Two guards dragged Amys along. Her head was down again and he still could not see her face.

"I want this slut dead! Dead! DEAD!" Gabatha cried, his voice rising hysterically. "Since I first set my eye on her she has brought me nothing but ill chance. Bring her to the water room!"

Gabatha himself jerked up a corner of the tapestry. Behind the woven scene was a small door.

The water room.

Enkidu could guess what it was for. He cried out in protest, but the eunuch was not to be caught off guard again. He stopped Enkidu at the first step.

One guard opened the little door. Two others shoved

the girl through it head first. A gasp escaped her—
but the sound of it was cut off by the slamming door.

"Hoist the sluice gate!" Gabatha cried, his voice
shrill with urgency and excitement.

A slave sprang to an alcove beside the door. There
was a circular crank there, similar to those used on
drawbridges. "Don't!" Enkidu cried at the slave.
"Don't turn it!" But he was impotent to stop Gabatha's
revenge.

The shrill screeches of women reverberated down
the hall. Ishtar was coming to the rescue! Or whatever she had in mind. But she had reached only
another room in this extensive house, and there was
still considerable scuffling.

"Open the sluice!" Gabatha cried again.

The eunuch held Enkidu while the slave at the
wheel gave it a full turn. He was forced to watch,
though there was nothing *to* watch, horrified, and
helpless.

There was no audible roar of water from the river.
Only a long, final silence. Enkidu realized dimly that
the walls and doors were too thick for those in this
hall to hear the lethal rush of liquid down the sluice
and into the chamber.

Gabatha broke the silence after some moments,
with a satisfied sigh. "Over so soon. Well, now it's
done. Now she's drowned, may my luck change!"

Enkidu, stunned, fought the full import. As in a
dream that did not concern him he saw Tamar step
naked into the hall, followed by her nude horde.
Even the eunuch gasped at these wild natural beauties.

The priestess spotted Enkidu. She spoke to him as
though they two were alone in the hall.

"Tammuz!"

NK-2 was in no condition to rejoin the battle with TM-R. The enemy would vanquish him in minutes if physical contact were maintained between the hosts. He had to get away!

Fortunately his host wanted no further part of TM-R's host. Guidance was easy for the moment.

Out! Out! Out! he urged.

CHAPTER 16

Enkidu, driven by horror, fled Gabatha's house. Tamar tried to hold him, but he shoved her away in his blind rush to escape, and lost her in the crowd of men and women filling the house.

A full moon rode high in the east, casting its pale yellow light and deep shadows upon the streets and the distant celebrants and the cubic houses. The Milky Way spread out above, a luminous, tattered veil, bringing to mind another night he had walked alone in the streets of Babylon. Now, as then, he felt an eerie camaraderie with that vision, as though the stars were something more than mere light to decorate and alleviate the monotony of night. He felt an unreasonable urge to rise up to one of those stars, and live there, joining with other entities. . . .

From one end of the street hooves clopped restively against the solid-packed debris and brick fragments. In the moonlight and the fitful glare of the torch of a passer-by he made out a bearded man in a faded soldier's tunic of foreign cut. And a pie-bald horse.

It looked very much like a Persian.

"Enkidu!"

He jumped, but it was not the horseman who had called. Tamar had wrestled her way out of the house, and now came purposely toward him, garbed as before. No—he saw now that she had donned a loose robe whose color was subdued in the moonlight, to the point of invisibility. Two or three of her women trailed her, pulling on similar apparel and studying the horseman with an interest that seemed reciprocal.

Enkidu waited dully as she approached. But he had a sudden, irrational premonition: he must not let her touch him. Something—perhaps his childhood *shedu* voice—was warning him of dire consequence . . . if.

"Enkidu—I'm going to be terribly busy now that the city has changed hands—"

"Changed hands?" He glanced again at the soldier.

"You don't know? Look around you. The Persian is here."

"Yes, I see him."

"I mean all the Persians. The host of them. Gobryas' men are inside the walls now—"

"Gobryas?" He edged away as she edged near.

"Cyrus' general. Cyrus himself will no doubt be here soon . . ."

Enkidu stared at her, jerked for a moment from his general state of shock. "They're *inside*? Where is the fighting? The pillage?"

Yet the Hebrew slave had said something—and

where there was one Persian, there could be a thousand more. He recalled how indifferent the residents of Babylon had seemed to the threat of Cyrus, though the man had already had impressive successes in the field. Could it be—could it possibly be—that Cyrus had kept Babylon waiting only in order to take her at the right time? That he had waited as one waits for a medlar—for that precise moment between ripeness and rot when one may with profit bite into the fruit?

The old wonder and awe of Babylon remained. She was a lovely, careless woman, who needed the guiding hand that her own ruler had failed to hold out to her.

"Elsewhere in the city, what there is of it," Tamar said, answering his question after a long pause. She, too, was contemplating the Persian soldier speculatively. "But no one is eager to go out and get killed over an issue already decided. So long as their homes and places of business are not looted, they will not give the conqueror much trouble, I think. Cyrus is not one to permit indiscriminate pillage."

"But what about the defenders on the walls, the soldiers? No army could pass—"

"The mercenaries? The Persian troops got around the wall somehow, and not by tunneling. Maybe they turned into birds and flew in. They're here, anyway, and the cone-heads on the wall are not breaking their legs rushing out to get themselves skewered, either. Not for townspeople who show no interest in defending themselves and who probably aren't good for their next wages. I daresay the wallkeepers will have to go to work now—for Cyrus."

She was still slinking toward him, and he was still

retreating. They were a good distance down the street now. "You'd better see to your women," Enkidu suggested. He just wanted to be left alone with his grief.

"I thought we might—" she began, but broke off when she saw that she wasn't going to catch him. So, with another easy about-face, she pulled her half-open robe about her. "Yes. I'm going to be terribly busy now. All those Persian soldiers hot from the campaign . . . we'll have to put the temple on double shift. A—a husband would only obstruct things now. I'm afraid I'm going to have to divorce you—"

If she expected that threat to change his mind, she was mistaken. "I understand," Enkidu said dully. "I wouldn't want to interfere with your religion."

For an instant total rage distorted her face. Then, so quickly that he wondered if he had imagined her anger, she was smiling graciously and waving an affectionate parting to him. She moved back up the street with her women in tow.

Perversely, now, he was sorry to see her go. It could have been a memorable experience. . . .

But not so soon after his real love had died! He must respect the worship of another person, however sensual and self-interested . . . but that did not require him to bury his love for Amys in the arms of the priestess of Ishtar.

His aspirations had been small as the world reckoned such things, he thought grayly as he tramped without destination up one New City street and down another. He could still hear the inebriated celebrants of the Harvest Festival. Those people would have an extremely sober awakening tomorrow!

Harvest Festival . . . the harvest of his aspirations would have involved the death of no person, the conquest of no city. He had wanted only to commune with his chosen god and to honor that god in the conduct of his life. He respected the ambitions of other people; if only others had seen fit to respect *his*! Even slaves, most of them, had choice of god and woman—both denied to him forever.

Why?

One god or another had smiled on the ambitions of Cyrus, and of Nebuchadnezzar before him, and of the old Assyrian kings before that . . .

NK-2 was safe for the moment. But his job was not done. He had to locate the galactic representative of Station A-10, and formulate some initiative to eliminate the enemy. The repair craft was due soon, and if TM-R intercepted *that*. . . ! In fact TM-R might have let him go again, deliberately, planning to pounce when he went either to his own craft or made contact with the repair mission.

TM-R had enormous leverage, for the host Tamar could influence almost any man in Babylon, including the Persian commander. He would have to do whatever was necessary here, then get out of the city before the enemy finally moved to eliminate *him*. If he found the other galactic, he could take him away too. Possibly together they could make an effective counterstroke, perhaps by investing Cyrus himself and having him execute Tamar for sedition.

His host was walking aimlessly when time was precious. It was time for new motivation. He had to check the nameless temple thoroughly, exploring everywhere with his penumbra.

But that was the last place Enkidu would want to go! How could he reverse that inclination, at least for an hour?

Perhaps through the man's own grief, unkind as that was. Unless he helped mitigate that sorrow at the same time— Yes. There *was* a relevant concept!

. . . Yet no god had seen fit to intervene to prevent the imprisonment and slavery and death of a young and gentle girl who had worshiped a god of mercy. Indeed, her road to oblivion had begun at the point where she expected her god to honor his commitments.

Could he have saved her by holding out against the torture? Would Aten then have intervened, however belatedly, on Amys' behalf?

No. A man had to do what he felt was right, and Enkidu had done that. If the genii were by their magic arts to give him back the last few days, he would renounce his god as quickly as before, and for the same reason. The only change he would make would be to fetch a dagger along for his visit to Gabatha, that he might slay the fat merchant before the beast slew Amyitis!

But how could that be justified in the name of mercy?

Was it thus that mortals were broken—by the worship of gods whose principles no mortal could fathom or honor?

He put this cold enigma aside. There was a single muddy marriage tablet imbedded in a prison wall that was worth more to him than all the machinations of—

The tablet!

She had been alive when she drew her signature and then passed the document back to him, pledging their union. That was all he could ever have now of Amys—the words of love she had written while near him, though prisoner.

THY LOVE IS AS THE SCENT OF CEDAR WOOD. . . .

He *must* recover it!

A Persian soldier stood outside the nameless temple. Other curly-bearded troopers guarded other places of value. Cyrus had indeed taken over the city. Would this sentry let him enter, or would he take Enkidu for a looter?

Enkidu rose to the occasion with a cunning he had not known he possessed. He marched boldly up. "What are you doing here?" he demanded with authority. "I do not know you."

The guard was impressed. "Go about your business, citizen." He had a heavy accent.

"My business lies in the temple. I am a Pretender," he said, making it sound important. "You—you're foreign, aren't you? A mercenary?"

"I am a Mede," the man said haughtily. "In the service of Cyrus the Conqueror. Just be glad I bother to speak your decadent language!"

"But Cyrus is outside the walls!"

The man fingered his beard. "That situation has changed." He reached impatiently for his dagger.

"Be off, before I forget my orders to treat you natives courteously."

Enkidu backed off—toward the temple door. "But no one has breached the walls," he protested, hoping the soldier would unriddle the mystery. "Babylon is impregnable."

"*Was* impregnable," the Mede said. "Now go! I can't have you getting underfoot." He waved his long dagger, and Enkidu retreated through the temple door.

The Persian troops, he realized, were good ones— well disciplined and not overbright. But how had they penetrated the city? This was a most unusual conquest!

He felt his way along the dark interior passage. Soon, traveling with more confidence as the terrain became familiar, he found the inside stair leading to the dungeons. The long period in these cells had educated his feet and fingertips. Less than a day and a night had passed since his residence. He passed the silent clock room. Presently he found the door to Amys' old cell, then his own. The very closeness of the atmosphere seemed homey now, almost pleasant. Certainly it was familiar! This was the place where love had come to him. Through this wall he had conversed with her, had come to know her. . . .

He loosened the key brick, fumbled for the tablet. His questing fingers discovered only ordinary bricks. Anxiously he removed them, first from the outer layer and then from the inner.

The tablet was gone.

But there was something else. Soft, woven material:

cloth. He drew it out, felt the long fine shape of it.
There was a hood, square sleeves . . . a cloak?

The marriage tablet gone; in its place a rich tunic.

It did not take Enkidu long to comprehend that the
cloak had belonged to Sargan.

NK-2 quested out, alert for the presence of the
enemy. But the environment was clear. Still, he had
to be cautious, for this could be an enemy trap. If he
invested too much of himself checking potential hosts,
and then TM-R struck—

Better to bring his own host close to any prospects,
so that he could check by restricted, concentrated
penumbra. Not direct physical contact, for if TM-R
lurked here, that would be disastrous. But close
noncontact, so that his field was most effective while
the risk of invasion remained minimal.

If he could just get his host to circulate, here in the
temple. . . .

Sargan. How understand such a man? He had committed savage and calculated atrocities. He had imprisoned countless pretenders, supervised their torture,
ruthlessly obliterated their honest, innocent faith. Only
after he had rendered them broken and godless had
he released them. All in the name of a god of mercy,
of whom Sargan deemed himself Chosen. Even his
own daughter, whose sole malefaction had been a
human compassion. . . .

Had this last act of his, the most evil transaction of
all, been too great a load for even his hardened
conscience? Obviously Sargan had come to this
cell, found the tablet, divested himself of his cloak,

and departed. Who could guess what jealous imperative guided him? Selling his daughter to Gabatha. . . .

He had no further business here. Sargan had deprived him of the last vestige of Amyitis. And yet—

There must be something of Amys here. There had to be! Some tangible token that she had once existed. Something she had touched. Something he could take and keep and cherish in lieu of the marriage tablet.

Should he search her cell?

No. He did not want to think of her in that filth and squalor. Anything he might find there would be associated only with her days of anguish and terror.

What about her seal? Sargan had evidently kept Enkidu's own seal in the clock-room. Could Amyitis' seal still be there?

Enkidu noticed with surprise when he reached the clock-room that he was still clutching Sargan's cloak. He laid it down on Sargan's chair, then proceeded to ransack the room. If he could find her seal. . . .

Nothing. There were parchment-rolls, but all were bare. These fragile records were easy to destroy, and the priest had set his house in order before vacating.

"Amyitis!" he cried, in the tone he had once used to invoke his god. But, like his god, she was not here.

There were footsteps in the hall. Someone was coming!

He must not be seen here—but there was only the one exit. He looked about the room for a place to hide, finding nothing. Then his eye fell on Sargan's robe.

In almost one motion Enkidu managed to slip into it, struggling with the voluminous sleeves and awkward cowl. He seated himself in Sargan's chair, pulling the cowl close about his face.

It was Amalek, who looked at the robed figure in obvious surprise. "I had thought you departed already," he remarked.

So Sargan had left. "Not yet," Enkidu ventured almost in a whisper, hoping his voice would not betray him.

Amalek, somewhat at a loss, informed him of the latest news. There were rumors that Nabonaid had been assassinated; that the invaders were commanded by a general named Gobryas; that Cyrus himself would arrive later for a triumphal entry into Babylon. However that might be, Amalek added in tentative relief, the Persians were no Assyrians; apparently the populace was not to be indiscriminately butchered. But Gobryas had already stipulated that no things of value were to be moved, on pain of instant confiscation. The temple treasures would have to remain here until such time as the Persians came to take inventory and levy tribute.

Enkidu merely nodded in the manner of Sargan and hoped that Amalek would go away. But the man lingered. "Your orders with regard to the pretender Amyitis have been carried out."

That much Enkidu already knew.

After a moment, Amalek added: "I have daughters of my own, as you know. I intend to raise them in unenlightened heathendom, and my son also. Perhaps in the Persian worship of Ahura Mazda."

At last he left. Enkidu relaxed and looked at the frieze. The wall flickered in the light of the single lamp and strange pictures seemed to form. He wondered whether Aten could be seen within that framework, were Aten not a false god. It was as though everything pertaining to him belonged in a different life—a life now vanished like the glories of Nineveh. There was nothing for him here.

There was nothing for him anywhere.

He remembered Tamar's comment that a god was very like a man.

Perhaps a god needed men for fulfillment of his divine existence, even as men needed a god in fulfillment of their mortal existence. Perhaps—

NK-2 wrenched himself out of it. He had been following his host's mental processes so closely, seeking the proper spot to nudge them in an advantageous direction, that he had started thinking like a man! Soon, if he were not careful, he would begin believing in the god Aten himself!

He had checked the native Amalek and found him void. Now he extended, alert for the enemy, seeking to locate the other natives of this temple.

Abruptly he encountered the expanding penumbra of another entity. He recoiled automatically before he realized that it was not TM-R.

It was another galactic. The station representative!

Enkidu realized that Dishon's torture had forced him to examine his simple faith in greater depth, and that faith had thereby vanished into the nothingness of illusion. But he had also lost part of himself. He was now a wiser but a lesser man. The elimination of his innocence had made him less worthy than before. For a time he had replaced the love of his unattain-

able god with the love of an unobtainable woman—
and now no vestige remained of either, and he was
empty.

He divested himself of Sargan's robe—and felt
something hard and cylindrical in a pocket of one
sleeve. He brought it out.

It was a seal, and it bore an intaglio design.

A butterfly.

"Thank Aten!" The words were out before he
thought. It seemed that he could never entirely give
over his faith, though he certainly could not accept it.
Gone were the old certainties, either of belief or of
disbelief.

He held up the seal and imagined it dangling between the breasts of a carefree young girl as she went
about her concerns . . . this seal, whose purpose was
to stamp the imprint of her existence on the clay
documents that were a part of every Babylonian's
transactions.

Its symbolism staggered him in a sudden flash of
revelation, and he wondered that he had never grasped
it before.

The imprint of the seal upon clay. It symbolized
the more subtle but unmistakable imprint of the spirit
on the clay of life. . . .

The seal existed after Amyitis herself had died.
The imprints it had made could endure after the seal
was gone. The imprint of Amys' spirit, her love,
remained on him regardless of her physical fate.

And the imprint of Aten remained upon them both,
whether Aten existed now or not. Whether he had
ever existed.

Perhaps Aten was not a god. Perhaps he was no

more than a *shedu*, an invisible spirit. Perhaps he had descended from those bright stars above Babylon, and touched just a few people, and departed. Now, because he was gone, he could be labeled false—but that was only one way of looking at it.

As meaning to writing, so was that spirit to its host. As the seal on the envelope of an important document, validating it—false if the tablet were broken, but true so long as it remained intact.

Enkidu's tablet—the tablet of his faith—had been broken. Yet he needed to validate that faith to no other person. Should he recover that faith, it would be as valid as before: his private tablet would be whole again. That was the difference between the spirit and the clay.

Somehow it seemed that if he could only heal that faith, recovering his god, all would be well again—*no matter what else happened*.

NK-2: I am NK-2, docked under duress equipment.

DS-1: I am DS-1, galactic representative, Station A-10.

NK-2: (appalled) Your host is . . . Dishon?

DS-1: Of course.

NK-2: You permitted your host to torture mine!

DS-1: This station is under siege by the enemy. There have been many ruses, many traps. I dared not—

NK-2: Why did you not send a galactic distress signal?

DS-1: (hesitating) It would have looked bad on my record.

NK-2: Do you think it will look better on your record to be charged with the deliberate harassment of stranded galactics?

DS-1: It is difficult to check every detail when under siege.

NK-2: That detail was the very validity of your mission! You denied the host of a galactic entity who had come to A-10 for sanctuary!

DS-1: The enemy is extraordinarily powerful. Had I made one mistake—

NK-2: One mistake! Your entire tenure here has been mistaken. You were a fool to permit the unobstructed landing of an enemy craft, twice a fool to withhold your distress call, three times a fool not to verify the identity of every potential host entering the premises, four times a fool to let the natives learn of Station A-10—and how could you ever have blundered so egregiously as to allow a galactic station to be *worshiped as a native deity?*

DS-1: We are required to blend with the population. The natives of this planet have extraordinary deistic identification. Your own host—

NK-2: Granted. My own host rationalized my directive along deistic lines. But that was an emergency situation. You are an established galactic representative trained to compensate for such tendencies. You have bungled horrendously, and have forfeited any right to your position. When I report—

DS-1 did not respond. His penumbra withdrew, severing communication. NK-2's own penumbra permeated the temple, locating his alternate host Sargan in the torture chamber with Dishon, experiencing great pain. But the host Dishon was closed as the native walked out of that chamber and entered the hall.

Suddenly NK-2 realized why. He had talked of being a fool—but he had been a fool himself to emulate native thinking! He had openly threatened to report DS-1's incompetence—when that entity's whole effort for the past seventy years had been to conceal his mistakes, even though by so doing he compromised his very mission.

So DS-1 was about to cover up again—by taking the most compromising step of all. He was bringing his host to attack NK-2's host. Galactic murder! The eunuch was far more powerful than the tortured scribe.

To make it worse, NK-2 lacked any real control over his own host. Both DS-1 and TM-R had had sufficient occasion to select and tame their hosts, but NK-2 had never established a proper liaison. Thus DS-1 had a double advantage.

Finally, NK-2's host was trapped here in the nameless temple. The eunuch, moving purposefully, had already blocked the lone exit-hall.

Like host, like entity! NK-2 thought ruefully. Ten times a fool—to walk into such a trap before threatening the galactic representative!

He disliked the necessity intensely, but he would have to make a deal.

NK-2: You and I together—we could vanquish TM-R. Then there would be no irregularity to report—

TM-R: Most interesting! Come to the Temple of Ishtar and—

NK-2 collapsed his penumbra so rapidly it hurt. Oh, no! The enemy now controlled this ambience!

There would be no deals—even if DS-1 found the courage to stand up to the enemy. Actually the station agent was already in such trouble that even elimination of TM-R would not suffice. And despite his probable fate, NK-2 was relieved not to have to compromise himself by promising silence.

Was this what TM-R had set up next? A death battle between the only two galactic entities on the planet? Surely the result would be an enemy planet; that required no oracle to foresee!

What could he do? Deal with the enemy? NO— that would be the worst betrayal of all. Actually DS-1 had collaborated with the enemy to the extent of suppressing the message of warning; perhaps that was why the siege had been subtle. TM-R was afraid that message would still be sent, the moment DS-1 felt himself in danger of oblivion. So it was a kind of impasse. Actual collusion between galactic and enemy was almost unthinkable—but in a prolonged and indecisive encounter far from civilization, certain degradation of standards could occur. As in this case.

The host Dishon was close. He was coming up the steps leading to the interrogation room: Enkidu could hear his footsteps. NK-2 remained trapped.

First things first. He sent an urgent directive to his host, one easily intelligible in the circumstance: *Danger! Hide! Defend!*

And the host, preoccupied with his own concerns, responded beautifully. He ran to the heavy door, pulled it closed, and slammed the wooden bar across. The other host could not enter. Not immediately.

But this was not enough. Enkidu might hold out for hours, but hardly for days. His resources, never great, were extremely low now. Only his intense deistic and romantic preoccupations maintained him in operating order despite his recent torture and fatigue. If Dishon was desperate enough to chop down the door, or even to set fire to the temple—

NK-2 had to gamble. He had to summon help, though he squandered all his remaining resources. The enemy penumbra prevented any normal contacts, but he could still needle to any previously checked potential host. It would exhaust his strength to motivate such an alternate through his penumbra alone— but he had no choice, now. It was a desperation move.

Yet who was there? Sargan was bound and helpless. Dishon could balk any of the other natives of the temple. And he had not checked any outside natives, except—

Unless—

If he were wrong—and that was the likelihood—

NK-2 would lose his penumbra uselessly. But if he could verify. . . .

He massed his energy and needled out, piercing the enemy ambience before TM-R could formulate a counterstroke.

And won.

It came upon Enkidu with a sudden fierce clarity: *She lived!* He had no tangible evidence, yet he was certain.

He looked about, dazed by the revelation. He was in the room of the water-clock, and someone was pounding on the closed door. In a fit of terror he had barred it.

Terror was irrelevant now. *She lived!* He had to go to her.

He unblocked the door. The slave Dishon charged in, a torture iron in his gloved hand.

Enkidu knew he should be afraid, for the eunuch obviously intended mayhem. But he had no intention of being balked now. She lived—and no man would interfere with their reunion. "Get out of my way, slave," he snapped.

Dishon hesitated, seeing Sargan's white cowl on the floor. The torturemaster could not know that the pale, shadowed figure standing in this room was not Sargan. But that would fool him only momentarily, for there was light enough. And the eunuch seemed to be guided by some unusual imperative.

Dishon raised the iron bar. It reminded Enkidu of the rod intended for Amyitis' eyes, there in Gabatha's cell. It was hot, but cooling; it had been minutes out of the brazier.

A film of holy anger passed before his eyes. No such instrument would be suffered again! He reached up and caught the end of it as Dishon struck.

Flesh sizzled, but Enkidu felt no pain. He did not let go.

Dishon fell back, astonished. Enkidu wrenched the iron from his flaccid fingers and held it aloft. He pursued the torturemaster slowly across the room while the stink of his own burning flesh irritated his nostrils.

Dishon backed into the table. The water-clock toppled and crashed with a jangle and splatter.

Enkidu dropped the hot iron. ''You are less than that to me,'' he said, and turned his back. He walked out.

CHAPTER 17

Pale dawn was upon the city. The inebriate throngs were gone at last. Persian troops patrolled the streets instead. An empire had fallen during the night!

He probably ought to care, Enkidu thought. But now there was pain in his hand, as though he had blistered it in a furnace; he remembered only vaguely how that had happened. Babylon's subjection seemed as unreal as all the rest that had happened this night.

How strange that there were no stones or spears or flaming arrows—yet the Persian had conquered. No slaughter of citizens, no razing of buildings, no sacking and looting and burning, no impalements. It hardly was a proper war!

As he started across the bridge to the new city, the tradesmen began to appear. There were many Persians here, too. A cart loaded with foodstuffs lumbered across the bridge, causing the skittish horse of a trooper to whinny and rear. Enkidu dodged back, then had to catch himself from falling over the edge. The rider cursed at Enkidu, thinking him to blame. Otherwise he was ignored.

In the growing light the river bed showed as an almost solid bank of mud.

But he had to keep going, lest his sudden, precious faith that Amys lived be lost. Let the mighty Euphrates sink to nothing; that hardly concerned him. Certainly the river was overrated. Could it ever have been very impressive! Why construct such a massive bridge?

He paused, startled by something obscure, then bent over and stared down. No, he had not been mistaken; the great river *had* fallen, even since he saw it last. The muddy pylons reached up out of gray muck festooned with weeds and rope and debris. Small boats were moored far from the tiny trickle of water remaining. A stale, tainted odor rose from the new mud flats. What had happened?

First the Persians had appeared mysteriously inside the impregnable city. Then the river had dried up. Twin mysteries. Could they be linked? Was Babylon truly cursed, as the Kebar Hebrews had eagerly foretold?

He stared out at the vanished river as in some nightmare between sleeping and waking, while another level of his mind pondered Amyitis and his certainty that she lived.

Abruptly everything fell together. The world jumped into focus.

*   *   *

The host had finally caught on. NK-2 could not stop him now, and had no need to. As soon as this business was finished, they could depart Babylon. . . .

He was running despite his weakness, fighting the jostling horses, the cursing men, dodging between a farm wagon laden with cackling poultry and the donkey pulling it, while the wagon's driver struck at him with a whip and the poultry set up an awful din of squawks. Enkidu untangled himself from the traces, scarcely aware of the commotion, and pressed on forward. He slipped around a herd of baa-ing sheep being driven into the city by shouting shepherds and barking mastiffs. He pushed wildly past or around or through all the slow-moving obstacles. On towards Gabatha's house.

Aten must have given him that faith in Amys' life—until his own observation and logic augmented it.

Close enough to the truth, this time! NK-2 thought. Maybe he *was* the spirit of a deistic entity. . . .

"I have business within," Enkidu informed the Persian soldier who challenged him outside Gabatha's house. It was amazing how rapidly Cyrus' host had multiplied in the past few hours.

The trooper's hairy face broke into an unpleasant grin. "A guest of Gabatha's? Enter, enter!"

Though the sun had barely cleared the horizon, the house seethed with activity. Servants rushed about bearing jars and baskets and there was a steady commotion within. The great courtyard swarmed with bearded Medes, and with women making them welcome. The fat merchant must be providing a banquet, sparing no expense for the invaders. Trust him to ingratiate himself with the prevailing powers!

But, oddly, most of the soldiers seemed more attentive to the preparations afoot in the center of the court than to the wine and the women. Enkidu looked where they were looking—and went sick inside.

Gabatha himself stood with feet planted in the middle of the court, directing the placement of a very long stake into a freshly dug hole.

"Set it loose," the merchant directed a couple of sweating slaves, "so that it can easily be taken out again once we fit it. Once we get our chief entertainer for today skewered, then you can set it up again and tamp it in solid . . . assuming you are not already on it."

Both slaves blanched. So did Enkidu, though Gabatha had not noticed him. What gruesome entertainment!

The stake set to his satisfaction, the merchant turned his eye to a group of slaves assembled at the far end of the court. He beckoned genially.

"Our Persian friends have expressed a desire for a skewering," he informed them, smiling. "Old-Assyrian style. What man of you will step forward to oblige our good friends? No volunteers for this simple task? You will not even have to stand on your feet, and you will have a lofty view of all the proceedings. . . ."

Enkidu rubbed his rear as he always did when thinking of impalement. He couldn't help it. Obviously Gabatha had someone in mind . . . *did he realize Amyitis remained alive?*

"Then *I* shall have to make the choice, I suppose. Now which one of you worthless servants can I most easily dispense with? Hul, step forth!"

Hul stepped forth, most reluctantly. He was a young boy with a scared face. Enkidu had seen him last night, bearing the first message . . . so that was how the merchant dealt with those who annoyed him by bringing bad news!

Gabatha eyed the boy appraisingly. "I have always wondered how you would look when elevated to your proper station. This is an excellent occasion to find out, don't you agree?"

The boy's Adam's apple dropped. The Persians guffawed—somewhat more heartily than the jest called for, it seemed to Enkidu.

Gabatha paused until the merriment subsided, then sighed with mock regret. "Alas, you are needed in the kitchen. Go!"

Hul did not need a second order.

"Azor, step forth!"

Azor was the elderly man who had brought the second message of distress. What a memory the merchant had for grievances, however trifling! But obviously he was only teasing these poor slaves for the entertainment of the guests. He *knew* who would grace that stake. . . .

It seemed, after leisurely preliminaries, that Azor was needed to see to the stabling of the Persian horses. He, too, vanished.

The faces of those who remained as Gabatha dismissed a third to his household duties were a study in quiet terror. The last to be queried . . . would not be dismissed.

Encouraged by his guests' pleasure, Gabatha continued his cruel game. No one paid any attention to
Enkidu.

He stepped quietly into a side hall and hurried
toward the back. A guard stopped him in the first
hall.

Enkidu wanted to shove the man aside and rush on
by, to Amys. But this would be folly. It was one
thing to get to this house, but another and more
difficult thing to get to Amys . . . without betraying
her life to Gabatha again.

"I have to—to see someone."

The guard took his arm in a grip of stone. "Yes
you do, citizen. Right this way."

Perforce, Enkidu accompanied the man down the
hall into a second and smaller court, where a monstrous Persian was directing Gabatha's servants in
preparations for what was evidently to be an all-day
feast. Servants scurried between the courts bearing
huge platters of savory mutton and stuffed poultry
and wines and breads. The guard propelled Enkidu to
a Persian officer who sat at an improvised table
dictating to a scribe. Apparently he was taking inventory of their host's very substantial properties. To see
that none were molested?

"A man who has to see somebody," the guard
reported, shoving Enkidu to a halt in front of the
table. The officer looked up.

He was an older man than any of the other Persians
Enkidu had noticed here: at least fifty, clean shaven,
gray at the temples but with a predatory sharpness of
feature and thick graying eyebrows.

"What is your business?"

What should he say? Enkidu decided to misconstrue the question. "I am a scribe—"

"Excellent! I can use you! Pick up a tablet and stylus. I will pay you one shekel a day for good notes."

Had Enkidu bluffed about his occupation, this sharp soldier would have made short work of him! But the last thing he wanted was to be detained in this place. "I—I mean to depart Babylon within the hour."

The officer lifted the tablet from the hands of his own scribe, holding it up for Enkidu to see. "Read—or you may depart this *life* within the hour!"

Enkidu read: "SLAVES, HOUSEHOLD—23. SLAVES, BROTHEL—42. PROPERTIES—"

The officer lowered the tablet, having verified Enkidu's ability. "Friend of our host?" he inquired casually.

It meant trouble, Enkidu knew. But he was through with temporizing, and he saw that little could be concealed from this pragmatic Persian. "Gabatha is no friend of mine! I came inside his door only to rescue someone from his dungeon."

The officer smiled bleakly. Enkidu suddenly realized that the man had been drinking, though he had himself well under control. "We saw to his dungeon. He had no prisoners there."

Enkidu's breath stopped. Then he remembered the tapestry that hid the entrance to the water room. The Persians would not know about that.

"So I cannot believe you, Babylonian," the man said, belching formidably. "Surely an enemy does not visit this house on such a happy occasion! Come—my men are weary with slogging in the silt of the river, since the garrison neglected to open the gates for us. The merchant is our esteemed host. He is our dearest friend. He loves all Persians—Medes, too. I insist you join us in enjoying the hospitality of this house.''

Enkidu decided he might as well be speared for a crocodile as for a lizard. The Persians would not let him go, anyway. ''I will never feast under this roof! Gabatha is your friend, not mine!''

''Are you implying you don't like Persians?''

''I care nothing for politics, or who rules Babylon. I don't have any feeling about Persians. But never will I associate with this murderer, this traiter, this refuse—this Gabatha! Only let me do what I came to do and I'll depart.''

The Persian sat back and appraised Enkidu. His head nodded slightly from the drink he had taken. ''You sound almost as though you dislike our esteemed host.''

Was there any way he could extricate Amys without revealing to this man that he had come for a woman? ''Yes.''

A servant brought the Persian a large jar of ale. He blew off the foam and quaffed the brown fluid from a mug. Presently he said: ''He had two eyes, Gabatha, when he visited Ectabana twenty years ago. He was my house guest, and he used those eyes to spy out my most valued relics. You may guess what followed.''

''Yes. He grew richer, you poorer.''

''But when Cyrus came, he had need for educated officers, and so I prospered after a fashion. Now it seems I am Gabatha's house guest, though he does not yet remember me.''

What would have happened to him, had he professed friendship for the merchant? Enkidu realized that he had had another narrow escape. "How long will you permit this man to impale his slaves for the amusement of your troopers?''

"Citizen, I suggest you come to this party.''

Enkidu declined. "I have no stomach for impalements, least of all wanton ones.'' Then he paused, comprehending. "Gabatha!''

"Our chief entertainer for the day, naturally,'' the Persian confirmed. "Are you sure you don't want to see his face when I impart this marvelous news to him?''

A cold shudder worked its way through his bowel. "I—it is fitting, but—I think not. Just let me release this prisoner and I will go away before—your ceremony.''

"The prisoner within the empty dungeon,'' the Persian murmured over his ale. "Your mind is a boat that floats a narrow channel, citizen. Who is this person?''

He had been foolish to hope he would not be asked this question. "Amyitis.''

"Ah, a woman. Our host has already provided us with a number of these convenient articles. Ishtar also has been most kind. But I assure you the tally checks; the merchant held no woman out. Are you certain she is not among the celebrants here?''

"The merchant thought her dead, and perhaps he is correct. That depends on how high the water level of the Euphrates was at the time she was flung into his water chamber.'' He decided to put the question more directly. ''That is how you got yourselves into the city, isn't it—by lowering the river in some way, so you could pass under the barricades?''

The man grinned. ''Let's just say we felt the need to fill the ancient northern reservoir—in case of drought. We had very good Hebrew labor—it was almost as though those slaves *wanted* Babylon to fall!'' Then his voice became sharp. ''Citizen, we have spun this story out long enough. You had better be able to show us where this woman is.''

''I—she is my wife!'' Enkidu burst out desperately.

Something moved behind the officer's eyes. ''Gabatha took your wife?''

Unable to trust his voice, Enkidu nodded. Would the conquerors have any respect for local marriage?

The Persian shook his head. ''He took mine, too. He obtained her in partial settlement of his claim. Later I learned he had hired her out as a prostitute at one of his riverfront establishments.'' He summoned a soldier. ''Take this man where he wants to go, to release a woman—and see that they get safely out of this house. Move!''

Meanwhile the officer started purposefully for the banquet court. He turned at the door to speak once more to Enkidu. ''Are you sure you don't want to witness at least the beginning of this day's entertainment?''

''Not unless my bride is dead.''

The Persian shrugged and Enkidu departed with the trooper in somewhat reluctant tow, for the hall of the tapestry.

CHAPTER 18

Impasse.

The host had at last united with his love, and the two would surely exist for many years in the rapturous and quarrelsome relationship that was native marriage. Both were scribes in a world that needed scribes.

DS-1 remained in control of Station A-10 and its galactic apparatus. The repair craft would soon arrive, but NK-2 would not be able to make contact, and DS-1 would let it think that the stranded galactic had perished before reaching the station.

Meanwhile the enemy TM-R remained, too powerful to eliminate individually, too dangerous to ignore. TM-R would discover the location of his craft and take it over and destroy it, if he attempted to return to send warning.

The natives were all too ready to interpret galactic

and extra-galactic entities as deities. As if the situation wasn't complicated enough already!

NK-2 paused and went over that thought again. He could not accomplish his purpose directly—but suppose he went at it indirectly, using that same deistic tendency of the natives? Building a real religion around Aten, the compassionate god—whose adherents would be bound to oppose the influences of the false god Ishtar, by whatever guise she appeared? Good against evil?

If it worked, TM-R might be destroyed. Then he could send his signal, and in a few more years he would be home. The enemy would have no base on this planet.

If it didn't work . . . he would just have to keep trying. Even if it took centuries.

The first thing to do was change the orientation of Aten. Make him omnipotent, eager to assimilate all worshipers, even the unworthy. Set up prophets to spread his reputation, arrange for appropriate miracles.

Even if it took millennia. . . .

Turn the page for an exciting preview
of the next Piers Anthony hardcover
coming from Tor in September 1985!

STEPPE

UIGUR

Alp slapped Surefoot on the flank and guided him toward the gorge. The barbarians probably thought he would head for the open plain, but they were about to discover that civilization was not synonymous with stupidity. Not entirely!

He eased the pace as he picked up the cover of the scattered trees of a large oasis. Surefoot would need his strength for the gorge!

It would be better to stop here and rest—but Alp could not take the chance. Once the pursuers realized he was *not* rushing directly south in blind panic, they would cut back, killing any oasis peasants who failed to point the way. That would be in a matter of hours—no more.

He would not have had even that much leeway, had he arrived in time to fight for his wife and child. But their demise had saved him, for he had seen the enemy standards at his tent. Too many to fight . . .

He broke out of the protective hollow and climbed the ridge. There was treacherous country to negotiate, and he was hardly fool enough to rush it. If Surefoot sprained an ankle here—

Shapes raced out of the late afternoon sunlight on either side. Kirghiz! They had anticipated him after all!

Alp knew that retreat was impossible. The savages were almost within arrow range already, and their steeds were fresh. To flee was to be cut down from behind—much as his Uigur countrymen had been decimated.

His dry lips drew back over white teeth. There had not been time for a general alert against him. At least some of these riders had to be from the horde that had overrun Alp's estate. His discipline had stopped him from attacking suicidally then—but the current situation, though bad, was improved. He could make his first payment on a very large debt of revenge.

So he charged. Not for the diminishing open spot ahead, the center of the barbarian pincers, but for the left group of

257

horsemen. There were four on that side—more than enough
to do the job, but not so many that he couldn't take one or
two with him as he went down. Perhaps three. They
thought the Uigur had forgotten how to fight, that he had
fled the massacre of his family because of cowardice . . .

The four Kirghiz rallied as he came at them, forming a
half circle for him to enter. Their bows were ready, but
with native cunning they held their fire until their target
was sure.

Alp grinned again—the bared fangs of the wolf. They
were right about the *average* Uigur, for his people had
grown soft in the course of a century of dominance over
the steppe country. Many had moved into the great city of
Karabalgasun, high on the Orkhon River, forgetting their
plains-riding heritage that had made these Turks great. The
Khagan, ruler of the Uigur, had adopted the foreign religion Manichaeism, and the nobles had turned to scholarly
pursuits. They had mastered the difficult art of writing, so
as to record the legends and history of the world. Thus the
Uigur's nomad power had waned while his intellectual
power waxed—and thus the primitive Kirghiz on the northern reaches had been able to rebel and prevail. The enemy
had sacked the capital city and brought ruin to the Uigur
empire.

And desolation to Alp himself. Only the need to make
his vengeance count as heavily as possible sustained him
now. He was one of the few who had maintained the old
skills while mastering the best of the new. He had no use
for Manichaeism, so he had been out of favor with the
Khagan. Only his resolute fighting posture had saved Alp
from the wrath of his ruler. He had remained technically
loyal, and the Khagan had needed sturdy warriors as officers,
so an uneasy truce had prevailed.

Now all that was done, with the Khagan dead and his
power obliterated. The Kirghiz intended to eliminate the
most serious remaining threat to their newfound empire.
And they had just about done it—they thought.

Alp's bow was in his hand, the first arrow nocked. He
had designed the set himself: the bow was larger than

normal and was braced by the finest horn available, with a gut string from the leading specialist. The arrows too were long and finely balanced. It had taken him years to settle on the ideal proportions for this weapon, and its elements had cost him much, but the superior instrument had been well worth it. He could shoot farther than any other man he knew, and with truer impact.

He fired, rising momentarily on his stirrups for better aim. The arrow made a high arc—and struck in the belly of the nearest Kirghiz. The man gave a horrible cry, quite satisfying to Alp, and dropped off his horse. "That for my son!" Alp muttered.

Immediately the other three fired—but one arrow fell short and two went wide. Alp's second was already in the air, and this time his aim was better. The point scored on the second barbarian's face, penetrating his brain. "That for my wife!"

Alp ducked down as Surefoot automatically responded to battle conditions and ran a jerky evasive pattern. The horse had been almost as difficult to obtain and train as it had been to design and make the bow—but again the effort had been worthwhile. Two more arrows missed—but at Alp's signal Surefoot reared and stumbled as if hit. The two remaining Kirghiz exclaimed with joy, seeing victory— and Alp's third arrow, fired from the side of his stumbling horse, thunked into the shoulder of one. The fool had sat stationary for an instant too long! "And that for me!"

Alp could take the fourth enemy easily—except for the five warriors of the other wing now closing in. Yet he could not afford to leave that man behind, free to take careful aim at the retreating target. Alp's bow was no advantage now, for he was well within the Kirghiz range, and there were no cowards or bad shots in the barbarian cavalry! The element of surprise was gone; the Kirghiz knew they faced a fighting nomad.

"Now that the amenities are over, we shall begin the fray," Alp said. "Uigur cunning against Kirghiz." He felt a bit better, for he had avenged his family for today. Tomorrow, if he lived, he would avenge it again—and so on, until the need diminished. Then he would seek another wife.

Alp touched Surefoot again in a special way, and the horse responded with the certainty of a reliable, well-loved friend. Surefoot leaped, landed, and tumbled, rolling all the way over before struggling to his feet. Alp's precious bow was flung wide.

The fourth Kirghiz clung to the side of his own mount, proffering no target, bow ready—waiting for the Uigur to show, dead or alive. But Surefoot rose and trotted on, riderless. The Kirghiz charged the place where the horse had rolled, expecting to dispatch the injured rider—and died as Alp's accurately thrown knife caught his throat.

Surefoot charged back. Alp fetched his bow and leaped aboard. *Now* he fled—and the five other riders were still beyond range.

Alp knew he was not out of it yet. The Kirghiz would surely gain as Surefoot tired, and all Alp's tricks would be futile the next time around. The savages were very quick to catch on to new combat techniques and very slow to forgive them. If he exhausted his horse by racing to the gorge . . .

He looked behind and saw the five pressing on determinedly, not even pausing to aid their fallen. He had no choice.

The gorge was a long crack in the earth and rock. It had been created, the legends said, by the kick of an angry jinn generations ago. Its shadowed depth was filled part way with rubble and the bones of enemies thrown there. The gorge extended for many miles, requiring hours to ride around—but most men spent those hours rather than risk the certain death of a fall into its narrowing crevice.

A good horse could leap it, though. If properly trained and guided. And fresh.

Surefoot was not fresh. He had barely held his lead over the five Kirghiz and sweat streamed along his sides. The enemy would be within arrow range the moment Alp slowed or turned.

There was still no choice. If he crossed the gorge, he would be safe to pursue his vengeance at his leisure. The barbarians' untrained steeds would balk, or fall short. If any did hurdle it, Alp could pick them off singly as they landed. That would be an easy start on tomorrow's tally!

By the time the rest circled around the crack, he would long since be lost in the countryside.

But first he had to hurdle it.

He urged Surefoot forward as the rift came into view. The mighty horse knew what to do. He was hot and tired, but he did not balk or falter. He leaped into the air.

Not far enough. The hard run had sapped too much of his strength, cutting down his speed at the critical moment. His front hooves landed firmly, but his rear ones missed. For a moment they scrambled at the brink; then horse and rider tumbled backwards into the chasm.

Who will avenge Surefoot? Alp thought wildly.

Alp knew instantly that it was not heaven, for his horse was not with him. Alp was uncertain of his own disposition in death, but Surefoot was heaven-bound: of that there could be no doubt.

Therefore Alp was in the hell of the chasm. That was the worst possible outcome—but at least he had the dubious advantage of recognizing it. In life he had prospered by his wits as much as his strength; in death it should not be otherwise. He need have no scruples in dealing with the demons he found here, whatever their aspect.

Their aspect was strange indeed! They wore costumes roughly resembling his own, but their tunics were not of true linen and their helmets were obviously unserviceable for combat. Which meant, again, that these were demons, mock-men, whose dress was mere pretense and whose purpose was devious.

Alp himself was naked now. Worse, he was weaponless. His bow, sword and dagger were gone, and no quiver of arrows clung to his back. Naturally the demons were giving him no chance to fight them. The average demon was a coward, skulking in shadows, seldom showing his ugly face in man's land.

One came toward him, carrying a helmet. The headpiece was far too cumbersome for practical use, being so broad and deep that it would fall almost to a man's shoulders, blinding him. Alp shied away, baring his teeth in an effort to frighten the thin-faced demon away.

This was effective, for the creature paused and backed off, though he was taller than Alp, true to his ilk.

Another demon moved, placing a hand in a box of some sort. Alp watched him covertly, in case he should be fetching a knife. But the thing only touched a round knob.

Coincidentally, Alp's power of motion left him.

Magic! He should have expected that, though there seemed to be no way to avoid it. He had hardly believed in magic when alive, knowing most shamans to be charlatans. Of course he had *professed* belief so as to stay clear of unnecessary complications. But this was death, and different laws prevailed. These creatures might be laughable as physical fighters, but in their own black arts they were matchless.

It was a necessary reminder that no entity could safely be held in contempt. The Kirghiz were too dull to master literacy, yet were formidable warriors. The demons could not compete with Alp physically but possessed the skills of another realm. If he hoped to survive this state, he would have to make a special effort to understand its laws.

The first demon, seeing Alp immobilized by the spell, now screwed up his courage and set the gross helmet over his head. Alp's sight was blotted out. He strove to break free but could not move. Still, he was not suffocated; evidently the demon did not realize that the prisoner's head was the wrong shape for such torture.

Actually, suffocation would be one way to escape this region. If he died here, he would proceed to the next level of the afterlife, never to return. Perhaps his fortune would be better, there.

No—it was not in the Uigur to surrender! Better to fight for *this* life—which might not be a bad one, once he escaped these demons. Perhaps this was no more than the initiation test: only the capable visitor managed to remain.

Something strange was happening. It developed slowly, like the barely perceptible rising of the sun at dawn—but like the sun, it spread its influence pervasively. Alp began to understand things about these demons.

They did not consider themselves demons. In their own odd language they were "Galactics"—human beings from far away, representatives of a mighty empire that spanned a much greater region than did the Uigur realm at its height. That empire extended over planets and systems and constellations—though these were concepts of such sorcerous complexity and incongruity as to baffle his mind. He knew them to be pretense and illusion nevertheless—because demons were things of the fundament, not the welkin. Soil-grubbers, not sky-flyers. So that much he could set aside as irrelevant.

Or could he? Again he had to remind himself that the rules of his own realm did not necessarily apply. Conceivably demons *did* master heaven, here—or thought they did.

The demons spoke a language of their own. Not Uigur, not even Chinese. Their speech had no writing. They had "machines" to do their bidding, these devices being jinn-like entities housed in metal, capable of phenomenal wizardry.

The demons were engaged in a war that was not a war but a game, in which those killed did not really die yet could not exactly return. Reincarnation was the only possibility—but for this they had to pay a fee.

It was too much! Alp closed his mind to this madness—but found there was no escape from it. The helmet was not a suffocation device after all; its torture was more subtle. It crammed unacceptable information into his shuddering brain, destroying his comfortable patterns of belief.

The helmet claimed it was actually a force-education device that was radiating demon-information into his head like a shower of arrows. True torture of hell!

Finally they took the thing off, but Alp remained frozen

in place. Had the spell not been on him, he would have
fallen to the floor.

"He should comprehend now," one demon said.
"Though you never can tell, with an actual barbarian."

So it was like that, Alp thought grimly. The Kirghiz had
figured him for a soft civilized fool, and these Galactic-
demons figured him for a stupid primitive.

"Release the stasis," another said. "We can't interrogate him this way."

So they meant to question him—and could not release
his jaw without nullifying the entire spell. Already he was
grasping the limits of their magic!

A touch of the box—and the spell was broken. So that
was the instrument: a machine! Alp was free—completely.
He verified this by flexing muscles that did not show:
calves, buttocks, back of the neck. All in order.

But he put his hand slowly to his head as if dazed.
When he acted, that magic box would be a prime target!

A Galactic stepped toward him, an ingratiating smile on
his shaven face. "Salutations, warrior."

Alp returned the creature's gaze dully. Demons were
always fairest of speech when they intended mischief! He
grunted.

"I knew it!" one of the others said. "Stupid. Can't
orient."

"Terrified, more likely," another said. "Primitives are
normally superstitious, afraid of sorcery. All his life on the
plains he never experienced anything like this in his narrow existence. Give him a chance. We've invested heavily
to fetch him here."

"Understatement of the century!" the third muttered. "A
time-snatch of a millennia and a half—we'll all be broke if
this doesn't pan out!"

"I'm in debt already," the last muttered.

A millennia and a half, Alp thought. Millennium,
correctly; the demon usage did not precisely match the
helmet language. Significant? In his terms, at any rate,
fifteen hundred years, or thirty lifetimes. But time stretched

two ways. Was it the period before man had arisen on the plains, or after man had passed?

"Speak, warrior," the demon in front said. "We wish to know about you and your society." There was that in his manner that suggested insincerity. The language of facial expression and bodily posture transcended man-demon distinctions.

"Ugh," Alp said, still feigning ignorance. They didn't want to know about him nearly as badly as he wanted to know about *them*! Obviously they were not omniscient, and they also thought they could lie to him, which meant they could be fooled themselves. What did they really want?

"All for nothing!" the first of the three demons said. "We gambled our entire Game fortunes on this ridiculous snatch from the past—and fetched a moron!"

The leader refused to give up. "You are from a great culture, warrior. We are your friends. Tell us who your leader was—*is*. Your king."

So the creature wanted information about the Uigur empire—not knowing that it had fallen or that the Khagan had been slain. Obviously the magic helmet could not extract information the same way it projected it. These were political spies of some sort who had an interest in worldly power. Why?

And the one behind had verified that Alp was from the demons' past—making these entities of the time after the downfall of man. They should know, therefore, the full history of the steppe region and have no need to ask him. Another indication that they were concealing the whole truth. This was no more and no less than he had expected from demons, whose nature did not change from year to year and whose purposes seldom aligned with those of true men.

The leader shrugged. "He won't respond. I suppose we had better return him to stasis while we consider—"

The Galactic nearest the spell-box reached toward it.

Alp launched himself, knowing he could wait no longer. He clubbed the leader-demon with the hardened side of his hand in passing, knocking it back, and dived for the box.

He was too late. The other demon's hand was already on it, turning the knob. Alp's body went dead.

But momentum carried him forward. He crashed into the box and the demon behind it. Both toppled over. There was a startled cry, a crackling sound, a moment of intense pain—and Alp was free again.

He saw a curtained window—but the remaining two Galactics stood between him and it. Alp had no bow, no arrows and no blade. He charged them anyway, kicking at one while butting the other. Then he leaped through the aperture.

Alp had not really expected to discover the plains of his homeland outside, for he knew the land of demons differed from mortal geography. In one region there was a magnetic mountain that snatched all metal away from men who rode by; in another the sun shone brightly at midnight. So he was prepared for something unusual here.

Still, he was amazed. The curtain was not physical, not of wool nor horsehide; rather it was a tingling surface like that of a chill river. The notion of taking a bath was dismaying! And beyond this barrier were no trees, *ger* or desert sands, but a complex canyon of many colors.

It had to be the nether region of the gorge he had fallen into, though he had never imagined it could be so vast and splendid! Bright boulders rolled along narrow channels, and lights rose and fell *inside* the opposite canyon wall.

No—his new understanding told him that the boulders were cars—wheel-less wagons able to roll uphill without being hauled by horses. The lights were in antigravity elevator shafts: magic hoists that carried men up and down without weight. Demon tricks, of course, called "science." He had no inherent fear of it, but he realized that he should treat it with extreme caution. A living demon killed men for the mere joy of it, but magic science acted without joy or sorrow.

Alp was naked, weaponless, and horseless. Was Surefoot here? He saw no bones. And of course he had already decided that his mount would not be here in hell, not even in the hell for horses. That was the nature of *man's* hell: to be without horse and weapon.

His appraisal of the canyon had taken only an instant, but already the scuffling sounds in the chamber behind made it clear that the Galactics were coming after him. That was the system of hell too: perpetual pursuit, and torture upon capture. But now he knew that not all demons had the same specific objectives; most likely the other demons of this realm had other warriors to torment and would ignore him. If he could kill the four assigned to him, as he had killed the four Kirghiz, he would have no quarrel with those outside.

Kill? Not precisely. His Galactics were associated with the Game, and in that context the act of killing did not accomplish the usual relegation to an afterworld. There were strange things about this Game—but he didn't have time to work it out now, though it was all in his helmet-sponsored memory. He had to move.

He ran down the channel he found himself on. Above it were other channels, and below it were more, like ropes stretched the length of the canyon. This was a street in a city—neither road nor town like any he had known in life. Karabalgasun was a city, and it had streets, but the houses were not tall and the roads were flat on the ground. The cities of the far places he had read about were similar: Changan in China, the Middle Kingdom; Babylon in the southwest.

Now he realized that the path itself was moving! He had stepped onto a woven mat being dragged along, and it was carrying him along with it, as though he rode the back of a monster serpent.

As he moved, the other demons on the pathway began to take notice of him. He would have observed them sooner had he not been distracted by the awesome depths of the canyon opening below him as he moved out. There was no bottom to it!

The females—dainty of limb, thin of face and fair of complexion—for demons—averted their eyes modestly. The males scowled. Nakedness was a taboo here, he realized—or

a mark of subservience. That was why he had been stripped.
Hell overlooked no torture! He had to get clothing, so that
he could conceal his status and pass among the demons
unrecognized.

"Hey, you!" one of them called in the demon-tongue,
Galactic. It was a guard, a police official.

Alp saw that the creature was armed, so he stopped. He
stepped into an alcove on the side, to get off the moving
belt. They did not use swords here, or bows, or even
daggers, but they had effective magic weapons nonetheless.
Most effective! He would have to plumb his new knowledge for details, because he was already aware that the
fighting instruments he had known would be almost useless in this situation.

"What stunt is this?" the guard demanded. "You drunk
or crazy?"

Alp knew he would have to make his first speech in the
new language. His own Uigur vocabulary would instantly
give him away. This demon was neither friend nor enemy,
but an officer of law charged with maintaining order in
hell. His question was rhetorical, as there was no alcohol
or insanity in this framework. A proper answer might
actually place the guard on Alp's side.

"I—suffered an accident," Alp said haltingly. "I fell—
and woke without clothing. I do not know exactly where I
am or how to return home."

The police guard squinted at him. "Put out your hand."

Alp did so. The demon slapped a disk against his palm.
Its nature was not clear, this was the first tangible gap in
the helmet knowledge. Had a swift arrow of information
missed his head?

"That's the truth, but not the whole truth," the guard
said, looking at the disk. "Care to try again?"

A magic truth disk! Now Alp understood. The information was in his mind after all, but he had not recognized
the concept. How fortunate he had not attempted an outright lie!

Actually, it would not be proper to lie to any of these
demons other than the four he fled from, for the others

were not his enemies. He could not condemn them all merely because they had the misfortune to be demons. Technically, he was now a demon himself!

"I am an Uigur subchief. My family was killed by barbarians. I obtained vengeance but died while escaping the Kirghiz, and now I am in hell without horse, weapons or dress." Actually the words he used were not precisely analogous to the concepts of his people, but more than a language barrier was involved. This language of Galactic seemed to have a plethora of terms relating to vehicles and ships, but almost none relating to important Uigur matters such as "stirrup," "bowstring" or "gorge." "I escaped the four demons assigned to torture me—and there they are!" he pointed.

The guard's round eyes widened. "That *is* the truth, as you see it—but there's little sign of derangement! Mister, you've been hyped! I'll nail them all!"

The demons saw the guard and tried to retreat, but he whipped out a portable stunner. Docilely they coasted down to line up beside Alp.

"Officer," the leader said respectfully through his obvious discomfort. "We're in Steppe. We were interrogating this man when he attacked us and plunged into the street."

"Steppe!" the guard exclaimed, grimacing beautifully. "I should have known. What in hell are you clowns doing on this level?"

So the demons admitted this was hell!

"Our equipment is here. We had no intention of coming into the street, but we couldn't let the primitive run loose—"

Alp kept silent. He was learning a great deal of value, more by the memories evoked by the dialogue than by the actual words. His new memory had to be drawn out in comprehensible segments to be useful. "Steppe" was not a land but a synonym for the Game—a game of life and half-death. A game that somehow involved Alp himself.

"He claims you kidnapped him," the guard retorted. "Game or no Game—"

"No, officer! We pooled our resources and fetched him

from the past. He's a native of the real steppe. We mean to interrogate him and ship him back—''

Back! Alp's face remained passive, for there was no sense in letting them know how well he comprehended. Back to life, and to vengeance among the Kirghiz—

No! This was *not* death, but a removal to another age of man. Back meant true death for him and true hell! Better to fight it out right here; if he won, he had new life, and if he lost, he would be no worse off than he had originally thought.

The guard checked the demon-leader's story with his truth-disk. Actually there was no sense in thinking of them as demons any more; they were in fact men, like him. "Very well," the official said. "Get him off the street— and see that you don't intrude on this level again, or I'll run you in! I know you're violating Game regulations."

"We appreciate it, officer!" the man said. "Now—"

Alp moved with a speed and certainty unfettered by either clothing or Galactic scruples. He snatched the stunner from the officer's holster, aimed it the way he had seen it aimed, and pressed the visible stud.

There was a snap. All five men stiffened and toppled as the invisible beam mowed them down. They fell across the moving belt and were carried away.

Alp lowered the weapon, for which he was developing hearty respect—and his right leg went numb. The device was still operating! He stumbled, balancing on his left leg while he fiddled with the stud. It snapped up, stopping the force—but his leg remained dead.

Other Galactics were coming toward him. Alp held the stunner well out of the way and ran awkwardly, clinging to the beltway rail for support. There was no pain in his stunned leg and no visible injury, but it would neither respond to his will nor support his weight. It had become a useless attachment that tended to drag.

He had to get out of sight! He put the stunner between his teeth, heaved himself over the rail and climbed down outside the belt channel, using both hands and his good foot.

There was a framework under the belt, buttressed by a pattern of beams. Alp clung to these, looking for a way down. He was in good physical shape, like any true Uigur, but climbing and hanging were not his forte.

There was no descent. The gorge reached down sickeningly, making a drop unthinkable, and the belt support stretched twenty meters in either direction before meeting vertical supports.

Alp was a horseman, not a bird. But there was no horse, and his leg still lacked sensation. He proceeded along the beams, passing from one to the next, hand across hand.

Now people on the belts below were looking up. He *still* wasn't hiding very well! He had to get away from here and get some clothes—before more policemen converged.

His arms were fast tiring. Alp hauled himself back up the side and fell over the rail with the last of his strength. He had been using his muscle instead of his brain, and that was bad.

The five stunned bodies had been carried away. He knew they had not recovered yet because his leg had not—assuming the effect of the beam were reversible. A lone man was riding the belt toward him. And in the sky, above the highest to the criss-crossing beltways, Alp saw a flying shape like a monstrous mosquito, its wings invisible. A hovercraft, his new memory said. More antigravity—an opaque concept.

He took the stunner from his mouth, aimed it at the lone man, and pressed the stud. The man fell forward, and Alp caught him. His leg gave way and they both collapsed. Alp made sure the stud had not locked down this time, so as not to deaden any more of his own anatomy, then turned his attention to the man.

He was narrow-faced, like most of the Galactics, and had the same burned-off hair style Alp had noted passingly on the men of the lower beltways. The four demons had approximated Uigur style tonsure, with the main mass braided and thrown back from the forehead; but it seemed other Galactics declined to maintain tresses of appropriate length.

Quickly he yanked off the man's tunic. The Galactic's bared skin was paler than Alp's own, and more hairy; the muscles were comparatively flabby, and there was some fat. Could this be a noble? Certainly the body was that of neither peasant nor horseman!

Alp put the tunic over his own head. The material was like quality silk, light but strong. There was also underclothing; Alp had neither time nor inclination to don it himself, but he did get it off the other. The man's genitals were unusually large: yes, surely a noble!

But an enemy noble, or at least not a friend. Alp let the man ride on down the belt, while he leaned against the stationary rail of the alcove. He was just beginning to fight with his brain.

The insect in the sky expanded into a floating machine. A police craft. Alp had suspected it, for his new awareness told him that only officials and police were permitted the use of hovercraft within the city proper. That was why he had acted so rapidly. But now he waited.

The craft approached the belt. The machine was hollow like a gourd, and two more guards were inside. One opened a hatch and jumped out on the belt. "There he is!" he cried. "Naked man!"

The policeman caught up with the body and hauled it to an alcove, using a small magic rug to make it float. The vehicle came alongside, and the two men passed the unconscious one inside. Still Alp did not move.

The craft departed, moving upward with no wings. At last Alp smiled. He had feared the ruse would not be successful, and that he would have to stun these police too—if it were possible to affect the one in the craft. Had they suspected his identity they could have stunned him without warning, finishing his fling at freedom. That was the gamble he had taken, not from boldness but necessity. It had worked—and almost too easily.

But now he had to secure his position in this world. He needed better clothing, and money or barter, and a horse—or at least a moving machine. And a suitable territory to roam. For these Galactics could not be stupid; he had fooled them once, but like the Kirghiz they would be on guard the next time. Their magical resources were far greater than his.

First, his hair. He possessed no knife to cut it short, so he would have to do it the hard way. He sat down so as to free both hands, taking a pinch of hair between his fingers with his left hand and a section of that with his right. He yanked. A tuft came loose, hurting his scalp despite his protective grip.

Alp laid the black strand down and quickly unbraided the remainder. Then, yank by yank, he dismembered his fine ebony mane, leaving a ragged pasture where there had been Uigur pride. Another torture of hell—and he had to do this to himself!

Sensation was finally returning to his leg. That meant the others he had stunned would be coming to. There would soon be a second alarm.

He placed the mat of hair in an inner pocket of the tunic; hair could be fashioned into rope when required. He hoped no blood showed on his head; his hasty barbering had been brutal in places.

Alp rode down the belt until he came to a crossbelt. He took that, then found a descending lift and rode that. The feel of weightlessness alarmed him, but he quelled his stomach. He felt more secure nearer the ground. While he travelled he used his brain some more, digesting his new information and seeking ways to use it.

This was a remarkable land. There were no true horses and few plains. There were more people here than in all of populous China. Machines did almost everything—even thinking and copulating. Men could still do these things, but the machines did them better. A machine could spawn a human baby if properly primed; this was called "hydroponic insemination" or something similar. Appalling—but so it had been for generations. And the stars in the sky were no longer specks of light on the dome of the night, but bright suns—and near many of these suns were other worlds like this one.

People were numbered. Machines provided their food.

A man was limited not by the strength of his arm and the accuracy of his bow, but by the amount of intangible wealth he possessed, reckoned in points. Naturally this made for extreme laziness. The Chinese were soft, while the hard-riding Uigurs were hard—or had been, before civilization had softened them and made them vulnerable to the Kirghiz. But among these Galactics the edge of war no longer necessarily gave the hard men the advantage; the machine weapons and magic were far too strong. So there was no natural halt to the process of decay—some year the machines themselves, like the Kirghiz, would rebel and take over. Alp well understood the process!

Meanwhile, there was the Game. The competitive nature of the minority of Galactics was sublimated there. The conditions of times past were duplicated—crudely—and history was re-enacted—approximately. A man's fortune and reputation in the galaxy was determined largely by his performance in this Game, and the most ambitious men participated. Even women! In the Game was all the action and lust and intrigue that the mundane galaxy lacked.

It took only a minute's thought to show Alp that he would be far more at home in the Game than in the "real" galaxy, for that mundane scheme was as foreign as hell to him, literally, while the Game—

The Game was Steppe. Uigur and Chinese dominated it. Its present stage in history was about the year 830, Christian Era. Alp cared not one sheep-dropping for Christianity, but he was satisfied to orient on its time scale for now.

Alp himself had been snatched from a time about ten years later—841. That was why the four demons—actually Game players—had used their machine to fetch him from the canyon just before he died at the bottom. His absence made no difference to his world, for he was dead there anyway. A complex concept of "paradox" governed that. The four players had hoped to draw information from him concerning the intervening years he had experienced—the years between 830 and 841. Information that would profit them enormously in the Game.

This was important, he realized, for they had gone to a

great deal of trouble for the sake of learning about those years. Why? Why should news of a decade matter that much? What good could it actually do them? Particularly when they could look it up in a history text?

No, they could *not* look it up, for these Galactics were illiterate! Their machines did all their reading for them, turning it into pictures on windowlike screens. They knew only what their machines told them.

And—the four demons did not know precisely *when* Alp was from! They had fetched him from their past, but they had had to take only the man whose removal could not affect their own history. So they had oriented on the bottom of the canyon, waiting for someone to fall—and few men *did* fall, alive, because it was in Uigur territory and Uigurs were not fools about canyons. Only the pressure of the chase had forced Alp himself to attempt that leap when unprepared. Probably he was the only man to die that way in twenty years—and possibly much longer. So the players might have wanted a man fifty years beyond Game-time—and had to settle for Alp. He was actually worth less to them than they supposed.

Yet surely they could ask the machines for what they wanted to know! That seemed easier than delving all the way into the past. The knowledge-machines still obeyed men.

No, they did *not*! Certain areas of knowledge were blanked from public awareness. This history of the steppe-country of Asia; of the Vikings of Europe; of the Moslem Arabs, the pre-Columbian Amerinds, and pre-European Africans. What these histories entailed Alp did not know, for the other names were unfamiliar to him. Those adventures could hardly rival the activities of the steppe, regardless!

But he understood the principle: for some reason the machines had been set not to give out these histories, thus keeping the Galactics ignorant. There were many such gaps in the record, his helmet-education informed him; some histories had been taught fifty or sixty years ago but not, since.

One gap was only partial: Steppe. Because Alp had studied the history of his own people, from Turk to Kao-Kiu to Tolach to Uigur—first a minor subtribe, then an increasingly powerful nation of nomads, and finally masters of all the steppe, equals of the civilized Chinese. Alp knew a thousand years of local events in fair detail. Surely there was more in the machines, following his own time—but that of course was blank to him.

Why was this historical ignorance fostered? To understand that, he had first to understand the nature of the Game.

Then it came clear, and he knew what he had to do.

The beltways and lifts did not extend into the upper-most reaches. Alp had to take an internal elevator—and there trouble struck.

An alarm sounded as he entered.

Alp leaped back before the closing doors trapped him. He had not had experience with alarms before, but he had a lifetime's experience with mischief. His reflexes seldom betrayed him.

Now he remembered: key transports were equipped with personnel scanners. And all human clothing carried identification codes. He had plucked out much of his hair uselessly, missing what was there in his new memory to see. Obviously the police had discovered their error and put out a bulletin for the clothing of the robbed citizen. The chase was on again!

If he continued to wear this tunic, he would quickly be run down, now that they had a fix on him. Their magic machines could sniff out an identity unerringly; better to have an angry jinn on his trail! But if he removed the tunic, he would be a naked man again—another sure mark. Either way, capture and death—because he was not a proper citizen of this universe.

But he had only a little farther to go! Once he reached the Game, he would have more than a fighting chance.

He ripped off his tunic and dropped it off the edge of the beltway, saving only his handful of hair. The cloth flut-

tered down, carrying the telltale identity with it. Of course
the police could identify human bodies too—but another
complex principle called "personal privacy" made that
difficult. A body had to be taken to the police station,
where the number on it could be brought out by the special
equipment there, for recognition to be certain. Even then,
there had to be special authorization before the information
could be circulated. The typical Uigur Khagan would never
have tolerated such restrictions!

Alp himself had no Galactic number—but since he would
be the only living man without one, they could readily
identify him. He did not know whether the alarms were set
to respond to the absence of any number; but in any event,
his nakedness betrayed him.

He still had the stunner. He flicked it on and off at the
next man he encountered. The citizen stiffened and would
have fallen had Alp not caught him. This one was small
and frail.

Alp hauled the tunic over the Galactic's head—and
discovered the body beneath was feminine. He had been
about to don this new apparel, knowing it would take the
police a while to catch up with the changed number, but
now altered his plan. There seemed to be no difference
between man-tunics and woman-tunics, but no self-respecting
warrior would wear female apparel!

This was the first Galactic woman he had seen up close.
Her hair was burned short and her body was slender, but
otherwise she was in no way inferior to the standards he
knew. Why had she dressed like a man? Or were the men
dressing like women? Had the long-haired citizens he had
seen below actually been women, or—his new memory
provided the term—transvestites? It was a sorry world
when women pretended to man's status—and got away
with it!

But that was the way it was today, he realized. There
were no requirements for the sexes. Some men preferred to
be overtly masculine, and some women splendidly feminine;
but the majority fell into a sexless anonymity. An anonymity he had emulated by reducing his hair; there would have

been nothing wrong with his warrior's braid! Every citizen's right to individuality was respected—and also his freedom *from* individuality. At least, this was so in public.

Alp dropped the tunic off the belt. Then he stripped away the woman's underclothing and dropped it over also. As the woman moved, regaining consciousness (because he had dosed her with the shortest possible stun), he propped her against the moving rail and let her travel on, naked.

Nudity: there was a major taboo showing up all the Galactics' freedom of individuality as spurious. Alp, sensibly, would rather go naked than wear a woman's tunic; these foolish people would rather exchange sexes than show their bodies. Of course, if Alp's own body were as flabby as what he had seen here, he might conceal it too . . .

Another citizen arrived, male, and Alp treated him the same way. Then two more came together. This was more difficult, but he managed. Then another woman, similarly processed. A line of people was moving down the belt.

Now the earlier cases realized their condition. Horrified, they fled to other belts and other levels, trying desperately to avoid contact with other people. It was a hilarious game of hide and seek. The sphere of nudity was expanding!

A police craft appeared. Alp rode down the belt himself, gesticulating as if in dire embarrassment. He was one of several—and the policeman could not distinguish him from the others!

Alp jumped into another elevator. This time no alarm rang. Good! He made it to the highest level and charged forth as though crazed.

But more police craft had assembled. Evidently they were taking no chances and were rounding up all the naked citizens. One flying machine oriented on Alp, gaining on him.

Alp dived for a special booth marked GAME ENTRY. "Sanctuary!" he cried as the police came up.

The door slid closed, and the clamor outside abated. "Identity?" a neutral voice inquired in Galactic.

"Anonymous," Alp said. He had rehearsed this dialogue in his mind during the chase.

"Entry fee?"

"Advance credit."

"Advance credit is not gained on an anonymous basis."

This was the crux. "I plead an exception. I am not a Galactic citizen."

"Your hand."

Alp held out his hand. Something touched it. "Intriguing," the voice of the Game Machine said. He knew it was the Machine, because there was now a superior quality about it, indicating intelligence. He knew the Machine would have the truth from him—if it so desired. He was at its mercy.

He also knew that machines did not care about human concerns. He was gambling that its disinterest in whether he lived or died was matched by its disinterest in the need of the police to capture him. The Game Machine could learn the truth about him—and not bother to give it away.

But it probed no further. "What indication is there that prospective winnings will be sufficient to repay such advance credit?"

"Technical expertise." The words came with difficulty, for both language and concepts were foreign. What he was really saying was that he would be a skilled player.

Now the police were peering in the transparent aperture, but they could not intrude until the Machine ejected him. He had to convince it to accept him into the Game!

"Of what nature?"

"Extrapolation of events." That meant he would be a lucky guesser. He could not claim to know the immediate future of Steppe—the past ten years of his own life—for then the Machine might suspect he had snooped on the program.

"One technical question."

"Agreed." As if he could refuse! This was another point of decision. If he could convince it that he was a good risk despite his anonymity, it would stake him to the minimum entrance fee of one hundred points. If not—

"What is the likely fortune of Wu-Kiai?"

Alp's hopes collapsed. "I do not know that name."

"Perhaps you know him as Uga."

Alp thought. "I do know of a chief by that name. A Uigur; a strong, violent man." He considered carefully. Actually he knew Uga very well, for that man had also been out of favor with the Khagan and had assumed much greater power when the Khagan died. But supposedly Alp was extrapolating, and he had to be cautious. "I believe he will rise high—but he lacks the judgment to be a really effective leader. No doubt he will die in battle."

"Here is a sampling of available parts. Make your selection."

Alp's pulse leaped. "You are extending credit?"

"That depends on your selection."

The Machine was candid! But Alp was half there.

A picture-screen illuminated. As the voice named each man, an image showed. This was followed by a brief description: current family and position and personality. The summary was fair; Alp had known several of these men personally. Obviously the Machine had done thorough research.

Could Alp himself be in the Game records? There was a nervous twitch down his back. At this historical date he would be but a stripling, as yet not come into his demesnes, as yet unmarried. But later he would be a chief . . . and perish in the gorge. An inferior part!

Credit was never extended for more than the minimum, which meant he could not obtain a really promising part. The quality of the part offered dependent on the amount of the entry fee paid. Yet even the least likely prospect could turn out to be a winner; that was part of the appeal of the Game.

Alp knew that more than one of these prospects had died in the decade following the present Game-time of 831. Naturally the Machine knew this, but the players did not. If Alp chose wrongly, he would "die"—actually, be ejected from the Game—very soon, with no chance to succeed in the manner that would earn him back his entrance stake.

Such figurative death would soon become literal, for him, since the police would be waiting outside.

"These are all Uigur," Alp said.

"Those are the most commonly desired parts of the moment," the Machine said. "There are many others. What group do you prefer?"

"Kirghiz." Alp was disgusted, having to consider a barbarian part, but he needed quick success.

"An interesting choice." Kirghiz parts appeared on the screen.

Was the Machine suspicious? It could not really find anything "intriguing" or "interesting," for it had no emotion. Such words could be signals of trouble. It had to know that the Kirghiz were about to supplant the Uigur in Steppe. But there was scant indication of this ten years before the actual overthrow.

"No, they are too barbaric," Alp said. "No future there. A Uigur is best, after all."

"As you wish." The Machine was giving away no hint!

Alp chose a literate Uigur subchief named Ko-lo: a man of some potential but little present importance. Alp now knew that literacy was rarer in the Galactic society than among the Uigurs. Illiterates did not favor literate parts, since they could not play them well, so this was an underrated attribute. Just what he needed: a potent if subtle tool for advancement.

"Here is your costume," the Machine said. Material spewed out of a slot: a loose robe falling to his calves, split at the sides and gathered by a broad belt. A short fur cape to cover his shoulders, and a fur cap. Not a real fur, of course. Wide trousers, that he strapped in at the ankles. He did the same for his sleeves at the wrists. Stout leatherite shoes.

Alp knew right away that this costume was no more authentic than those of the four demons who had brought him to this time. The underwear was similar to what he had removed from the men and women on the belts, the boots were not suitable for riding, and the belt chafed. But it was a reasonable approximation, and once he wore some dirt into it he would be able to wear it comfortably.

There were also weapons, at last! A bow in its ornate sheath that hung from his belt before his left thigh. A quiver of arrows, that rested across the small of his back, with the barbs to the right. A dagger and a short sword, both in good sheaths.

He was in business. The Game Machine had admitted him on credit, which meant it thought he had a reasonable chance to repay. His choice of the part must have been the decisive factor. Apart from the literacy he had taken Ko-lo because he had never heard of that particular chief nor his family, and was almost certain the man had not existed historically. That meant the part was open: no specific historical fate awaited, and it was up to the player to improvise.

His memory had told him that a few such parts existed, so that the Game would not be completely fixed. There had to be leeway—room for individual initiative, along with the strict programming of established characters. No one was supposed to know whose fate was predetermined and whose was self-determined; all were mixed together in the Game. Every player could believe that he had free will.

Of course, being a free agent was no guarantee that a player would profit. Most washed out even more rapidly than the average. But a smart—and lucky—man's best opportunity was here.

This part of Ko-lo was a subchief: better than the minimum fee normally brought. That meant that immediate hazards existed that would shorten the span of play. The Machine did not say this, but in practice a peasant with a likely long life could command a higher entrance fee than a chief who was about to be executed.

But Alp did not intend to depend on either luck or the largess of an "intrigued" Game Machine. He happened, by the freak of timesnatch, to be thoroughly conversant with the history of the real Steppe—including particularly the ten years following the present Game-date. If the demons had thought they could profit from such information, why not Alp himself?

"Bare your arm," the Machine said.

Alp bared his left arm and lifted it. There was a momentary pain as light flashed. "Your Game identity number," the Machine explained.

Alp looked. The light had burned a tattoo into the skin of his forearm. He was no longer anonymous!

A panel opened opposite the entrance. Alp/Ko-lo stepped out into the great Game of Steppe.

For a moment the beauty of it made him dumb. As far as he could see, the grassy plain stretched. There was not a tree or tent anywhere—nothing to interrupt the charge of a good horse. Even the door through which he had come was gone; there was nothing behind him except more plain. Glorious!

First he checked his weapons. He drew out the bow. It was not of the type he ordinarily used, being metal and plastic—plastic was a Galactic invention: a substance somewhat like dried gut, but shaped with greater versatility—rather than wood and horn. But it had good weight and spring, and the string was of sturdy nylon—yet another imitation material. The Galactics seemed to have a fetish about avoiding animal products. So it was a facsimile—but a serviceable one.

Alp whipped out an arrow from the quiver, brought it over his shoulder and nocked it in the bowstring in a single motion, as the fighting Uigur always did. And halted, amazed.

The shaft of the arrow was not solid. It was made of a beam of light. Only the head and feather were substantial—and these not very. The tip was no more than a paper shell that would collapse instantly on impact, and the nock was actually set into the feather: it should tear apart when fired. Yet the arrow as a whole had an odd firmness, and the head remained before the feather no matter how he spun it about.

How could the arrow act solid—when it was made of

light? Tractor beam, his memory said, but that hardly helped.

Alp touched the shaft with one finger. Yes—that finger went numb. It was a stunner!

Carefully he returned the strange arrow to its quiver and drew the sword. It was similar: a thread of light in lieu of a cutting edge. But his experience with the police stunner—which weapon he had left in the entrance booth as a prerequisite to admittance to Steppe—convinced him that these instruments were sufficient. They would not kill—but they would incapacitate as surely as the real weapons would have.

He struck the air with his sword, shadow-cutting. He could handle it. Any player receiving a "lethal" strike would "die"—and be ejected from the Game, a loser. He could then re-enter by seeking new admittance, paying the fee, and assuming a new character. If, in the course of his prior parts, he had amassed sufficient Game-credits, he would be ahead; if not, he would have to produce the fee from his own resources. A wealthy man could afford to lose many times. But Alp himself had to prosper within this one part. His first loss would be his last, because of the waiting extradition to the hell of the chasm.

Alp found a sharp edge on the handle of his dagger and used it to mark the other weapons inconspicuously in Uigur script. A routine precaution. He brushed back his hair.

Hair? *His braid was back!*

The work of the Machine again. Players were made up for each part, so that others could not tell what they had originally looked like. Alp did not remember going through make-up, but—here was his hair, spliced as though never cut.

One more succinct reminder: he had only an idiot's notion of the capabilities of Galactic magic.

Meanwhile, the Game beckoned. The sun was high. It was noon, and the day was hot. He could relax, for all he had to do was stay alive and he would have many years' respite.

Years? Suddenly he remembered another thing about the Game: its time was not the same as that of the galaxy. The Game time scale was accelerated. Every day here was equivalent to a full year in the historical world!

So the theoretical life of a player from birth to a death of old age was in the neighborhood of seventy days. And most parts were much shorter, for they started at early maturity and often were terminated violently. Each Game-hour was a historical fortnight, and each Game-minute six hours, and each Game-second six minutes.

The Game sun did not move faster. Actually, these Galactics claimed the sun did not move at all, at least not the way it obviously did. They thought the sun stood still while the plains and seas and mountains whirled around it. This was yet another idiocy he would have to contemplate at leisure. For the moment he had to grasp the nature of the Day that was really a year.

This was noon midsummer—and about twelve historical hours had passed in the two Minutes Alp had taken stock. Dusk would be the fall season and night would be winter. Spring would come at dawn. He had to find a place to stay before the snows came.

That increased the other pressure on him. The dangers that had cheapened the value of the part would strike in hours or even minutes, rather than days, because of that acceleration of the time scale. And he had to make his political move within ten days—before his decade's foreknowledge was outrun. Otherwise he would have no advantage over the other players.

He was in a much stiffer exercise of his ingenuity than he had supposed. He couldn't do much, alone on the steppe. He had to get a horse and make contact with Game-Uigurs—soon. Every day he delayed was a full year wasted!

Yet he had to waste a few minutes more. In Game-parlance, Minutes—to show their historical gravity. One day was twenty-four hours; one Day was a year. He had to formulate a strategy that would ensure his survival and bring him the greatest profit within ten days—Days. That meant achieving a position of leadership among men—and he had no immediate idea where to find them.

There was something even more urgent than leadership, however. Alp found a good sandy place and scraped a small hole in the ground. Barely half a handspan down he encountered bedrock.

Surprised, he excavated further and inspected it. The underlying material was rocklike in its hardness but was not actually rock. More metal, perhaps. Something manufactured by man or demon. So this was not real steppe.

Well, why not? This was all the stage for the Game. Underneath were those multiple layers of Galactic civilization. He must never forget that none of it was genuine, however cleverly crafted.

Meanwhile, there was his urgent business. This sand was shallow, but it would do. He squatted and attended to it, then carefully smoothed the sand over so there was no indication.

It was the longest time, historically, such an act had ever taken him.

Supposedly the Game steppe land was similar to the original geography. But not literally. The Game-steppe spanned the galaxy. This was a large canvas indeed, covering all the skies of the night, far too vast for him to comprehend fully at the moment. Smaller regions were mapped as planets—rather, planets represented cities and oases. Horses—he paused, fighting confusion as he integrated his two sets of experience—horses were space ships. Carts that spouted hot wind and flew from star to star.

So this plain was no more literal than the hours of the Day. The whole thing was a mockup, perhaps intended to give him the feel of the Game—or to lull him into a disastrous complacency. The true stage was condensed in time and magnified in scale, and the visible plain was no more than the patch of soil covered by one fresh horse-dropping.

Why should a new player be set apart like this, on foot and without provisions? Was it a handicap, a hurdle, something for him to prove himself against? If so, it was ridiculously feeble by native Uigur standards; Alp had known how to forage from the land since childhood. This land differed from his own, but he could eat grass if he had to, and if there were any wildlife at all—

No—the isolation could be a measure of protection from exploitation by established players. Every new player represented competition or opportunity for the old; suppose there were those who laid in wait to dispatch or enslave the novice? That made sense; it was good nomad logic. The neighbors must be hostile, and this accounted for the cheapness of the part.

Alp grinned in the way he had. He nocked another arrow with the skill that few Uigurs and no Chinese could match and sent it flying at a shrub on a hillock thirty meters distant. It struck a little beyond; it was sleeker and lighter than those he was familiar with, but its flight was true. He fired another, and this time scored directly.

He might be a complete novice in the Galactic city, but he was only a partial novice here in the Game—and he could fight well. He doubted that the majority of players were really adept with their weapons. Affluence and ease tended to corrupt, and these Galactics had much of each.

But the players had to interact! They had to travel from city to city—planet to planet—or remain forever encamped at one location. The true nomad did not reside alone without horse or cattle. He was part of a tribe, sharing its protection and obligation. It would be pointless to set a man down too far from such a tribe—but perhaps dangerous to place him where others would discover him too rapidly. Probably placement varied, making contact random—but still, it had to be near some locus of activity, or there would be no Game.

So he had to find that locus, before it found him. And join it on his own terms. Even if he had to dispatch a few tribesmen first, to make his point.

Where there were sedentary people or camping nomads, there was fire. Where there was fire there was smoke.

Alp looked at the sky, carefully. It was clear. No clouds, no smoke.

Of course this was the galactic year 2332 his new memory said, and the planet was governed by contemporary conventions. Pollution was a crime. So no horse dung, no wood fires. Therefore no smell or smoke. But—

There it was! A faint streak of cloud, typical of—of the condensation pattern following a space ship moving through atmosphere! The Galactic equivalent of smoke—or the dust raised by a running horse.

The streak pointed to the south, assuming his brief survey of the sun's elevation had oriented him correctly. Therefore there was a stable there. But Alp checked the sky carefully for other signs before acting. Did many horsemen come to that oasis? Were there other places he might go, more profitably?

He found no other indications. That one, already fading in the sky, would have to do. Had he not been alert, he would have missed it—as perhaps most players did. It was distressing being afoot, and it made him feel insecure and lonely for Surefoot. But he had ground to cover in a hurry, and he would do it.